Zae blinked. At times like this, when the course of events took a turn she wasn't expecting, she felt like a clock that had just started to run down and would be fine again after a bit of winding. While it was a relief to see that, once again, Appleslayer's wary instincts had been correct, Zae felt strangely betrayed. There had been something endearing about the guide who didn't know the city.

Three men and a woman in leather armor and shrouding hoods converged on them, weapons drawn. Rather, they converged on Keren—she had the big sword, and had held Kala's attention. Zae and Appleslayer hadn't registered as a threat. This was something Zae could use to her advantage; she retreated a few steps and dropped her hand to her side, palm back, signaling for Appleslayer to wait. She called upon Brigh to bless her allies, and saw courage surge through Keren and the dog.

Keren drew her long, straight-bladed sword up into a parry, deflecting an attacker's sword with a clang of angry metal. "I don't know what you think I have, but I swear to you I don't have it. We're just here to train."

"Unlikely," Kala said, drawing a sword from the folds of her robe. "We've been waiting for the Knights of Ozem to get involved. How convenient that they always arrive at the same place. So. Lead us to the artifact and we'll spare you. Defy us and we'll kill you both, and the next knights they send after you, and the next."

THE PATHFINDER TALES LIBRARY

THE PATHFINDER TALES LIBRARY

GEARS OF FAITH

Gabrielle Harbowy

A TOM DOHERTY ASSOCIATES BOOK
New York

This is a work of fiction. All of the characters, organizations, and events portrayed in this novel are either products of the author's imagination or are used fictitiously.

Pathfinder Tales: Gears of Faith

Maps by Crystal Frasier and Rob Lazzaretti

A Tor Book
Published by Tom Doherty Associates, LLC
175 Fifth Avenue
New York, NY 10010

www.tor-forge.com

Tor® is a registered trademark of Tom Doherty Associates, LLC.

[[CIP DATA TK—TOR TEAM WILL INSERT]]

Tor books may be purchased for educational, business, or promotional use. For information on bulk purchases, please contact the Macmillan Corporate and Premium Sales Department at 1-800-221-7945, extension 5442, or write to specialmarkets@macmillan.com.

First Edition: April 2017

Printed in the United States of America

0 9 8 7 6 5 4 3 2 1

To Dad, for the Car Games. Playing *Star Wars* pilot-
and-navigator together showed me that make-believe wasn't
something I was required to outgrow.

To my teacher, Austin "Larry" Lawrence, for introducing his
third-grade class to these amazing worlds.

To Ed Greenwood, for encouraging me to navigate them.

Inner Sea Region

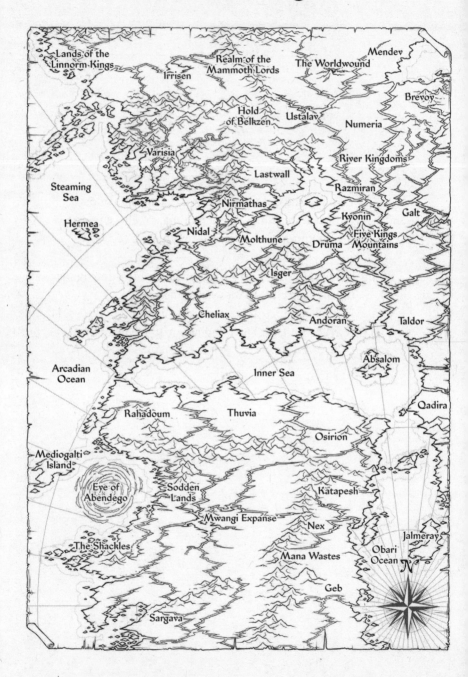

Absalom

1

Don't Eat the Messenger

Zae

Once upon a time, there was in the city of Vigil a brave young man named Darrin, of whom all the bards sang. For Darrin had slain a powerful demon lord, tamed a savage dragon, and deposed a corrupt and evil king—all before lunchtime."

Zae—gnome, healer, devotee to the goddess Brigh—paused to blow a stray azure-blue curl out of her eyes. Her audience of one looked as proud as a boy could look with his face still red and puffy from crying. He listened with rapt attention, gaze fixed on the metal ring through Zae's lower lip. When she'd gotten it, years ago and after her ears had filled up with similar rings from lobe to tip, she hadn't thought it would come in handy as a distractor of young patients, but between the shiny metal that moved when she spoke and the tale she was weaving, Darrin was barely aware of her hands or the sturdy pliers she lifted from her tray of tools.

"And so it was that, on his way home from these noble deeds, the victorious hero's thoughts were full of knighthood and glory and jewels. Thus was one last foe, a fierce serpent with fangs of iron, able to sneak up on our hero unawares. Oh, the viper's fangs did sting, but they were no match for the knight, who steeled up his courage and pulled out the fang on the count of three."

She paused to meet young Darrin's eyes, and he nodded gravely.

"One . . ." Zae said. "Two . . ." She pulled hard with the pliers and the nail slid out with protest, leaving an angry wound behind. Abandoning the pliers and nail on her tray, she took the boy's foot between both her hands, whispering a prayer. Before Darrin's mind could catch up, before he could gather his breath to scream, Brigh's divine blessing was already flowing through Zae's hands and into the wound.

"Three."

The wail died in Darrin's throat and his expression turned perplexed. This was Zae's favorite part of healing: the part where the body was expecting pain and preparing to react to it, then found itself tense with energy that suddenly had nowhere to go. For the split second before they relaxed, patients always made the most spectacular faces.

Zae beamed at her brave young charge and offered her hand to help him down from the examination table, murmuring thanks to Brigh under her breath. Darrin landed solidly on both feet and tested his weight, still expecting pain where there was none. Then he beamed back. At age seven he was already taller than Zae— who, as a gnome, stood barely more than a regal three feet—and he seemed to be enjoying the novelty of that, too.

When the two emerged from the treatment room into the parlor, Darrin ran to his aunt for a tight hug. "Look, Strella! It's all better!"

"Please, let me give you something for your trouble." Strella, barely more than a child herself, handed Darrin his shoes and reached for her coin purse. "And for not telling his parents about this. They trusted me to mind him."

Zae shook her head and lifted her hand, displaying the shield marked on her right palm. "I took the oath to protect and defend citizens of Vigil. I heal all Oathbound—and their children—free of charge. And of course I'll protect you, too, and not mention this to Arrin and Dora . . . this time."

The girl's arm tightened around her nephew's shoulders. It said a lot about Strella's upbringing that Zae's assurances only seemed to make her more uncertain—as though silence offered freely was a weaker thing than silence bought.

"Have you been in Vigil long?" Zae asked on a hunch, and wasn't surprised when the girl shook her head.

"No, in fact. I was raised in—what's that noise?"

It was an odd name for a town, Zae thought, but when she listened for it, she could indeed hear a noise. Clanking and whirring filtered in from the front yard, interspersed with the energetic growls that meant Appleslayer, Zae's dog, was happily at play.

Zae followed her young patient and his aunt out the front door of what had once been her home and clinic both, and was now just the latter. She lived a few streets away now, with Keren, and had kept her treatment room apart from their lodgings at Keren's request. The day they'd adopted Appleslayer, Keren had come home to find Zae doing surgery on him in Keren's kitchen, and after that a line had been drawn.

Appleslayer was a sled dog breed, pure white with a black nose and black lips that made him look like he was perpetually smiling. He was large for a dog, and sturdily built, prompting Keren to remark that Zae could practically ride him. Zae, in response, had tried to clamber up on his back. The dog surprised them both: upon accepting a rider, his whole bearing transformed from a playful tail-wagging companion into a serious mount ready for direction. He'd been trained for this, it seemed, and that had settled the matter.

Like Zae, Appleslayer was full of energy. True to his breed, the dog was always eager to pull a sleigh through a blizzard; more specifically, this dog was always ready to run, to attack a bushel of unattended fruit, or to carry his gnome into battle. The fence couldn't have kept him in if he'd wanted to leave, but he was content with his new life and seemed happy to have his own patch of grass to bound around in. He'd already been fully grown into his sturdy feet and rounded ears when Zae had found him a year before, but he still had a puppy's ever-present desire to play.

At the moment, he was rearing up on his hind feet and pouncing with a happy bark, the way a fox might leap on a mouse. His prey glinted bronze in the afternoon sun, and as Zae moved closer she could see that he'd caught some sort of little clockwork construction, only about a quarter as tall as Zae herself.

"What's he got, Aunt Strella?" Darrin asked. Zae was wondering the same thing.

Strella took Darrin's hand and steered him to the front walk. "Whatever it is, I'm sure Miss Zae can handle it." She glanced up at the midday sun and then at the gnome.

Zae had seen that sort of glance before. "Absolutely. Go on home before anyone knows you've been gone."

Zae took a seat on the front step and whistled, then snapped her fingers next to her ankle. "Bring it over." Her tone, while not angry, left no room for argument. The big white dog got to his feet, trotted over to the gnome, and obediently dropped his prey into her lap. It was a bronze orb, dented by his strong jaws and slick with dog slobber. Machinery was visible through the hole that had previously connected it to the parts now strewn through the grass.

"Good boy!" Zae shifted the orb into one hand so that she could pet Appleslayer's head with the other—and casually wipe her hand dry on his thick fur. He nuzzled her fingers for a moment, then sat back and looked at her expectantly. "Go on," she said, and he scampered off. When he'd retrieved another piece, he flung it skyward with a snap of his neck and immediately bounded off after it, catching the severed mechanical arm before it could hit the ground.

Rubbing Appleslayer's head hadn't done much to help the state of Zae's hand. If anything, it had made matters worse, adhering white fur to her damp fingers. It was just as well; this was a job to take to her workshop, anyway, and she could dry the object properly there.

The workshop was the other room attached to the sitting room. It had been her bedroom once, but was now given over to tools, metal, and gears. As befitting a cleric of Brigh, the goddess of clockwork and constructs, Zae's personal philosophy dictated that living things and machines had much in common: they had a peak operating condition at which everything ticked along smoothly, but sometimes things happened—whether accident, injury, illness, or just normal wear and tear—that made their performance less than optimal. Engineering and healing, then, were much the same for Zae. Even though they sometimes employed different tools, they were both about fixing what was broken.

Zae appreciated the aesthetic of orderly clutter, but she preferred to keep her workshop optimized in a tidy fashion. Tools were arranged by function, and parts were stored in drawers along the walls. Rather than interrupt her work to walk to a cabinet and back, she had created a track for her worktable so that it could always be nearest to the appropriate tools. A complex pulley system could also raise the table to the higher shelves, while a rolling ladder and extendable platforms at any shelf could do the same for Zae. That system still needed some refining, though, and was rarely used: Appleslayer had discovered that he could release the brake with a paw and herd Zae's ladder around the room, so alternate anchoring technology was the next project in her queue.

A thick cloth was sufficient to dry the clockwork head, and after a brief examination Zae clamped it down and set to work on it. Its construction spoke of quality and skill, and tiny maker's marks had been struck into each piece, perfectly aligned and consistent. The gears were milled precisely, each tooth the same as every other, and the soldering was all but invisible from the polished exterior.

Jammed inside was a thin metal tube, spring-loaded to pop out of the top of the little machine's head. Zae had already had her suspicions as to the construct's origin and purpose, but now anticipation fluttered in her stomach.

The tube's compartment was supposed to be cylindrical, but Appleslayer's jaws had rearranged things more than a bit. It was the sort of intriguing puzzle Zae loved. Carefully, she removed each component and dismantled the head, taking copious notes and labeling each piece. In less than an hour, the dented tube was in her hands. Inside, as Zae had hoped, was a crisp parchment scroll held closed with a golden waxlike seal in the shape of a gear.

Zae held it, stretching out the moment before discovery.

"I'm not going to ask what Apple's playing with out there." Keren's contralto voice was music to Zae's ears. She spun, grinning up at her knight, who lounged in the doorway with her arms lightly crossed. It was later than she thought, if Keren had already removed her white-and-gold armor, bathed, and changed into a casual tunic and breeches. Her shoulder-length brown hair was mussed and still damp. She had an easy bearing, and what Zae thought of as a young and gentle soul in a warrior's solid body, all muscle and efficient planes, as if her build itself had no tolerance for the extravagance of curves. Even her chin was no squarer or more pointed than it had to be. Only her lips showed a sensual fullness, and the honey color of her eyes seemed to brighten when she smiled. Keren had been a soldier all her life, and Zae rejoiced quietly to herself whenever she succeeded at drawing out Keren's playful side.

"He's playing with the construct that brought this." Zae held up the scroll, wiggling it. "I think this is what I think it is!"

Keren crouched beside Zae to meet her at eye level and offered her hand, which Zae took and squeezed. "You haven't opened it yet?"

"I was savoring the uncertainty."

Keren laughed and leaned in, nosing soft blue hair aside and nipping Zae on the gently rounded tip of her ear. "Come on, Pixie. Let's see it."

Zae took a slow breath, eased the seal up without breaking it, and unfurled the scroll, holding it for them both to see. Too excited to read the whole thing at once, she skimmed for the words "Clockwork Cathedral" and "accepted," and relaxed only when she found them. She turned toward Keren with a fierce hug and a happy kiss. "Praise the Bronze Lady and her mysterious ways! Now we'll both be studying in Absalom."

"Congratulations! This couldn't have been more timely. Tonight we celebrate. First thing tomorrow, we pack."

A couple months prior, Keren had requested a transfer to Absalom for advanced training—the Knights of Ozem had a large presence there, with both a church of Iomedae and a training hall for paladins, knights, and their companion steeds. Keren had trained Appleslayer in the art of combat as well as she could, but her experience was with training horses, not dogs; along with Keren's own studies, the sturdy sled dog was also to receive advanced battle training. As for Zae, she could settle in anywhere, since healers were always in short supply, so she'd have been happy to move with Keren no matter the destination. Attending Absalom's prestigious Clockwork Cathedral, however, had been a dream of hers for years, so she had seized the opportunity to apply. An academy for artificers, clockmakers, and constructors of constructs, it was the best institution of its kind in the entire world. Anyone could request to attend, but the cathedral was selective about its applicants; its admissions standards were mysterious but rigorous.

"It says there's a whole group dedicated to crafting healing devices. I've never been part of a group before!"

"I'm so proud of you." Keren shifted and pulled Zae closer, rewarding her with another, more serious kiss, toying with the brass ring in Zae's lower lip. It seemed the celebrating part of their evening had begun.

After the first round of celebrations in Zae's workshop, they had adjourned home for an evening meal and more celebrating. The gnome always rose early; after her morning prayers, she peeked her head into the bedroom. Keren's soft brown hair was still splayed across her pillow, and blankets hid the rest of her.

"You're going to be late," Zae admonished. "The day's going to save itself without you."

Keren murmured something unintelligible and rolled onto her back, squinting up at Zae for just a moment before letting her eyes flutter closed again. "Today waits for no woman. All right." She sat up, if reluctantly, and stretched. "Are you packed?"

"Not yet."

"Mm. Then hurry. I've got prayers and drills this morning, and we're to meet the Precentor of Magic at noon."

Zae blinked. "Is there something I'm missing?"

"Last night, I said you'd need to pack today."

"Well, yes . . ."

"Because we need to leave today."

Zae blinked again. "I'm sure I'd have remembered that part."

Keren swung her feet out of bed and drew Zae into her arms. With Keren seated, they were nearly the same height. "We were celebrating. I didn't want to burst the mood." She drew back. "But we need to leave today. There's been a strange buzz around the order. Something big is going on, people are on alert, and the Watcher-Lord himself wants me in Absalom sooner rather than later. So soon that he's arranged for the precentor to teleport us over."

Zae felt a flutter of excitement in her stomach. "I've never been teleported before. Don't they reserve that for extreme situations?"

"They do. It's an honor that they're offering it to us."

"Is it that the roads and seas are unsafe, or . . . ?"

Keren shrugged. "I don't know. Be ready when I get back, and we'll find out."

Zae made a face. "I guess that means we don't have time for more celebrating?"

Keren offered Zae a hand. Their fingers entwined, bringing together the matching rings they wore—Keren's inheritance from her father. "Or it means we can get back to celebrating sooner." Keren squeezed her fingers. "This is the start of something new for both of us. I love how cozy our life is, but we haven't had a new adventure in a while."

Zae hesitated. "Not to break the mood, but after Ennis . . ." When Keren and Zae had quested to the Worldwound to find Keren's estranged brother and tell him of his father's passing, they had arrived too late to save him from the demonplague. "Failing Ennis—failing *you*—was the worst new experience I've ever had. I do crave novelty, it's true, but recovering from that and making a cozy life together has been my adventure. It's what we've both needed, I think."

"Yeah," Keren murmured into Zae's shoulder. "I've been thinking about that too."

"Then let's put failing behind us, and embrace whatever comes next." Zae untangled her fingers slowly, not wanting the contact to end. "Which for you is getting dressed for prayers and training, and for me is packing and closing up shop for a while. Let me know when you're ready for me to play squire."

To Zae, packing was not an ordeal, but a fascinating challenge. Her machining supplies and completed gadgets were the most obvious necessities, of course, so they went into her pack first.

She paused with a hand on her surgeon's kit; would she have time to do healing on the side, along with her studies? Possibly not, but if Keren was to be training too, there would be the usual souvenirs from sparring matches for Zae to attend to. As long as she had to bring the satchel, to secure the more delicate potions and sharper tools, she might as well not unload anything from it.

Clothing she packed sparingly, choosing function over quantity. At least teleportation meant that neither she nor her clothes would be road-weary upon arrival. And if she had forgotten anything, it was a safe bet that the biggest city in the world would provide access to reasonable replacements. When she was done, her necessaries and clothing had all compressed into a single pack just smaller than Zae herself. She might not have been able to carry it, but she knew her human companion could. Appleslayer needed only his riding saddle and grooming kit. When Keren returned and brought out the saddle, Appleslayer dropped a dented piece of construct-guts at the knight's feet and pranced around her, tail wagging hard enough to stir a breeze.

Keren nudged the mechanical leg with her boot. "I hope the Clockwork Cathedral considers their little messengers expendable."

"If they're expecting the construct back, I'll tell them honestly that my dog killed it." Zae paused, struck by a new thought. "What if the whole school is full of those things? He already thinks they're toys. That would be an awkward start."

A slow smirk lifted a corner of Keren's lips. "On the bright side, you'd get really good at fixing them."

2

Welcoming Committee

Zae

Veena Heliu, the Precentor Martial for Magic, was often described as fiery for reasons that had nothing to do with her red hair. She was deep in an argument when they arrived, her raised voice audible from the other end of a long marble hallway. Pages wearing indoor boots of soft leather shuffled past silently, carrying scrolls in secure tubes and not making eye contact with Zae or each other. Keren, by contrast, had the conspicuous jingle and clank of armor to accompany her every step.

Zae couldn't distinguish Veena's distant words through their echoes, and she was almost disappointed when the yelling cut off abruptly upon their approach, replaced with the sibilant hisses of angry whispers. From the set of Keren's jaw, this wasn't normal; Zae surmised that whatever the source of the buzz Keren had mentioned, it had not been resolved overnight.

Zae had never been inside Vigil's Crusader War College, but Keren's father had taught here, and his children had grown up within Castle Overwatch's walls. Zae and Appleslayer followed as Keren led the way with the familiarity of muscle memory rather than recent experience. She tried a couple times to make conversation, but Keren's face was drawn tight and Zae left her to her own thoughts.

"Keren Rhinn! Right on time." Most people towered over Zae—she was used to that—but she suspected Veena Heliu could tower over people even taller than the sorcerer herself. She radiated such power and certainty that the air was alive with it. Zae looked around, but saw no one else; whomever Veena had been arguing with had left, if they'd ever been physically present at all.

"Reporting as summoned," Keren answered, stopping sharply at a respectful distance. Veena was a half-elf, and though she was not Keren's true aunt, Keren had referred to her as "Auntie Veena" on the walk over. There was no sign of that informality on Keren's part now. "This is Sister Zae, Cleric of Brigh."

The precentor nodded curtly toward Zae, then surveyed Appleslayer, who stood alert at attention in his polished saddle. "And this is your mount, ready for his combat training." More often than not, the people Zae encountered were surprised to see dogs in such a role, but Heliu's life revolved around the art of war and the duty of defense. Her lack of surprise was no surprise. A note of approval hung in her voice, which might or might not have been Zae's hopeful imagination.

Appleslayer's plumed tail twitched back and forth once in a single low, uncertain wag.

Heliu held out her hands, one toward each of them. "Are you ready?"

Keren hesitated.

"Speak freely, Crusader."

Keren cleared her throat. "Excuse me, ma'am, but I'd requested to be briefed on the reason for the fast transport."

"I didn't receive orders to brief you. I'm afraid your request's been denied from higher up."

Zae looked between the two women. Keren always accepted command decisions, even when they left her conflicted—and Zae knew when she was conflicted, because the bottled-in frustration came out in the safety of their home—but Zae had also seen Keren's *can't we work around this?* face enough to recognize it now.

"Well, thank you all the same," Zae said to defuse the silence. "I would be excited to spend weeks on a boat, but I'm sure Keren's glad to be getting to where we're going."

"Quite so," Heliu answered. "I'll be taking you into a private park. It's discreet, unchanging, and no one pays much attention to how many people are wandering around there. I must return immediately to my duties, so I won't be able to direct you to the Seventh Church myself, but someone from the church will be there to meet us."

They both took Heliu's offered hands, and Zae and Keren each buried their free hands in Appleslayer's fur. The sensation was slight—just an odd weightlessness in Zae's stomach—and then it was over. Her feet were now on grass. Whereas they had left at noon, they arrived in a place where the sun was noticeably lower in the afternoon sky. A copse of trees at the edge of the park made an almost accidental clearing that would be difficult to stumble upon by chance. In different circumstances, it would have been a perfect spot for a moonlit tryst.

Zae checked herself and her companions. No limbs seemed to be out of place. Veena had already disappeared again. Appleslayer whuffed softly under his breath, and Zae shook her head. "No exploring for now. Stay close."

When they stepped around the corner and into the larger park, they found an expanse of lush green meadow dotted with people lounging in twos and threes. In front of them, sitting on a stone bench with a small leather-bound book in her hands, was a woman dressed in the robes of Iomedae.

"I leave you to it." Veena nodded toward the initiate, and exchanged quiet words with Keren. Zae was too distracted studying her surroundings to pay attention.

The priestess stood and tucked the book away into the folds of her robes as Zae and her companions approached, greeting them with a warm smile. Roughly the same age as Darrin's aunt Strella, she had straight honey-brown hair and a particular intensity Zae had often seen in people who were strongly devoted to their gods.

"Welcome," the woman said to them, gaze lingering on the white and gold of Keren's armor. "You must be our new arrivals from Lastwall."

"That we are." Keren held up her left palm in greeting, displaying the sword-mark there. Zae and Keren both bore the shield on their right palms. While Zae had her odd gear-shaped birthmark on her left hand, Keren had received the sword-mark of Iomedae on that palm to identify her as a Vigilant defender of Lastwall. "Crusader Keren Rhinn, and this is Sister Zae. Thank you for meeting us. We're pleased to be in Absalom."

"My name is Kala, initiate of Iomedae. It's a pleasure to be of service to the Knights of Ozem, especially in these trying times. Shall we?" Kala gestured to the path.

They walked along a quiet wooded trail at an unrushed pace that surprised Zae, considering how hasty their departure from Vigil had been once all the gears were in motion. Kala addressed Keren while Zae and Appleslayer followed behind. Keren stole a look over her shoulder, eyebrows drawn in momentary concern, but Zae smiled assuringly in response. She didn't feel slighted. If her organization had greeted them, Zae would have expected the attention to be hers, but it was a pleasant day, with a breeze stirring the tops of the trees, and she was content to walk with her dog, enjoy the weather, and muse about what studying at the Clockwork Cathedral would be like.

"What's the name of this place?" Keren asked.

"Oh! I should be a better guide. I'm sorry. It's always so exciting to meet new people. This is the . . . well, Greenery Park. We'll be heading west into the center of Absalom from here. It's the best route at this time of day."

Her hesitation sounded like embarrassment, so Zae said, "City planners are strange creatures. Seems like a redundant name for a park, doesn't it? Does the temple have you on guide duty often?"

"Oh, not often. Well, not until recently. All these servants of Iomedae flocking into the city. I do quite enjoy meeting new members of the order. Not *new* new, I mean, intending no offense to your possibly extensive and decorated service, but new to me."

They followed a wide carriage road out of the park and entered the bustle of a city headed toward evening. "You mentioned these trying times?" Keren asked.

"Are those *camels*?" Zae blurted at the same time. While there were a few horses and donkeys to be seen, camels seemed to be the customary beast of burden and transport here. Zae had never seen a camel in person before, and something about them struck her oddly. Maybe it was the spindlyness of their legs, or the long, questing necks, but they just didn't look like they'd been assembled according to an optimal design. Appleslayer stopped in the middle of the road, sniffing the air, and took a few steps toward a narrow side street, whining under his breath.

Zae followed him and peered down the street. She saw an aged pub sign creaking over a narrow doorway, and a shadowed dead end piled with rubbish beyond. She snapped her fingers by her thigh. "Come on, Apple. I know the camels stink, but I need you to stay close."

The dog whined once more, grumbled under his breath, and trotted back to Zae's side. She rubbed between his ears. "Good boy. I know it's all really interesting, but we need to keep up with Keren."

When Zae returned with Appleslayer at her side, Kala was still describing the various troubles the city was facing. Keren, who had never lived in any city but Vigil, listened patiently while the initiate rambled. Zae, who had spent time in several cities, knew the issues to be mostly generic. Sewers not keeping up with rising population; crime in the poorer districts; too much distrust of certain officials and too much trust of others. Meanwhile, there was no mistaking their passage across some invisible border into the next district to the west—buildings were suddenly closer together and more people crowded the streets, all with different destinations. A knot of chaos resulted, which for Zae manifested as a sea of knees and thighs. She noticed armor, leather and metal; women in soft breeches or simple dresses with minimal ornamentation; and very few shoes that had seen a brush or cloth in recent memory. These were commoners by and large, with a few servants shopping for their masters, and a few lawkeepers maintaining order or soldiers doing their own errands. She hopped up into Appleslayer's saddle and then, while stopped at a corner, stood atop it with Keren's arm for balance, at last catching a glimpse of the peaks of market stall tents.

"What's this place?" Zae asked.

"Ah, this? This is the Gold District."

A passing servant with a broad basket at her hip bumped into Kala and looked at her askance. "It's the Coins, actually," she said, and then moved on.

Kala cleared her throat, ignoring the imposition, but Zae exchanged a glance with Keren. A translation error, perhaps, though Kala didn't have any particular foreign accent that Zae could place. "Whatever you call it, it's the trade quarter, if you will. Anything can be bought and sold here, at any time of day or night. Is there something like it where you come from? Lastwall, wasn't it? They never tell me anything about the arrivals, just when to be at the meeting point."

The constant questions were having an effect on Keren's bearing, though Zae knew no one else would have noticed the shift in her armored shoulders. "Have you always studied here in Absalom?" she asked, redirecting the initiate.

"Oh, I've only arrived recently, myself. It's the home of so many miracles, you know. Legendary for its concentration of relics, too.

I've heard that practically everything of religious significance probably finds its way here eventually. Have you heard that?"

"I hadn't, actually."

"Well, apparently it's true. The Pathfinder Society has its headquarters here, and securing relics is one of the many things it does. And there are so many museums! Both public and private collections. This truly is where antiquities are traded and where history lives."

"Speaking of living history, are you taking us directly to the church, or to our lodgings first?" Keren asked. The row houses here weren't exactly crumbling, but they looked like drunken old men in the small hours, propping each other up as they stumbled home from a tavern. It would be interesting to stay in one of them, Zae thought. She imagined them smelling of booze on the inside and swaying slightly around last call.

"Oh, to your lodgings of course, so that you can freshen up before you present yourselves to the church. You'll be staying just west of here, in the Foreign Quarter, where most of the city's guest housing is. I brought you this way because it's just so important to know where the markets are in a new city, don't you think?" Kala returned her attention to Keren. "Everything can be bought and sold in the Coins."

Keren nodded. "As you said. It's very good to know; you have our thanks."

Kala pressed her point. "Everything."

"Indeed, Sister."

"So, if you were searching for someone who'd stolen something, perhaps to sell it, this might be where you would look. Wouldn't you say?"

Zae knew the expression that now crossed Keren's face. For a moment, she wore the same one. "I daresay you know the city far better than we, Sister." Keren was only that formal when she was choosing her words carefully. "Surely a city this large has many crevices for people who don't want to be found."

"Yes, surely. But where are they sending *you* to look?"

"Look for what?" Zae asked, nudging Apple to keep up. Kala didn't spare her a glance.

"It's all right." Their guide shifted closer to Keren. "I know why you're really here. I so desperately want to help, but I'm a new initiate so they've got me just escorting the seasoned ones in. I don't get to see any adventure for myself. Take a little pity on me and let me live vicariously through your mission. The other groups have all told me where they're being sent . . ."

"I didn't think it was exactly secret," Keren said, and Kala's posture straightened expectantly. "My mission is to train at the Tempering Hall. I'll be deepening my understanding of my faith, studying the Acts of Iomedae, and—"

Kala waved her graceful hand. "There's no need for such pretense."

"Pretense?"

"Your cover story is practiced to perfection. It's completely believable. But I mean your *actual* mission, of course. The . . . artifact. You know."

"I'm sure I don't," Keren said. "Perhaps you've confused us with another traveling party."

Kala smiled a smile that was just on the forced side of amusement. "Anyway, it doesn't matter. Tell me, in—Lastwall, did you say?—is torture a part of your training?"

"The giving or the enduring?" Keren answered, her voice just a notch too tight to be joking. Kala tossed her head back and laughed.

"Oh, you're lovely. The enduring, of course."

Keren stiffened again, and Appleslayer's muscles tensed as if he'd caught wind of an unpleasant smell. He knew how to read Keren's body language as well as Zae herself did, or perhaps an actual scent signaled her wariness to the dog's sensitive nose.

"Yes, yes, you're very loyal. I can see why they chose you." Kala turned a corner, leading them down a narrow alley that ended at a crumbling wall. "But unfortunately, that loyalty means you're of little use to me. I've given you plenty of chances to answer me freely, but those answers will be carved out of you if need be. No one can hold out against torture forever." Four shadows dropped from the low roofs on either side of the alley. "This is your last chance."

Zae blinked. At times like this, when the course of events took a turn she wasn't expecting, she felt like a clock that had just started to run down and would be fine again after a bit of winding. While it was a relief to see that, once again, Appleslayer's wary instincts had been correct, Zae felt strangely betrayed. There had been something endearing about the guide who didn't know the city.

Three men and a woman in leather armor and shrouding hoods converged on them, weapons drawn. Rather, they converged on Keren—she had the big sword, and had held Kala's attention. Zae and Appleslayer hadn't registered as a threat. This was something Zae could use to her advantage; she retreated a few steps and dropped her hand to her side, palm back, signaling for Appleslayer to wait. She called upon Brigh to bless her allies, and saw courage surge through Keren and the dog.

Keren drew her long, straight-bladed sword up into a parry, deflecting an attacker's sword with a clang of angry metal. "I don't know what you think I have, but I swear to you I don't have it. We're just here to train."

"Unlikely," Kala said, drawing a sword from the folds of her robe. "We've been waiting for the Knights of Ozem to get involved. How convenient that they always arrive at the same place. So. Lead us to the artifact and we'll spare you. Defy us and we'll kill you both, and the next knights they send after you, and the next."

Zae curled her hand into a fist; Apple, recognizing the wordless command, sprang forth with teeth bared.

"Tezryn—behind you!" one of the attackers shouted, and the robed woman turned. She slashed at Appleslayer with her sword, but the dog sprang out of range. He circled and made a lunge for Kala's calf. The dog had enough bulk to throw an unprepared opponent off balance and enough herding instinct to shuttle enemies toward Keren's blade, but Kala sidestepped, raising her sword to parry Keren's attack. No matter how many times Apple engaged in combat, Zae was always fascinated to see him employ the same leaping and bounding maneuvers that were trademarks of his breed's energetic play.

Zae ticked over the spells she had prepared that morning, without having known she would be teleported to Absalom or dropped into the middle of an alley brawl. She now knew several things about their guide: not only was she not a cleric of Iomedae, but if her first instinct was to strike out with a blade rather than a spell, then she likely wasn't an aspiring priestess of any god at all. Meanwhile, something odd was tickling at her senses, something about the way the rest of them moved that wasn't quite right.

Kala—no, Tezryn—dodged Keren's next attack, but that put her right in the path of Appleslayer's teeth. He latched onto her hamstring, jerking his head from side to side. Keren neatly sliced the back of Tezryn's other leg, bringing her down, then turned her attention to the closest attacker, matching him swing for swing.

Appleslayer released his prey and turned toward one of the other shadowy figures, a fury of sharp teeth and strong paws, nimbly ducking swords and unarmed swipes. He would come in from behind to keep an enemy turning and distracted, and then Keren would take the foe down with one fierce swing. He and Keren fought as one, seamlessly aiding each other with each foe. While Apple's emotional devotion was to Zae, he was equally loyal to Keren. She had trained him well, and their rapport was a beautiful, fluid dance that just happened to result in a certain amount of blood.

But this time, it didn't. Keren sliced a man's arm clean off, and it fell twitching without the trademark arterial gush. Zae cursed herself for not realizing it sooner, and called upon Brigh to bring down her holy wrath upon the attackers. The maimed man fell, and the others cringed and staggered at the sudden assault of light. Though remarkably whole, they were not alive. And neither was their leader. She had struggled to her knees at the periphery of the fight, but she cried out and curled herself into a tight ball under the assault of power.

Appleslayer and Keren tore through the attackers one by one. Their blows rang against Keren's shield. When all of them were on the ground, Zae finished them with another surge of holy power. The initiate, however, had worked her way to her feet somehow, and was stumbling toward the mouth of the alley. In a fluid movement, Keren freed her shield from her arm and threw it like a skipping stone. It scuttled across the cobbled street and cut Tezryn's wounded legs out from under her, sending her sprawling. When Keren pushed the leader onto her back, she was glassy-eyed but snarling.

Keren reversed her grip and held her sword over Tezryn's throat, two-handed. "What do you want from us? Tell me!" Her hands were steady and the swordpoint didn't waver, but Zae knew her well enough to hear the hurt in her voice.

When the mock-initiate only grinned at her with bloody teeth, Keren brought the blade down with such force that it struck all the way through the woman's throat and impacted the pavement beneath. Tezryn gurgled, and was still.

Zae started to call Appleslayer back to her, but the dog was approaching Keren, so she held her tongue. He sniffed at the knight, tail low, pacing around her like an anxious child while she checked the other attackers to make sure they'd been put down for good. Now that they were still, peeking into their hoods showed skin stretched tight over starved cheeks, and the teeth within their parted mouths were longer than they should have been.

Tezryn was dead without a doubt, but that didn't put Zae at ease. She pressed her fingers to the guide's forehead, then brought them to her own nose. The scent was faint, but it held notes of rosemary and clean linen. "Undead, and disguising it," Zae said. "Unguent of revivification, I think. And she's definitely not Iomedae's priestess. She concealed both her appearance and her aura." Beneath the vestments, she wore the same leather armor as the others.

"Are you sure she wasn't just alive and evil?"

"Positive. I called Brigh's light down upon the undead, not the living."

"So the others . . . ?"

"Probably not under her thrall, but likely she told them where to go for a good feast. None of them bit you, did they?"

Keren shook her head. "Apple bit one of them, though. Should we be worried about that?"

"I don't know. I don't think so, but better to be safe than dog food." Zae motioned the dog over to her and extended a hand. Apple sniffed cautiously at her fingers. They still smelled of the ointment, Zae realized. She wiped her hand on her coat and gave him her other hand instead, whispering to Brigh and sharing a soft, warming light from her fingertips through Apple's fur, concentrating on following the warmth all the way through him. She encountered none of the sorts of obstacles that would indicate disease or corruption. "He's fine."

"Which means that our real welcoming party . . ." Keren and Zae exchanged a long look.

Zae mounted up on Appleslayer's saddle while Keren took the vestments of Iomedae from Tezryn's corpse and re-shouldered their supplies. "Apple, that alley you were curious about. Can you lead us back there? Good dog!"

As they hurried away, Zae took a quick glance back over her shoulder. Figures were already emerging from the shadows and creeping toward the corpses. Zae had seen squatters and street gangs scavenge what they could from the dead in the seedier quarters of other cities. It felt a little strange to her, knowing that it was happening, but it worked in her favor; there would likely be little left for the attackers' masters to find.

In the alley with the pub sign, Apple's nose led them through a heap of rubbish to the dead end and a broken, upturned crate, underneath which was bundle of bloodied rags that had once been fine cloth; it must have been the actual Kala's underdress. Keren cursed and turned away, but Apple stayed by Zae's side while she peeled back the stiffening fabric. There was little flesh to be found. Small scavengers hovered, drawn by the blood and determined to find a scrap to eat.

"Get, you!" she heard Keren shout, followed by a scattering of refuse and a scuffle of many tiny feet. Half a dozen rats scampered out of range of Keren's sword, but didn't flee from sight, unwilling to give up the chance of a meal. Keren crouched over the cloth, her expression set and cold.

Zae gave her a moment, then asked, "What do you think they wanted so badly that they'd kill a priestess just to ask us questions?"

"I don't know," Keren said grimly. "But we're going to find out."

3

SPECIAL DELIVERY

KEREN

Keren pulled one of the empty sacks out of her travel pack and stretched its drawstringed neck to the fullest. Sacks were for holding things, and that was exactly why she brought extra when she traveled. They could be used for foraging, for storing purchases to take home, or for sorting belongings so that a party could separate. It felt undignified to collect the desecrated vestments of a servant of Iomedae into a rough-spun sack, and she thought briefly that her cloak might be a more appropriate vessel, but she put that discomfort out of mind. She had been trained against sentimentality when there were casualties to attend to, and when she let her practicality take over from her emotions she could concede that cloaks were designed to be worn and sacks were meant to hold things. Zae, misreading her hesitation, stepped forward to take the rough fabric from her and hold it open.

Keren accepted the help gratefully. "This wasn't a spur of the moment thing."

"No, it wasn't. Tezryn, that's what they called her?" Zae looked back over her shoulder, as if she might still be able to see the other alley. "She had a bevy of ghouls at her disposal. Probably drew them up from the sewers or someplace, told them where they could find an easy meal if they waited."

"With an acolyte as an advance for good faith. So to speak." Keren frowned. "Someone knew we were coming and where we were being met, and wanted to intercept us. Now I really want to know why we were given quick transport."

"Then the best thing for us to do is get to the temple, and hope that some answers might be waiting for us there."

They walked toward the mouth of the alley and looked back the way they had come. Keren knew where they were relative to what she had seen of the city, but she was disoriented as to direction—which had probably been Tezryn's intent. "Now we just have to *find* the temple, without a guide."

"If it's any consolation," Zae said ruefully, "we've got better odds on our own than with the guide we had."

Keren sighed.

"Also," Zae added, "my acceptance letter came with a map."

It was the first promising thing Keren had heard since Lastwall. "All right. Help me secure poor Kala's things to Apple's saddle."

"That's awfully impersonal. Here. If you take the lead, I'll carry her. Them. The . . . bag."

Something caught in Keren's chest, and for a moment she felt she might burst with feeling. That Zae did this of her own initiative, for someone of Keren's order whom she had never met . . . She didn't know if what she felt was closer to love or to pride, but traveling either of those paths would lead to the sort of misty-eyed moment they didn't have time for.

Zae produced the map and Keren took it from her. It was more an artist's rendering than a guide, but it showed all the districts of Absalom in their correct relative positions, none the same color as its neighbor. "It looks like there's a main road that leads to the Ascendant Court in the center of the city. That's the district with the churches."

"That sounds right. And look, Keren—it *is* the Coins, not the Gold."

The Clockwork Cathedral's map led them through a hectic central marketplace, though without the run-down desperation they'd seen earlier with their false guide, and then continued northward into a quieter, more orderly district. Marble buildings stood sentinel on either side of a wide, clean lane. Here patrols were more numerous, too, strolling along in their uniforms and matching cloaks among the common citizens and the clergy in the colors of their gods.

Keren scanned the left side of the road while Zae scanned the right. A stately cathedral of white stone loomed up ahead, and on it a large stained-glass window depicting the holy symbol of Iomedae glowed in the late-day sun. "That's got to be it," Keren said. As they approached, she nodded to two guards in Iomedaean livery on either side of the doorway—a human and a dwarf, both too well-armored and watchful to be stationed there just for ceremony.

"Crusader Keren Rhinn, Knight of Ozem, Vigilant Defender of Lastwall. We're expected."

The guards stepped aside. "Enter, and be welcome."

Keren bowed her head in thanks, and they continued into the church.

It was hard to say which hall of worship felt more imposing, the Cathedral of Sancta Iomedaea in Lastwall or the Seventh Church in Absalom. Keren was more certain of a divine presence here, she decided, or at least the presence here seemed to be paying closer attention. It rippled out of the tapestries that lined the walls—eleven of them in all. It teased her nose with the scents of old scrolls and the echo of incense. And it radiated from the central altar at the end of the long hallway, and the robed, dark-skinned figure who waited there.

"Welcome. I am Yenna Quoros. The Precentor of Magic sent you?" The ornate trim on the priestess's vestments indicated a high rank, and the sternness of her face showed the discipline that had earned it.

"Yes, ma'am. Crusader Rhinn, from Lastwall. This is Sister Zae of Brigh. I'm afraid we bear bad news regarding the initiate sent to greet us." Keren took the bag from Zae, held it a moment, and then offered it toward the cleric.

Yenna took the bag; her lips tightened when she saw the bloody robes inside. "Tell me from the beginning."

Keren nodded. "Zae and I were both set to travel to Absalom by conventional means—she's to study at the Clockwork Cathedral, and her dog and I are to train at the Tempering Hall— but I received word from Precentor Heliu that we should teleport without delay. She said that there would be a representative from the church to greet us in the park, and there was. She was dressed as an initiate and said her name was Kala, and she asked a lot of questions about why we were sent, and where we were sent to look, and she mentioned an artifact. She said she was our guide, but she didn't actually know the city very well. And when it became clear to her that we didn't know what she was on about, she signaled an ambush."

"Also," Zae added, "she and her companions were all undead. She was using a cosmetic to hide it."

Yenna's frown deepened the lines of age on her face. "I see."

Keren remained at attention, mind racing, while the priestess turned to summon an acolyte. She handed over the bag and murmured quiet instructions. It wasn't Keren's place to make demands of her superiors, but she prayed with all her might that Yenna's next words would be anything other than "that will be all." Veena Heliu had not briefed them before the oddly hastened trip, and that made Keren suspicious enough already that something serious was happening somewhere. If they got no answers on the receiving end either, now that they'd stepped right into whatever it was, Keren would . . . well, she'd do nothing. She knew that. She'd accept the wisdom of her superiors and stay out of it, and go about her training. But she'd be frustrated. She had never met Kala, but Kala had been a fellow servant of Iomedae, and that was enough.

Yenna did not dismiss Keren. "Let's continue this in private."

Keren silently thanked Iomedae, dipped her head in reverence to the statue, and followed the priestess through a side door that opened onto back hallways and offices.

When Yenna's lead widened, Zae shifted closer to Keren. "So this is the Seventh Church?"

"Yes."

"What happened to the first six?"

"That's not what it means. This is the church where Iomedae performed her Seventh Act—the calling of the Undenying Light."

Yenna stopped at an empty room and gestured them in ahead of her. "In here, please. Is there anything you need?"

Keren shook her head slowly, trying and failing to turn her focus back to her own needs, but Zae said, "If it's not too much trouble, ma'am, some water for my dog? We didn't have a long trip, but it's been an eventful one all the same."

"I'll have someone see to it." She ushered them in but didn't follow, continuing down the hall at a quick pace instead.

It was a modest, simple chamber, possibly meant for solitary prayer. There were no windows, but wall sconces gave the room gentle magical light. For decoration, a statuette of the goddess was mounted on the wall between two narrow tapestries of white and gold, and the furniture was minimal—a writing desk with a chair in front of it and a chair behind it. A silent acolyte appeared with another chair, waving Keren off when she tried to help. Keren sat, then stood again and paced the small room. The priestess had seemed displeased, but not surprised, by the evidence of Kala's death. Keren wasn't sure what to make of that.

Appleslayer shook out his fur and settled down by his gnome's feet to groom.

Two more acolytes arrived, one carrying a tray with a pitcher of wine, glasses, and a plate of fruits and cheeses, and the other bringing a carafe of water and an empty bowl. Zae set the bowl beside Appleslayer and poured the water for him before pouring wine. When she handed Keren a glass their fingers brushed, but not for long enough.

Presently, Yenna returned and closed the door. In the soft conjured light of the inner chamber her features appeared gentler, though Keren saw streaks of white marbling the black of her short hair. Yenna sat straight, looking tired but unbroken—not even particularly ruffled. She took no refreshment for herself.

Definitely not surprised, then.

Keren set her glass back on the tray, armor clacking with the bend of her elbow. "Thank you, ma'am. I'm ready to be brought up to speed." It was a calculated risk, breaking protocol to ask someone so far superior in rank to tell her what was going on, but she told herself that if Yenna had wanted to leave them in the dark she would have simply sent them on their way.

Yenna nodded shortly. "You want information. There's little I can give you. Just advice: be prepared and alert. Your introduction to Absalom was unfortunate, but probably not an isolated incident."

"Why is there such open hostility against the order?" Iomedae was the goddess of justice and honor. While there were evil gods whose congregations included undead like the ones they'd faced, picking a fight with Iomedae would be near suicidal for them.

"Not against the order, as such. Go about your tasks as planned, both of you, just keep your eyes open."

"So this wasn't an attack against Zae and me personally, or against the order, or against Iomedae, but we should expect it to happen again." *I would like to know what I was nearly killed for, since I was apparently sent into it open-eyed by someone I've known and trusted since I was five.* It wasn't something Keren could say out loud. At the same time, she could still choose the nuance of her words to make her dissatisfaction known. "With respect, ma'am, we'll be able to give better reports if we know what sort of information would be most helpful to you."

Yenna pursed her lips. After a few moments, she folded her hands on the writing desk. "You said this false guide questioned you about an artifact."

"Yes, ma'am."

"All right. Here's the situation: We are currently searching for a particular artifact, and so is another interested party. We have our resources and they have theirs. We know they've been watching us; you are not the first new arrivals to be approached. The specifics change each time, but this is a sharp escalation in their tactics. I presume their agent followed Kala toward your arrival point, lured her off and killed her to take her place, and waited. When she saw you arrive, escorted by a high-ranking official, she assumed you were involved."

Keren took a moment to digest this. "But you're still using the same arrival points, despite previous . . . encounters. Did the precentor know what she was delivering us into?"

"Yes. With no disrespect to you, we're using any unrelated travel to Absalom to our advantage, so that we can distract the opposing party from our actual investigators. Every distraction helps. They may be bringing reinforcements into the city, too, but so far we think their force is fairly small, and we aim to spread them thin. So if they dispatch someone to spend several hours watching the park, there's somewhere else that they're *not* watching."

"And they know you're looking for it too, so they're trailing anyone wearing Iomedae's sigil in the hope that we'll lead them to it?" Keren surmised.

"That's basically the shape of it. Expect to be followed. Trust no one who asks you about your business here, or who cozies up to you for any reason. If you identify the spies watching you, do not engage them; leave that to us. Your position is strategic, so let's keep our advantage for now. And for your own sake, the less you know, the more honestly you can claim to know nothing."

Keren and Zae exchanged a glance. Keren recalled the random woman in the Coins who had corrected their guide, and wondered how random that had truly been. Had that been another agent keeping tabs on the first? If so, then Tezryn's demise would already be known to the rest of them. She related this to Yenna. "Should we still go about our business?"

"Yes, absolutely. We're following up on many rumors and leads; you can aid us best by continuing as you've begun: if they consider you involved, you'll be a helpful distraction, leading them down dead alleys."

Keren winced at her phrasing, but only nodded. "Let them follow us, and don't engage."

Yenna didn't seem to notice Keren's wince. "These people are not afraid to die, and they have a variety of poisonous defenses they employ to take their enemies out with them. If cornered, they might explode, or dissolve to acid, or spread virulent disease."

"Tezryn used no such defenses."

"Theirs is a highly compartmentalized order, with different cells having specific functions. The agent you met was likely supposed to sound out whether you were informed and report back, not to take your life."

"She's right," Zae said, nodding slowly. "She said she was going to torture it out of you, which means she had to take us alive . . . or leave us alive. Promising us to those ghouls was supposed to frighten us into talking. We were ghoul-food only if we didn't know anything."

They shared a few moments of uncomfortable silence. Keren didn't feel she needed more time in which to contemplate the various possible means of her own messy demise, but if Yenna had wanted to impress upon her the importance of not setting out on her own personal undead-hunting mission, she had succeeded. "Thank you for the warning, priestess. I will do my best not to engage."

"Good." Yenna rose to her feet. "Settle into your lodgings and report to your training sessions tomorrow as planned. Keep an eye out for people watching you, but don't acknowledge them. If you have any further incidents like today's, report them directly to me."

Keren rose as well. "Yes, ma'am. We'll help you recover the artifact however we can."

"Let's not overreach. We have our top investigators on the chase. Just do your best to not get killed, Crusader."

4
Location, Location, Location
Zae

Once Yenna left, the acolytes provided Keren and Zae with provisions and maps, and they made their way back down the main hall of the vast cathedral. At the cobblestones just outside, however, Keren let out a startled cry and fell to her knees.

Zae rushed to Keren's side. "Keren? What is it? Keren!"

The knight didn't seem to notice her there. She stared into the distance, tears glinting brightly in her eyes. Zae scanned their surroundings for shadowy foes, then hurried to check Keren's back and arms for projectiles.

"Don't worry, miss." The dwarf who had admitted them into the church joined her at Keren's other side and rested a knowing hand on her shoulder. "Happens all the time."

Keren, oblivious to them, pulled her sword and knelt more deliberately, bowing over it in prayer. When Zae met the guard's eye again, he jerked forward and up with his chin.

Ahead, mere blocks away, a gigantic white glacier of a temple rose to a single spire's point far above them. Zae suddenly had a hundred questions all at once for the two guards, but decided to start with the most practical one.

"We haven't formally met. I'm Sister Zae of Brigh, and my dog is Appleslayer. And you?"

The grizzled dwarf bowed smoothly, without as much as a creak from his armor. "Sword Knight Barent Arjun. My companion is Corin Elias."

"Sword Knight Arjun, this large edifice that has my companion speechless is . . . ?"

"That's the Starstone Cathedral. Raised by the great god Aroden himself at the founding of Absalom, and where our own Lady Iomedae ascended to her godhood."

"And . . . you said many people do this? With the falling, and the praying, and the tears?"

"Usually more tears than this, but yes."

"All right. So, here's my question." She stepped around Keren and put both her hands on her beloved's shoulders. When Keren was aware enough of the gnome to meet her eyes, Zae continued. "How could you *possibly* have missed this when we came in?"

Barent's smile was gentle, and his own glance toward the cathedral was full of reverence. "More easily than you might think. Just give your knight a minute and she'll be fine."

Keren's wide eyes seemed to offer their agreement. Reluctantly, Zae eased back a few steps. She and Barent rejoined at the doorway, watching in companionable silence.

It was several minutes, all told, before Keren sighed, wiped her eyes on her cloak, and got to her feet. "I was so focused on delivering the body, and finding the church, and what might happen next . . . I guess I was barely aware of anything else."

Corin, the human guard, smiled. "It's more common than not. Don't worry yourself over it. If I may, I recommend going up to the edge and letting yourself be awed a few moments more. Get it out of the way now, so that it doesn't strike you at an inconvenient moment."

Keren bowed her thanks, and Appleslayer, recognizing Keren's bow as a gesture which signaled that they were soon to be departing, came to attention and wagged his plumed tail.

Zae settled herself in Apple's saddle and they started off. The gnome waited until they were around the corner from the church, following Yenna's map, before speaking. "Do you want to pass by the cathedral now, like they suggested?"

Keren shook her head. "I think I want to get where we're going and have a long bath."

"I know that look. It's the one that means your brains are full."

Keren grinned wanly. "More full than I expected. I mean, Iomedae was a Knight of Ozem before she ascended. She trained at Overwatch, just as I did. She walked the streets of Vigil, same as I have my whole life. So why is it that being *here*, walking the streets she walked and seeing the sites of her holy acts, is so much different? All right, that's the place where she ascended to godhood. That's pretty overwhelming. But to me, when I've slept in her barracks and trained in her yards?"

"Because it's new?" Zae offered. "Those things have always been landmarks for you. These things represent a part of her life you've never traced before. Besides, in Vigil she was a mortal. After Absalom, she was a god. Don't you think that's going to feel a little different to you?"

Keren didn't answer, dipping her eyes as if the map was suddenly fascinating. "I think we turn here."

When Keren evaded a question like that, it was never wise to press her on it until she was ready, so Zae tried to come up with something else to say in the meantime. Their path led them out of the Ascendant Court and into the winding streets of a more residential area. Row houses stood gleaming like ladies at a ball, in contrast to the tired, leaning buildings they'd seen on the outskirts of the Coins. "That whole thing about where they're housing us— what Tezryn said—that was a lie?"

"I think so. There is a Foreign Quarter, but it's on the other side of the city. We're on the border of the Merchants' Quarter, which is where the Clockwork Cathedral is. It looks like it'll be a convenient location for both of us."

"The order doesn't house their visitors near the church?"

"That's what I expected, too. Maybe it's cheaper out here."

Zae glanced around. "Maybe with all that's going on, they want us to be away from interested eyes. Like the ones a block back—did you see them?"

Keren shook her head. "If they want us to be decoys, hiding us away from interested eyes doesn't make sense. And I did see those eyes, but I think they were just interested because they were children and you're a gnome riding a dog with a saddle."

Zae had to concede that this was possible.

"Here, I think this is our street."

A crescent of stone row houses huddled together around a cobbled courtyard, sharing their side walls in common. At the courtyard's center was a lumpy bronze statue of, as near as Zae could tell, a precarious tower of overripe oranges. To add indignity, the statue turned out to be a fountain. Zae dismounted, wincing.

"What is it?" Keren asked. "Do you sense evil?"

"No . . . but I think I've just detected ugly."

Keren and Appleslayer went ahead with the keys while Zae examined the fountain. No angle of viewing improved its odd visage, which Zae was surprised to find mildly reassuring. She might have been obligated to feel ashamed if the sculpture had resolved into the likeness of someone famous or important.

Delaying also gave Zae the opportunity to scout out the neighbors. One elderly woman across the street came to her window and parted the curtains, watching Keren unlock the door. A young man with long braids paused in the sweeping of his family's stoop to do the same, canting his head like an interested little bird.

Zae supposed Keren's wisdom might still hold true. These were probably just people who lived here, as naturally curious about strangers as Zae was about them.

She dipped her fingers in the fountain's cool water. "Public artwork always enhances a neighborhood, don't you think?" she asked the boy with the broom.

"If you call that art, you're touched in the head," he answered.

"I've been accused of worse."

The boy looked confused but didn't offer any further conversation, so neither did Zae. She found herself wondering again what made the missing artifact so important, but there were more immediate things needing her attention. Drying her fingers on her breeches, she went off to help Keren unpack.

Inside, the flat reminded Zae of a home she'd briefly occupied in Wispil, though scaled up to human size. The front room was spacious and rectangular, with a hearth built into the left-hand wall, a dining table pleasingly centered, and a parlor to the right. Straight through, past the table, was an archway with a rounded-top door, currently open to a single bedroom. Appleslayer had already made himself at home under the table, resting with his front legs extended in front of him on the floor and his tail thumping eagerly, as if waiting for his dinner.

"Cozy, isn't it?" Zae asked him. He responded to her voice with a pleased whuff.

"Impressive," Keren answered from the doorway. "I was expecting barracks, or a dormitory. This is very generous. I certainly wasn't expecting this much privacy."

Zae glanced meaningfully toward the front window. "Yes . . . if you can call it that." She shook herself and joined Keren in the bedroom, climbing up on the bed to act the squire and help Keren out of her breastplate. "The neighbors are curious about us. I hope the last guests of Iomedae to lodge here weren't drunk and destructive, with wild parties all night."

Once her torso and arms were free of the armor, Keren stretched. She unbuckled one leg while Zae started on the other, "No, Justice, Honor, and Order usually aren't rowdy neighbors."

She sat heavily and patted a bare patch of quilt beside her, but Appleslayer leapt into the invited spot before Zae could take it.

"It looked like Justice, Honor, and Order were about to get rowdy this morning, when Veena wouldn't tell you anything."

Keren sobered and answered with a sigh. "Well."

"Well nothing. Talk to me. What was that about?"

Her knight frowned. "Something's going on, Veena knew it, and all I asked was to be sent into it prepared. How do I best serve honor and order: by keeping my mouth shut and honoring my superiors' orders even when it feels wrong, or by pointing it out when their orders aren't the best way to promote the edicts we serve?" Keren caught herself; Zae could practically see her shutting off the flow of words. "I'm sorry. I'm being petulant now. I just get so frustrated because I feel like I should be doing both those things at once."

This was not the first time they'd had this particular conversation. It had been the source of Keren's desire to transfer to Absalom in the first place. "No, it's fair to be frustrated. It feels like no one else around you has the same conflict of faith, between what you're ordered to do and what you feel is best, and you wonder if it means there's something wrong with you."

Keren nodded dully.

"I understand," Zae said, "but have you considered Veena's perspective?"

"That I've got to go into situations unprepared, to harden me enough to eventually send other people into situations unprepared?"

"No, that you've got to learn *why* people are sent into situations unprepared, so that you can eventually make decisions about whether to prepare people or not."

"All right. Why did she send us unprepared?"

"Because Veena knows you and believes in you, your intelligence, and your judgment. She knew you'd be able to handle yourself. You wouldn't have been able to fake that level of confusion. She knew you were safer knowing nothing and getting sent to the weak ghouls by someone who underestimated you, than knowing something and getting led right to the interrogators who would have been convinced that if you knew a little bit, you knew more."

"But—"

"Your Auntie Veena used you as a decoy because she trusted you, not because she didn't."

Keren rubbed her forehead. "I know that, on some level. It just doesn't resonate inside me. It feels like everything I survive without information just reinforces that it's all right to give me orders instead of information. I've been showing them what I'm made of all my life, but all they see is that I haven't died yet."

"Well, you're here now, so that's all about to change."

"All?"

"Not the not-having-died-yet part," Zae hastened to add.

That, finally, brought Keren a smile.

5

ALIVE AND TICKING

ZAE

Zae woke before Keren, as always, and crept out of the bedroom with the leather roll that contained her holy gears. These were the polished bronze cogs and tools with which she prayed to the goddess of clockwork and artifice.

Never having been formally educated in engineering—or anything else—she wasn't sure which spells to prepare for her first day of schooling. She used her best judgment, and with each spell she ticked her fingernail down another tooth of the gear she wore as a pendant. Delaying poison was always handy. Mending objects. Healing wounds. Detecting undead, if the previous day had been any guide. But what else?

She kept her healing kit in a square canvas satchel that had started its life as a gambeson. Its sturdy fabric and hard padding made it an ideal carryall for small vials. Each vial of potion, tonic, and spell component was fitted individually into an impression molded to its shape, and secured with a loop of canvas. A beltlike closure made each loop adjustable and easy to open in a hurry, but unlikely to come undone on its own. The bottles themselves were mostly opaque, coded by color and etched with runes and symbols that Zae could recognize by feel. Additional compartments held cutting tools, bandages, and other surgical instruments. Some were the traditional sort, like scalpels and suturing thread; others were her own inventions, or tools that, though originally improvised out of need and desperation, had thereafter made themselves indispensable.

By the time Keren was awake, Zae was dressed in her best leather breeches and long, brass-buttoned brown leather coat, with a white ruffled shirt peeking out between the lapels. She brushed her blue curls back and secured them with a comb, then made sure her satchel held her goggles and the acceptance letter.

"Have fun at clock school," Keren offered, and Zae beamed widely.

"You have fun at Iomedae school. And Apple, too. Train him to do fantastic things."

Keren touched Zae's nose with her fingertip, then tugged lightly on the ring pierced through the gnome's lower lip. "He'll be juggling on horseback by the time you get home tonight."

The way to the Clockwork Cathedral seemed straightforward, but Zae wasn't going there directly. The school was divided into cognates—student-run informal organizations that generally gathered their members around a particular theme. Based on her interests, a cognate had been suggested for her. She wanted to construct medical devices, and to her surprise, she wasn't alone. The healing cognate went by the name "Alive and Ticking," and was headquartered a few blocks from the cathedral in a shuttered old tea shop called Green and Gold, in the Merchants' Quarter. Its faded sign showed leaves in both its signature colors, with a twin-spouted teapot pouring water over both of them at once.

The door opened smoothly at Zae's push, without the foreboding creaks she expected from the rickety-looking entrance. Her entrance triggered the faint chime of a bell.

For all that the shop looked long-abandoned, Zae couldn't spot any dust. Everything seemed to be deliberately placed, and she wondered how many of the teapots and tins contained clockwork toys—or traps. Her fingers twitched toward them, but when the door closed behind her with a second faraway chime, a glint of light at her feet drew her attention away. A thin glowing silvery trail had appeared beneath her boots and now wound its way between the shelves to create a path.

Nothing else seemed to offer her any direction, so she followed it. The trail directed her past the rows of pots and tins of all shapes and sizes—the whimsical, the practical, and the beautiful all shelved together with no discernible rhyme or reason. She lifted a lid and peeked inside. Nothing. She tried a few more, but all the pots she opened were disappointingly empty. She decided to quit before she stumbled across one that wasn't.

The path, meanwhile, had grown insistent; the pale silvery light turned orange and schooled around her boots like hungry fish. Kneeling, she discovered that the path was made of luminous powder, and that a series of very fine, very shallow tracks notched the scuffed wooden floor. When the tracks rose nearly flush with the floorboards, moved by some unseen device, the clear powder in the tracks was pushed upward and activated somehow, following the carved patterns to make intricate designs. The track must have been flexible, to rise bit by bit, triggered by her step and knowing where she had paused. She was tempted to step off the path to see what it did to direct her back, but she worried that stepping off the path would mark the failure of some initiation test. What if the trail would simply give up on her, her only chance lost? She had dreamed about this opportunity for too long to allow that to happen.

Zae's magical senses detected nothing malicious about the path or the powder, so she steeled herself with a deep breath, straightened, and followed. The path led behind the former shopkeep's counter and she hesitated, conscious of violating the personal space of a long-gone proprietor. The powder turned bronze, the color of Brigh, as if to reassure her that it would be all right, so she pressed on. When she turned the corner, the path came to an abrupt end at a closed wooden door behind the counter.

Zae rested her fingers on the ornate lever-style handle for a few moments, savoring the anticipation. Then, she pushed down on the handle.

It was locked.

She tried it again, and this time, despite the adrenaline pounding in her ears, she listened.

Not locked. No. It was jammed.

Well, then. Locked and jammed were completely different things. One said, "Stay out!" and the other said, "If you can fix me, I'll let you in." And Zae was good at fixing things.

She set her satchel down on a plain, non-glowing span of floorboard, pushed her acceptance letter out of the way, and reached past it for her roll of tools. "Let's see what we can do about you."

Removing the door lever was the first step. The screws holding it in place were well hidden, flush with the surface and covered with paint to obscure their grooves. Zae had to scrape them clean first, and only then could she fit a tool to them and, with significant strength, get them loose.

Without the screws, the assembly came away easily. She set it aside, carefully placing the screws where they wouldn't roll off.

Inside its housing, the mechanism of a door latch was usually simple. Not this door latch. It was nothing short of clockwork, which made it the first real, solid proof that she'd come to the right place. Something swelled inside her. Some combination of joy and adventure and joy at *having* an adventure.

Zae put on her goggles and flicked tiny levers on the sides to amplify their magnification. Now she could see the tiny gears more clearly. They were exquisite, and markedly similar to the gears in the construct that Apple had torn apart. She traced their workings from one to the next until she made her way to a particular gear with teeth too worn to catch against its neighbor.

With a surgeon's precision and patience, she took apart the entire structure, setting everything down in careful order so that she could put it back together, until she got to the worn gear. She measured it. It was a nonstandard size, and with just the tools in her leather roll it would take her quite a while to make a new one. Unfortunately, it wasn't a matter of just fixing it. With the teeth so worn, there was no material at the edges for the next gear to find; there was no way for her to build it back up, with the tools she had at hand, that would be structurally sound enough to last.

The gnome sat back. Frustration teased at her, but she treated it like the worn gear and refused to give it purchase. She'd made things with odd-sized parts before. There had to be something in her bag that would work, even if it wasn't a perfect match.

She started laying out all her supplies in a neat spiral on the floor, digging past the acceptance letter in her satchel to feel for bits and various types of containers. She kept her healing supplies in vials, her tools in pouches, and her machining components in tins, so that she could at least find the right kind of thing by touch. After the fifth or so time she jostled the parchment out of her way, she finally took it out and set it aside. It rolled, just a little, halted by the recessed track in the floor.

The seal on the parchment was gear-shaped, as Zae had noticed when she'd first opened it. She had assumed it to be wax, but now that she examined it more closely she saw that it was only coated in a thin layer of wax. Even if she'd been careless with it, it wouldn't have snapped like a proper seal. Its design, which she'd assumed was purely ornamental, was an outer ring with a smaller cog inside it. A miniature gear, just the right size for an overly convoluted miniature lock.

Carefully, the gnome freed the seal from the paper and snapped the inner ring free from the outer. A bit of buffing made it smooth and ready.

It fit.

With excitement buzzing through her, she forced herself to go slowly, putting the lock back together in the precise manner in which she'd taken it apart. When it was ready for its frontplate, everything fit back together perfectly. Zae tightened the final screws, put away all her things, and then gingerly tested the handle.

The door swung open on silent hinges, and the newest member of Alive and Ticking started down the stairs.

6

TEMPERING

KEREN

Keren fastened her cloak over her armor and set out with Appleslayer toward the Tempering Hall. She knew she didn't need the full suit to protect her against wooden swords, but after the welcome they had received the day before, she wasn't willing to leave herself completely vulnerable. As a compromise, she protected her torso, arms, and legs, but left her helmet, gorget, and pauldrons at home.

Her sword was a comforting weight at her side. While she was under orders not to engage, Tezryn had proven that whoever the other people seeking the artifact were, they were not under the same sort of constraint. This feeling of having her hands tied by mortal restrictions, yet not being certain whether following orders or breaking them would earn the displeasure of her god, was precisely the discomfort that had brought her to Absalom. She hoped to find a path of service better suited to her temperament.

The fountain Zae had remarked upon the evening before still looked like a sad pile of rotting oranges with water trickling out the top. It was clearer now that it was supposed to be a sculpture of artfully arranged stacks and bags of coins—representing the Merchants' Quarter, no doubt—but Keren knew she would never be able to see anything but oranges in the curved and wrinkled surfaces.

None of the neighbors on the quiet crescent were out and about, and the only sounds were distant ones; Keren wondered whether she was leaving home too early or too late to mingle with the locals. A shift of light across the way caught her eye, but when she looked toward the neighbor's front window where she had seen it, the curtains were closed.

Though perhaps only newly closed.

She followed the map they'd received the night before, retracing her steps with Appleslayer by her side. It was strangely quiet without Zae, and it was a menacing sort of strangeness. She was surprised to find she'd grown so accustomed to Zae's tendency to take place names literally that she was doing it herself. She passed a pub called the Smug Owl, but it was less amusing to contemplate what an owl might be smug about without the gnome by her side.

Keren skirted through the edge of the Coins, avoiding the central marketplace but passing a few street vendors and shops that were already open. She bought a doughy pastry stuffed with nuts and savory meat, and a few cubes of meat for Appleslayer. He ate quickly and nuzzled her hand to see if there was any more. She took her time, working on her pastry as she walked. The outskirts were quiet, and they took a leisurely pace.

The Tempering Hall, training ground for paladins and other holy warriors, was similar in architecture to the Seventh Church across the street. White, tall, and imposing, it glowed pink and orange with the last remnants of dawn fading to daylight in the clear sky.

She wondered how Iomedae had felt, returning from her test and seeing these streets, these buildings, with new eyes. She wondered how much ascension had changed her. She couldn't imagine godhood doing anything *but* changing a person.

"Rhinn . . . Any relation to Julian Rhinn, perchance?"

Keren strode beside her new trainer, Appleslayer padding along obediently at her heel. She had known this would come, but hadn't expected it so soon. "He was my father."

"He taught me battle strategy at the War College. A fine man and a devoted knight." Evandor Malik was blond, thick with muscle, and gentle of face. He didn't seem surprised that Keren had used the past tense, and that at least was a relief. Keren had been raised among soldiers and knights, and was comfortable with their outlook on death. A typical townsperson generally assumed that other people experienced no changes in their lives while they were out of sight, and simply carried on until seen again; there was a default assumption that they were alive and unchanged until proven otherwise. A soldier had to accept that anyone they had fought beside, trained beside, or drank beside might have fallen in battle at any time since. Word of a comrade's death, therefore, might not be welcome, but was never entirely a surprise.

"And now you're going to be training his progeny, so you've come full circle."

"Indeed, the thought occurred to me," he said, and Keren caught the faintest hint of a smile. She wished she could say she recognized him from the War College, but so many soldiers had gone through her father's classes. She could only be certain that he had not been in her year.

"Do you train the combat mounts, as well?" While Appleslayer was technically Zae's mount, he was also Keren's battle companion. The Tempering Hall trained all manner of beasts for combat, and if the signs were correct, combat was something they were sure to see again soon.

Evandor led Keren to an open archway toward the end of the long hall, and gestured for her to enter. "Not I. This is the way to our stables, where your lively young chap here will be receiving his training."

Keren knelt to ruffle Appleslayer's ears and meet his trusting gaze. "Listen and obey, yes?"

The dog parted his jaws, tongue lolling out in a smile.

"Good boy." She stood, gestured for Apple to heel, and continued on.

The hallway led to an interior courtyard, where an elven woman in leather armor was practicing lunges with a wooden training sword against an unarmed opponent. Though the courtyard was ringed with occupied horse stalls, the unpleasant odor Keren associated with stables was strangely absent.

"Sula Charish," Evandor said. "Houndmaster. She's one of our best."

They waited for Sula to finish sparring. The woman's movements flowed like water, with a confident grace that could wear down rocks or opponents with equal tenacity. Much of Keren's prowess was rooted in her strength and endurance, but Sula's was in her reflexes and speed. Keren found herself wanting badly to spar with the trainer, yet fearing it at the same time. The unarmed opponent anticipated her moves, dodging and weaving, but after a few minutes it was clear to Keren that Sula was holding back. It looked more as if they were dancing a choreographed routine.

Something subtle changed, nothing that Keren could identify any more precisely than just a feeling in the air, and the dance became a fight. Sula's movements were still fluid and sure, but now her opponent was flustered, hesitating a bit too long here and only barely rolling away from the wooden blade there. She tapped him across the back and a voice called, "Hit!"

It belonged to another onlooker, one whose stillness Keren hadn't noticed behind the motion of trainer and trainee.

The bout ended with a clasp of hands and a few exchanged words. The unarmed man strolled toward the onlooker, nodded to him, and exited through a door at the far side of the courtyard. When Sula put up her sword and turned to them, it was clear she'd been aware of their silent presence for some time. At Sula's gesture, Keren walked Appleslayer over to her, where the elf extended her palm for his inspection. Up close, Keren looked for beads of sweat on Sula's forehead or chest, but saw none. It was as if the bout had been no more than a stretching exercise to her.

Appleslayer's plumed tail wagged fiercely, and he sat sejant—his front upright but his haunches on the ground, like a great heraldic lion—with the quiet whuff he made under his breath when he was deciding whether or not to bark in earnest.

Sula dropped to a partial crouch and put her hands out, palms toward the ground. Apple immediately mimicked her pose, barking happily. The elf grinned at him, and Keren felt some small pride in the dog that he recognized the invitation to play. Sula lunged toward him and he bounded back, then circled her in ridiculous leaps and hops. She feinted a few more times, watching his reactions carefully, then leapt after him and started a brisk game of chasing, tackling, and chasing again. This was rougher than the dog could play with his little gnome, and he ran and played at his full capacity, wagging and bouncing and returning for more each time she let him go. Keren knew how to train horses, and had been able to teach Apple a few of the basic commands, but she hadn't spent enough time around dogs to know how to play with them. At least, not like this. Now, she was resolved to learn.

While they ran about, the man who had refereed the sparring circled the ring to join Keren and Evandor. He was slight, all wiry muscle and smooth skin, a little taller than Keren, with black hair so thick that it held itself in a plait down his back without need for a clasp. He wore garments of simple white and brown cloth and his feet were bare. A rough, undyed canvas satchel hung over his shoulder.

"Crusader Rhinn, this is Omari," Evandor said. "Omari trains at the Irorium, the arena dedicated to the god Irori, over in the Foreign Quarter. He finds our ways too crude to train here, but he brings over his brethren for sparring practice."

"It's mutually beneficial," Omari said. He had sized Keren up from across the ring, and apparently felt no further need to look at her. His sharp gaze followed the elf and the dog. "You armored crusaders don't get much practice with opponents who fight unarmed, and if we're to learn to dodge a sword then we are honored to learn from the best. Houndmaster Charish teaches animals to fight, so who better to teach humility to overconfident men and women?"

"You're suggesting your students are dogs?" Keren asked.

"I believe that comparing ourselves to dogs is one of many ways to know ourselves better."

Irori was the god of perfection, Keren recalled, and everything about his servant reflected him. She wondered if she reflected Iomedae so clearly.

Keren had never seen Appleslayer worn out before, but eventually he flopped over onto his side, tongue lolling and barrel chest heaving. Sula stroked his coat and murmured something to him that made his tail thump happily against the ground, then brushed her hands off on her thighs and approached the three humans, her breath barely quickened.

"He's a gem. Where did you find him?"

Keren considered tempering her answer for a moment, but decided that Sula's response to the unaltered truth would be interestingly telling. "Undergoing surgery in my kitchen, in Lastwall. After which he destroyed a basket of apples, which is how he got the name Appleslayer." The trainer's face remained impressively neutral, so Keren continued. "My companion is a healer. She stitched him up, and I helped train him as her riding dog. He's got some combat experience, and he's a good mount, but I've trained him as far as I can—he's no a horse. I'm happy to turn him over to someone who specializes in dogs."

To Sula's credit, her only reaction to the story was the slight lift of one eyebrow. "I'm happy to work with him. Come by when you're finished for the day and we'll chat. Evan, don't work her so hard that she forgets."

Keren turned to Evandor in time to see that faint grin pass across his face again. "You have my word. Shall we?"

Keren exchanged farewells and followed him from the courtyard. To Keren's surprise, he led her not to another training yard, but toward the street.

"Given up on me already?" she asked, only half jesting.

"Hardly. We're going for a walk."

"A walk?"

Something in Keren's expression made him laugh. "It's not a trap, Rhinn. Just a walk. You're not as simple a creature as the dog. I'm not going to just teach you tricks and hope they'll come in handy someday. First we discuss. Then we move into the field. So. I know what you're looking to learn. Now I want to hear it in your words."

Keren couldn't fault his logic. She stepped out into the sunlight, squinting while her eyes adjusted. "I've been trained in mounted combat and foot combat. I'm a Knight of Ozem, dedicated to Iomedae in word and deed, but I'd like to . . ." She made a gesture with her hand, but even she didn't know what it meant, so it was futile to think Evandor might interpret it.

Yet, he did. "In word and deed. But in spirit?"

"It brings me shame to say it, but I've never felt that spiritual connection for myself. I believe in her, I devote myself to her. I was born to do so, and I don't regret my path. But the more I see how Zae—my companion—communes so fully with her god, and channels her holy energy . . ."

"And so you've made your pilgrimage here, to where Iomedae ascended, to find that kind of connection."

Keren nodded. "Partly. And even here, I feel immense awe, but I don't feel . . . Her."

"Partly, you say. And the other part?"

"It's hard to say this without feeling like I'm either whining or a heretic."

"Go on."

"I find . . . Increasingly, I find that I don't see eye to eye with my superiors on matters of strategy or resource allocation."

Evandor rubbed his stubbled chin. "Those are their words, not yours. Don't talk to me as a diplomat or a subordinate. Talk to me as Keren Rhinn."

Keren dipped her head. "I can't turn off my thinking mind to follow orders, and I know our Lady wouldn't want me to. But it feels increasingly that it's what's expected of me. I can't serve heart and soul when I don't trust that the mortals in charge are ordering the best course of action. And when there's a rift between my interpretation of what's right and the interpretations of others, I get stubborn, and then I feel guilty about being stubborn. I've been so well trained to follow orders that I hesitate to trust my own instinct anymore, but if I can't trust my superiors and I can't trust myself, how can I operate at my best?"

"If you were in charge of a unit, would you feel the same?"

She hesitated, giving the question serious thought. "I'm afraid I would. I'd still be fighting the battles I'm told to fight, rather than the injustice I see. Does that sound hopelessly arrogant?"

"I'd say it sounds too timid."

Keren blinked. "Sir?"

"You say Iomedae doesn't speak to you, yet you feel an indefinable wrongness about standing watch and following orders. Have you never considered that your unease might be a sign from her that you're meant for other things? Your dilemma is not unique, Crusader Rhinn. There are those who thrive as a small part of a larger body. It makes them feel complete. But others feel as you do, and thrive with autonomy. There's no shame in it, merely a different path to honor. We'll work together to find out how you might serve her best."

Shame flushed Keren's cheeks. A soldier didn't blush, but there it was. "Yes, sir. Thank you, sir."

"Well, now. There are a few routes open to you. Tell me, for what purpose do you want to be her conduit?"

Keren paused to set her words in order, but only briefly. They were already loud in her heart. "To root out the enemies of the order. Waiting for them to come to us . . . I don't think it's what I'm made for. Defending Lastwall, keeping vigil over the Whispering Tyrant and the orcs of Belkzen—it's all important, I'm not saying it's not."

"But you're a crusader, and you yearn to crusade."

"Yes, sir. But when my brother left for the crusade against the Worldwound, it angered my father and they never spoke again."

"Ah. And that looms over you when you have these thoughts." They reached a corner, and the knight indicated the way with his hand. "Very good. We'll examine this further. But first, there are things you should see."

"What kind of—"

The two knights turned, and the Starstone Cathedral now loomed tall at the end of a broad avenue. Keren had not taken the guards' advice and gone to stare at the cathedral the night before, but even if she had, she doubted it would have at all diminished the queasy awe it inspired in her stomach in its full daylight splendor: massive and gleaming white, with spires that stretched confidently toward the heavens.

"Well, that, for one." Evandor seemed unruffled, and was staid enough not to mock her for being overwhelmed.

Keren shook her head, still transfixed. "How long does it take before you can walk past this every day like it's a normal thing?"

"'Normal' is a bit generous, but after passing it for about a month, you start to expect it. It still affects us, but the ways in which it affects us evolve. You'll find the same, especially as your training progresses."

"I'll have to take your word on that for now."

"Fair enough. Now, I know it's a tall order, but I need you to tear your gaze away and look at what's in front of you."

Keren made a face, but brought her focus down to street level. Stretching before them was a crowded market bazaar with tents and booths lining both sides of a broad avenue. A constant rush of sound grew louder as they approached. "Street fair?" she asked.

"Permanent fixture. This is the God's Market, and it's where vendors try to make coin off the tourists, the pilgrims, and the hopefuls."

"Hopefuls? So people still try to take the Test of the Starstone?"

"Oh, yes. Many of them. The Avenue of the Hopeful, the street that feeds into this market, is where the aspirants live and gather their followings while they prepare for the test. Farther down that way, there's a whole shrine that's just the names of the fallen. It's incredibly sobering. Of course, every aspirant believes themselves the exception and is convinced they'll be the next new god, even though only three people in history have ever succeeded."

"I wouldn't take those odds," Keren agreed. They joined the crowd and let themselves be swept along at a snail's pace. The scent of grilling meat combined with the sweat of bodies and the faint salt of the sea. Some vendors worked the crowd and interacted with the passersby, while others stood in the shade of their tents and let young children hawk their wares for them, their high voices cutting over the din of the crowd and leaving the stall-keepers free to converse with more serious customers.

Evandor set a browsing pace, and Keren took the opportunity to peer into stalls as well as to watch the shifting crowd.

She saw statuettes of many of the gods, holy water, religious clothing and texts. Some of the vendor stalls were minimal: portable carts, or blankets, or tables open to the air. Others were more showy, with tents and banners, or actual reinforced roofs for shade.

To her right, a stall sold enameled replicas of the Starstone Cathedral, and boxy canvases with sketches and painted scenes of the market and its centerpiece. To her left, a vendor was proudly offering a handkerchief used by Cayden Cailean himself—unwashed, of course, and stiffened with the ascended god's mortal snot. Keren willed her expression to remain neutral. Inwardly, part of her was repulsed, but part of her wanted nothing so much as to find Zae and tell her about it.

Another tent, emblazoned with a large sign that read "Estelle's Last Hope Mercantile," also featured supposed relics. Keren had to concede that it was *possible* that a newly ascended god might not have need for his worldly belongings, and might not care if his home was looted by scavengers eager to make coin on his last mortal goods . . . but the spiral of petrified orange peel on the near shelf was unlikely to actually be over a thousand years old, and was more likely the remains of a snack purloined from the fruit seller across the way. There seemed to be no rhyme or order to the contents of each stall; they appeared merely to be whatever bits and bobs the seller could get his or her hands on.

"Jarid," Evandor greeted the stall's rotund merchant while Keren browsed. "Staying out of the Graycloaks' hair?"

"As always, Sword Knight. As always. Oh—may I interest you in this fine artifact of your own goddess?" He rummaged under the table. "I've been saving this for someone truly devout such as yourself. Ah, here. This may look like a simple scrap of scarlet cloth to you, but I've had it verified from three scholarly sources that this, my friend, is a piece of Iomedae's own sock. For you, her devoted servant, I could pass it to your safe keeping for a very reasonable price."

Without touching the sweat-stained rag, Evandor leaned over as if examining it closely while considering it too holy to actually touch. "A rare find indeed," he agreed, straightening, "but undoubtedly too rich for a stipend such as mine. You honor me by showing it to me, friend."

Undeterred, Jarid stowed the rag back where it came from, and gestured grandly to a stoneware jar. "And do you know what this is?"

"Cinnamon from Calistria's own cupboard?" Keren ventured.

"No, dear lady. This is a Bloodstone of Arazni! Yes, the very spleen of the Lich Queen herself. And for the Sword Knight, an excellent bargain."

Keren didn't make eye contact with Evandor; she couldn't trust herself to keep her expression schooled. "Fascinating. You truly have an impressive array of rare and precious goods." But since Jarid was on such familiar terms with Evandor, it was obvious he was toying with them deliberately. He bowed in their direction and excused himself to lure in another pair of more serious customers.

They moved on. "I don't understand. How can the enforcers let them operate, peddling fake artifacts as the real thing? Isn't this all offensive to the gods?"

"The hawking is a formality only. All this is just amusement; spectacle for the crowd. I doubt anyone, even the newest visitor, thinks any of these are real. They're novelties, sold to those who are amused by novelties. Real artifacts, on the whole, aren't for sale in the open air. Which is not to say that nothing here is of value. Plenty of these goods are real magical items. If nothing here had value, no one would buy and the market wouldn't survive. It's a matter of knowing where to shop. The flashier tents and stalls have the flashier goods. The smaller, nondescript tents are where you'll find the real magic."

Keren noticed a shift as they neared the cathedral, from stalls selling artifacts of ascended gods to sellers of potions, boons, and lucky trinkets meant to assist the ascending hopefuls themselves. "You mentioned Graycloaks?" she asked.

"The city watch of the Ascended Court. Here in the heart of the religious district, order is maintained by atheists who proclaim no allegiance. They wear unadorned gray to further stress that their loyalty is to no god."

"They must find this all absurd, then."

"Some look upon it as the desperation of the gullible. Others simply find it a good way to make a living."

"What's the desperation of the gullible, Sword Knight?" a gentle male voice cut in alongside them.

The speaker was human and slight. She recognized him immediately as Sula's observer from the courtyard.

"Crusader Rhinn, you remember Omari."

"A pleasure," Keren said.

"And likewise. Enjoy your tour of Absalom Rhinn. And your wooden swords. Be sure to come by the Irorium when you're ready for a real challenge."

"Are you still here, stealing my people? Haven't you ascended yet?" There was no malice in Evandor's voice. Omari laughed.

"When the time is right, and not a moment before." He bowed gracefully to both of them, winked at Keren, and backed away into the crowd. She scanned the market for him, but couldn't see where he'd gone.

"There's undoubtedly a story there," Keren said.

Evandor's laugh was robust and genuine, coming from deep in his belly. "The Tempering Hall isn't just for Iomedaeans. As I mentioned this morning, Omari came to us for training several months back, but lost patience with us and moved to the Irorium. Some of Irori's followers can be—how should I say this—ambitious about achieving enlightenment. It seems contradictory to me, but Omari embraces it. So he helps to train the unarmed fighters against us, and us against them."

"And he plans to ascend, you said?"

Evandor wandered toward a stall selling extravagantly expensive potions in cut crystal bottles. "He plans to try."

Keren picked a bottle at random and held it up to the light. Though it was difficult to see beyond the intricate bevels of the bottle, the pale blue liquid swirled with darker tendrils of suspended color.

"Oh, a good eye." A wizened halfling woman walked along the tabletop, inspecting the potion with Keren. "This one's for a cat's swiftness and grace. Quaff it and you'll be across the chasm without so much as a running start."

Keren set the bottle down. "It sounds wonderful. I'll be sure to keep it in mind." She left to rejoin Evandor before the seller could try to convince Keren of her need for it. "Are those potions just water with dye in them?" she asked him. "Some of them aren't even well mixed."

"There's a bit of potion in there. Diluted, of course, but enough to show an aura to anyone who tries to detect their magic. That's not to say that the potions do what she says they do, mind you, but as I mentioned, the people who are serious know to look beyond the showmanship to find the genuine articles. Ah. Watch yourself, now. Everything else we've seen might be exaggerated, but the pit really is as endless as they say."

Without realizing it, Keren had walked with Evandor nearly to the very edge of the street. It ended abruptly at a smooth curve of pavement that fell away to nothingness. Beyond a vast blankness that looked impossible to cross was the grand Starstone Cathedral, even more majestic in its unobstructed proximity. Keren tried to follow the wind-roughened cliff face of the endless pit downward with her eyes, but the cathedral's island at the center of the city defied her gaze. Before she had a chance to give heed to her vertigo, Evandor was already guiding her back from the edge.

"It's the spectacle," Keren said. "That's what you brought me here to see. How hopeless the quest for ascension is, and how much effort goes into making it something people can believe in. That if your mortal life is beyond hope and you have nothing left to lose, you can be the one to beat the odds and find all the power and glory you lack, with a thousand strangers cheering you on. That's why there's no railing. If you're foolish enough to get so lost in the dream of it, you've earned your fate."

They were silent for a few moments. Keren imagined she heard the wind howling through the endless chasm, but in truth she heard nothing but the dim roar of the market crowd at her back.

"That's the perspective your father would've taken away from it," Evandor noted. "Here's another: Iomedae breached this chasm. Look at it for yourself. Stripped of all the trickery and superstition, our mortal minds can only comprehend the impossibility of this task. So, in a metaphorical way—and a concrete one—this gap that seems so wide is only the first of an unknowable number of divides between we mortals and our gods." He touched her lightly on the shoulder. "Your first task is to contemplate that vastness. Mind that you don't fall in."

7

GREEN AND GOLD, AND ARTERIAL RED

KEREN

The clinks of small hammers on metal and the clicks of ratchets reached Zae's ears first, followed by the low, warm sound of comfortable chatter. No one stopped talking or gawked her way when she appeared at the turn in the stairwell, but one person, a young and beautiful halfling with tousled dark hair, extended his arm toward Zae and then curled it grandly back toward himself, summoning her inward. Everything was distorted in her vision, as if this really was all a dream. Then she realized she still had her goggles set for magnification, and eased them up off her eyes and into her azure curls.

About thirty people of all shapes, sizes, and ages milled about in a cellar that was as big as the upstairs, if not larger. Some sat around tables, looking over parchments decorated with diagrams and plans. Others worked on handheld devices alone or in small groups. Some wore colorful clothing, and some the drab garments of students and market-workers. Others wore the vestments of Brigh—the same sort of brown leather coat with brass buttons as Zae herself was wearing.

The halfling who had welcomed Zae down the stairs was still watching her with a coy smile even though he was involved in a conversation with three other students. She joined him, and the knot of comrades automatically flowed apart just enough to make room for her.

"Congratulations and welcome," the halfling said. His voice was more melodic than Zae expected, pleasantly rich with a lilt she couldn't place.

"Thank you!"

"Did you like the path?" The halfling pointed down. Zae's boots were rimed with the powder; its glow was quickly fading to nothing.

Zae laughed. "It was very nice! Is it the paper or the ink that the spell detects?"

"The ink. Pretty clever, isn't it? If you're looking for other first-timers, don't. It's just you today. This place works more on a continuum than a formal class setting. The machine keeps running while different parts are swapped in and out."

Zae could visualize this very easily in her head, and she grinned. "So swap me in."

The halfling laughed. "Come along, then. I'm Rowan."

"Zae," the gnome answered.

"Pleased to meet you. Where are you from, Zae?"

"Lastwall, most recently."

"Most recently?" Rowan winked. "Running from the law?"

Zae considered that for a moment. "Running *with* the law, more like it."

"Can I ask about your hardware?" Rowan touched his own lower lip, then pointed at Zae's. "Decorative or functional?"

She laughed, having forgotten the bubbly personalities of halflings, and brushed her hair aside to reveal the similar rings marching close in a line all the way up each ear. "There was a bet. I was keeping score with these, and after both ears I ran out of room."

"Congratulations and welcome!" a new voice cut in, before Rowan could respond with more questions. The dwarf was older, grizzled, with a voice that sounded like gravel worn smooth by time. His coat sported a brass button with the likeness of Brigh, just like the top button on Zae's own coat, and colored beads shone in his beard. Zae liked him already. "Renwick Graystone. I'm the leader of this cognate. Welcome."

Zae introduced herself. "You're faculty here?"

"Just an advanced student. There are five of us; we teach the rest of you, and also take more advanced courses of our own."

"It might be years before you see any actual faculty," Rowan added. "But don't worry. We're in good hands."

"Yes. I can certainly see that." Zae glanced toward Renwick's imposing hands, and was glad to be his ally.

"Did you bring a device?" Renwick asked.

"I brought a bunch."

"In that case, show me one you made to meet a specific need."

Zae quickly fumbled in her bag for it. "It's not a healing device, exactly, even though it's been used as one several times." She was set to continue with the story of how and why she'd made the divination orb that she now cradled in both hands, but at a gesture from Renwick she held her tongue and merely offered the plain bronze orb to the dwarf.

His smile was gentle, and his chuckle sounded like a trickle of granite easing loose from a distant mountain. "Discerning what it does and how you made it is my task now. Look around and get settled, while I spend some time on what makes this tick."

Zae hadn't realized that a crafted device would be her placement exam and interview rolled into one, but it made sense to her in afterthought. While she wished she'd known and had a chance to refine her device, she supposed it spoke more clearly of her abilities as it was. All the same, she felt a little lump in her throat as she watched Renwick carry it to a table, pull a jeweler's loupe down over one eye, and start his examination of her work.

"Duck!"

The shout from across the room pulled Zae from her spiraling thoughts. Without hesitation, she hit the floor. Rowan landed atop her in a jumble of cloth and limbs.

The audible whine came first, then a solid thunk.

"All clear." Where the warning had been a shout, this was a whimper. The room was a susurrus of clothing and expletives as thirty or so people rose from the floor, all looking around. A willowy elven man, the only person already upright and moving, was prying a circular saw blade out of the wall and cursing at it in several languages.

Rowan surveyed Zae from head to toe to make sure she was all right, then nodded. At such close range, all Zae could notice was that his eyelashes were extraordinarily long.

"Quick reflexes," he noted, brushing imaginary dust off her shoulders. "That's good. You'll need them. So, where were we? Oh! I was going to introduce you around a little."

Zae was pleased that Rowan's own curiosity led them first to the table from which the saw blade had flown. "Ask questions and look closely if you want to. Nobody worries about working on things in front of each other here because there's no ownership of our plans or inventions."

"Is that unusual?"

"It's a quirk of our cognate in particular, though some of the others have picked it up from us. The year I started here, there was a nasty rash of competitiveness that led to secrecy, that got, well, extreme. Distrust spells death when we're making things that people are supposed to be able to share and saves lives with. So we decided anything that helps to save lives should be available to anyone who can make it or use it."

Zae wasn't sure how she felt about this. She liked the idea of getting credit for her designs, but had never thought about what the logical extreme of that sort of mindset would be in such a close setting as this one. "Brigh encourages us to share what we know," she answered, supporting Rowan's premise without necessarily agreeing. She brushed the gear on her pendant with her palm, imagining she felt the warmth of approval in the birthmark that sprawled over the heel of her thumb.

Rowan beamed. "Exactly. Oh, and we're not completely healing-obsessed. If you come up with something that doesn't have a healing application and you want to try it out, you can still do that. It's a focus, not a mandate. Anyway, sometimes things that aren't designed for healing can still be used for healing."

The elf who had retrieved the saw blade was at a table with a woman with a bird on her shoulder. Their heads were bowed over a hand-cranked table saw that followed no schematic Zae had ever seen. As they watched, the elf jerked back from the saw, shaking out his hand and muttering under his breath.

"Or to make you *need* healing," the woman said. She was ready with a slender potion vial and a small square of cloth, and she offered these to the elf. He shook his head stubbornly and returned to his repairs, so she set items on the table within his reach. The whole exchange had the air of a longstanding routine. "Who's your friend, Rowan?"

"Zae, meet Ruby Tolmar. She's been here about a month. Ruby, this is Zae, who's ousting you as Newest Student."

With her long black hair tied back into a wavy fall down her back, striking blue eyes, and full red lips, Ruby looked like a classic illustration of a princess from a children's book, even in the casual homespun tunic and plain linen skirt she wore. But what captivated Zae even more was the mechanical hummingbird that shifted on the woman's shoulder with a brief whirring flutter of wings.

"Who's *your* friend?" Zae asked, nodding toward the bird. "She's beautiful."

It was intricate and lifelike beyond anything Zae had ever seen, and Zae had seen a lot of constructs in her day. At a glance, she could see at least eight shades of metal variegating the feathers, from a rosy pink gold through deep burnished brass. And the eyes, and the simple liveliness of its expressions! She found herself wanting to sit and watch it preen idly for hours.

A month, and Ruby had already created something so delicate and intricate. Zae suddenly felt less proud of her simple little orb. Was she even in the right place?

Ruby reached up to stroke a finger along the construct's narrow head, earning her a nuzzle. "This is Ouru, my familiar. I inherited her from my mother." The bird ignored them and groomed itself, clacking metal beak along metal wing through the movement of tiny gears. Zae's breath came a little easier now; the novice student hadn't constructed it herself.

"What are you working on?" Zae asked.

"Repairs," Ruby's companion responded dryly.

"We're trying to seat a healing spell in the mechanism of the saw, so that if it detects blood the blade stops spinning and the saw heals the wound that stopped it. But apparently we don't have it secured well enough. Get the blade going too fast and when it stops, momentum sends it flying. I think it just needs . . ." While her partner worked on returning the blade for another test, Ruby sketched out some improvements on a piece of parchment.

Zae stared at what she could see of the drawing for a moment, knowing that her own gears were turning visibly. "So, the blood triggers the stop, and the stop triggers the healing spell?"

"Almost," Ruby answered. "The blood triggers both those things at once."

"That's quite clever!"

"Not till we get it working. Now it's causing more injuries than it heals." She smiled at Zae. "But I think we've almost got it."

The elf interrupted with an explosive sigh and rapped his knuckles on the table. "More creation, less conversation. Or do I need to do this all myself?"

Rowan touched Zae's elbow with a slight hint of pressure meant to guide her away. "We'll let you get back to it."

"Pleasure to meet you both," Zae called over her shoulder. She had more questions, but she could see that it might be better to ask them another time.

They moved on, flitting about the room in a way that made Zae think of Ruby's bird flitting its wings. Just about as Zae was feeling saturated with new names and friendliness, Rowan gestured toward the edge of the room with a dramatic flourish. "Next stop, the sideboard."

"The sideboard?"

The sideboard was, indeed, just that. A shelf against the wall held a samovar and a precarious tower of cups and saucers. "One of the benefits of setting up in a former tea shop is never-ending tea. Renwick gets twitchy if you have tea on the table with an active project, but you can drink it here or take it to a table where no one's currently working."

There were a lot of rules in her cognate, Zae thought, but at least they were all rules that made sense. She glanced around the room, counting other tables and peering a bit more closely at their active projects. This inevitably led her gaze toward Renwick, who had her divination orb in halves and was studying some of its moving parts with two long tweezers.

"All right," she said. "What next?"

Rowan followed Zae's line of sight, nudged her shoulder with his, and took her by the hand, threading through the tables toward the opposite wall, like a ferret that had just caught a glint of light. "Best for last," he said. "The Gallery of Unfortunate Devices."

A glass-fronted display case which Zae, at a glance, had assumed held tools and works-in-progress, was actually a tour through the cognate's failed inventions. Each one was positioned proudly, with a small card proclaiming its intended function and its inventor's name in neat script. "The, um, unintended consequences are written on the back," Rowan said. "Some of us felt they ruined the aesthetics of the concept."

"More like, it's too embarrassing?"

Rowan coughed. "Like I said. Aesthetics."

Zae scanned the cards for familiar names. "Do you have anything in here?"

Rowan's cheeks flushed pinkish and he pointed to a monocle in an ornately filigreed silver housing on a lower shelf. "My first attempt. It's supposed to detect magic."

Zae canted her head and looked closer. Her fingers itched to open the cabinet and hold up the lens. "But it doesn't?"

"Oh, no. It does. Too well. It's built around a magic-detection spell, so . . ." He trailed off, waiting for Zae to make her own leap of reasoning. It hit her, and she straightened slowly.

"So . . . it always detects itself?"

Rowan beamed. "It's actually great with children, or the really drunk. You can convince them that there's magic *everywhere.*"

Zae laughed, and barely stopped herself from clapping with glee. "It's like a museum."

"It may very well become one, someday. Here . . . This is my latest." The halfling removed what looked like a mechanical worm from his pocket. "It's for leaving a trail for someone to follow. Not very elegant, I know. This is just my proof of concept. Anyway, it fragments off, and then each piece magically leads you to the next piece, until—" He straightened and cleared his throat.

"Not a bad device, Zae of Brigh," she heard from behind her. She whirled about, face to face with Renwick, who held her own orb reassembled in his hands. "Constructed on the go, I believe?"

Zae's nod was jerky, as if her head was so nervous that it stuttered on her neck. "On a boat," she supplied, cursing herself inwardly for the defensive note in her voice.

Renwick handed the device back as carefully as he'd taken it from her. "Your theory is sound, but your gears are imprecise. You cut them by hand, with a template, yes?"

"Yes." Those out-of-her-depth feelings started creeping up on her again. "And . . . on a boat."

He laughed. "It's all right. They're perfectly good for hand-cut gears. Have you done any hobbing or milling?"

"Not in years and years."

"Well, then your first lesson will be on the mill." He invited her to walk with him. "A gear is only as precise as its template. If one tooth on the template's a bit off, then all your gears will follow. The advantage of milling is that each tooth is cut with the same blade, so they'll always be precisely the same shape . . ."

The feeling of incompetence faded as Renwick instructed her. He spoke to her as an equal, and taught her the same way. Soon she had her goggles back down over her eyes and was creating gears that met his standards. Satisfied, he called one of the other students closer to watch her; Fidialory was another gnome, also a follower of Brigh, who looked barely past the age of maturity. A shock of purple hair sprouted from his head, just long enough to stand straight up on its own, and artful smudges of kohl made his eyebrows appear fixed in arches of surprise. He looked like he'd put his tongue to a motor. Zae idly wondered what that would feel like.

There was so much novelty here in this workroom, and yet so much familiarity, too. It had been many years since she had been in a room with other crafters like herself—since the little house in Wispil, now that she thought of it—and it filled her with an odd sort of warmth and confusion and fear that she might wake up and find herself the only one of her kind again. Being the only one of a thing was comfortable, something she was used to—even took enjoyment from—but it was a comfort she was willing to give up for the novelty of belonging.

She didn't realize her attention had drifted from the metal-cutting machine until pain blossomed in bright lights across her vision. Zae was familiar with the sting of air against a wound, but this was far beyond a simple sting. Reflex curled her fingers away from the blade and the raw pain shot up her arm all the way to her jaw.

Calmly, very slowly, she set the unfinished gear aside and reached into her satchel with her uninjured hand. The gear was slippery with blood—of which there was suddenly quite a lot—and Zae felt that certain mental numbness that sets in to lessen pain. She knew that the numbness always made rationality twist around on itself, but that didn't stop her from deciding that the mess on the workbench was by far the worst part of all of this.

"Oh no. Are you all right? Wait, wait!" the other gnome cried. "Glivia!" He beckoned to another of the students and a dwarf wearing green-lensed goggles came running so eagerly that Renwick snapped at her to take more care.

Glivia held out both hands to ask wordlessly for Zae's. She offered it, palm up. Glivia took it gently, turning it this way and that without touching the injured finger.

"Zae! What happened?" Rowan was at her side, wringing his hands. He looked like he might faint from concern, if not from actual squeamishness.

"It's not as bad as it looks," she assured him.

Glivia had done something to the pain. Now it only hurt when she curled her hand, so she abruptly stopped curling her hand. The dwarf was cleaning the wound with a feather-light touch, bent over it to keep it from her view. Zae studied the intricate braids that wove Glivia's blond hair to the back of her head.

"You've got quite a shard of metal lodged in here. Would you mind horribly if I asked you to leave it? I'm working on a project that uses metal to reinforce bone, and Renwick won't let me implant anyone yet. Will you be my test subject? Can I study how it heals with the metal in it?"

"Let me see it?" Zae asked.

Glivia moved aside at her request. In general, it was a good habit to shield a patient from anything too gory, but Zae knew she could handle it. Now, calmly, the gnome considered her finger. It had been a clean puncture. The shard, sharp at its point and all along the edge, had gone straight in through the fleshy pad of her fingertip, and it felt like the metal was thick enough that it probably wouldn't bend and force her pinky crooked. Though she took a few moments to turn over the request, she already knew what her response would be; the other student's enthusiasm was too joyous to deny.

"Can I heal around it?" Zae asked.

"Of course! Actually, allow me." Glivia wasn't a follower of Brigh, so her magic had a different flavor to it. It felt more like bricks reinforcing a wall than bronze heated in the sun.

Zae whispered a soft prayer to Brigh, thanking her for allowing another healer's touch. In moments, her fingertip was smooth and whole over the metal splint, though she still couldn't bend her finger and if she touched it she could feel the firmness beneath the skin. "Thank you. That was well done!"

"You're all right?"

"Of course. A sharp tool isn't really yours until it's drawn your blood. This means the workshop accepts me, that's all."

Glivia exchanged a grin with Rowan, who said, "Oh, yes. You'll fit in here just fine."

8

PENNIES FOR YOUR THOUGHTS

KEREN

Keren prayed to Iomedae for guidance at the edge of the pit, contemplating the unfathomable chasm and the Starstone Cathedral beyond it. Some Zae-esque part of her mind was still surprised there weren't more railings or other barriers around such a huge and obvious hazard, but she stood by the reason she had surmised to Evandor: Absalom, and even the gods themselves, didn't suffer fools gladly. They didn't step in to save people from themselves.

When hopefuls took the test, they had to traverse the chasm through some inventive means; if they succeeded, a bridge formed itself across the chasm, by which they could return to the mortal world in their new ascended state. Thus, there were three bridges, one for each ascended god. Keren had yet to step foot on Iomedae's bridge, but she made her way onto one of the others, contemplating both the pit and the Starstone Cathedral from the halfway vantage point. She couldn't even conceive of trying to cross the expanse without a bridge; she had never been afraid of heights, but she had also never stood over anything that was essentially infinitely high before. She was glad that at least the bridges had railings.

The Ascended Court district itself let her know when the noon hour arrived. One nearby cathedral's bells pealed the hour, and then others joined in. She closed her eyes, listening to the pantheistic song of call and response, and opened them when footfalls approached her. The bridges were open to all, but only a very small portion of the milling crowd ventured out onto them.

The vibrations of steps, which she could feel in her feet, were different from the vibration of the bells' song, which she could feel in her ribs.

Keren's shadow barely pooled around her boots, with the sun almost directly overhead. The feet that halted near hers were not Evandor's armored boots, but instead clad in aged leather. There was no specific moment where she decided to lift her head and turn on her heel, but instinct guided her and she spun. A dagger glinted right where she'd been a breath before.

Keren drew her sword and took a step back from her assailant. He was human, alive, youthful, and clad in a blousy tunic that mostly hid a close-fitting shell of leather armor underneath. Dark haired, clean-shaven, he fit so well with the noonday crowd that Keren could have passed him by several times already and not noticed him.

He feinted toward her. She backed away another step, and before he could take another swipe with his dagger two guards in gray cloaks were charging onto the bridge. Trapped between them and Keren, he had no way out but down. The boy peered over the edge, but didn't take the chance.

He offered no resistance to the Graycloaks. They searched him, finding several coin purses with their strings cut.

"Which one is yours, ma'am?" one of the guards asked Keren.

"It's not—" she started to protest, but the thief pointed one out with his chin.

"That one. The tawny leather. My apologies, ma'am. My brother and his friends said I had to, if I wanted to run with them. They said pick her, she got no stones." It seemed an odd thing, to confess to a gang initiation in front of the guards, but perhaps it was a lesser crime than outright assault. She wasn't familiar enough with Absalom's laws to know. She studied the boy's face more closely for hints of guile or remorse. When he caught her eye, he winked.

One of the guards pressed the pouch into her hands, and before she could find her voice to protest that it wasn't hers, they had turned the young man, taking him away. Nothing about this made sense. Why her? Why approach her in isolation on the bridge and not in the press of the crowd? She could only think that he had wanted to be caught; he'd wanted to hand her the pouch in a bold, public way. Why wouldn't he have just planted it on her person, if so? And the wink . . . the wink was so strange and brazen that already she was wondering if it had been her imagination.

This felt very wrong indeed. She hefted the purse, feeling its weight, and listened to it jingle with coin. Maybe this was some sort of an elaborate set-up to entangle her with the true owner of these coins. There could be a mark of ownership inside the pouch. Well. She wasn't going to inspect it out here. She set off toward the Seventh Church with purpose.

The scents wafting from the stalls on the way back up the avenue reminded Keren that she hadn't eaten since dawn. She had no desire for food but her hands and knees were shaking and the smell of meat made her stomach rumble. Most of the stalls had drawings of their varied goods, each with a price beside it. Keren pointed at a picture and handed over coins of her own—*not* from the strange coin purse—in exchange for grilled meat on a stick. Delicate spices and savory marinade couldn't hide the gamy flavor of what Keren suspected might be camel. She ate it slowly on her way back to the Seventh Church, playing the quick fight and the boy's wink over and over in her mind.

By the time she arrived at the church steps, the meat was gone and she was feeling more control over her limbs again. The two guards from the previous day recognized her and allowed her through in silence. She asked the first initiate she saw to tell Yenna Quoros of her arrival. Instead of standing idly and waiting for the priestess, Keren knelt before the statue of her goddess and passed the few minutes in prayer.

"Crusader Rhinn."

Keren stood. "Ma'am. Can we speak?"

Yenna spread her hands, as if to say *we're speaking already.* "What is it, Crusader?"

"I was approached at the Starstone Cathedral, ma'am. My assailant tried to make it look like a robbery gone wrong, to make sure I couldn't refuse this." She held out the purse with the cut strings. "If I'm being set up for something, I would prefer to open the pouch here, with you and the goddess as witnesses."

Where the priestess had seemed to be humoring her a moment before, now Keren had her complete attention. Yenna's silence stretched through several moments, and each felt as long as the Starstone chasm was wide. Then she sighed and turned. "Come."

Keren followed her back through the hallway to the same room they'd spoken in before. She gestured for Keren to sit and closed the door.

Keren sat, but Yenna did not.

"Let's see this pouch."

"Yes, ma'am." Keren opened the cut strings, widening the neck of soft leather, and then upended it slowly onto the writing desk. Coins spilled out, mostly thin copper coins of small denomination. They were stamped with the seals of different nations, and Keren recalled that Absalom rarely minted its own pennies, but rather redistributed whatever small coins were brought into the country by trade. To Keren's untrained eye, there might have been enough to buy a round of ale with; certainly not much more than that.

Yenna closed her hand around some sort of charm and murmured under her breath. She sorted through the coins, shifting them around on the desk in abstract eddies and swirls.

Keren, meanwhile, turned the pouch inside out and examined it for odd marks. "KF. And a sunburst sword like Iomedae's symbol."

Yenna's lips tightened. "Kala's pouch. You were right to bring it here. I'll make sure it gets back to her family." Out of the flattened pool of coins, the priestess plucked one penny, and then one more. She shifted the rest of the pile aside and set her findings down, turning them over to inspect both sides. Without another word, she swept the pair of coins into her palm and left the room with them. When she returned just a few minutes later, she was empty-handed.

"Is everything all right?" Keren asked.

"Those two coins have scrying spells set on them. I didn't want to say more in their presence."

Keren could have carried the coin purse with her and said any number of things in front of it, in public or in private, with no awareness whatsoever that she was being overheard. "What happens to the coins now?"

"Now, the high priestess will either destroy them, remove the spell, or use them to supply false information to their owners."

Keren sat back, suddenly finding herself irrationally distrustful of the remaining coins, too. "It doesn't make sense to me, why he'd be so blatant about it instead of just planting them on me. They're hardly effective for him now."

"It was a warning. They're showing us how easily they can access us, so that we know they could do it stealthily at any time. Did he say anything to you during the exchange?"

"Just that he'd been put up to it by older boys, and that I'd been his mark because I didn't have the stones."

Something Keren couldn't recognize crossed Yenna's face and abruptly fell back behind her calm exterior. "Are you certain that's exactly what he said? Stones, multiple?"

"I . . ." Now that she tried to think back on it specifically, she couldn't recall if he'd said multiple stones or if she'd just assumed it; the kind of stones mentioned in an insult usually came in pairs. "Ma'am, I'm still a target, and they mean for me to know it. I can report back to you more accurately if I have some context to work in. Let me and Zae be your eyes and ears, not just your distraction."

"Thank you, Crusader, but we have more experienced investigators already handling things."

Yenna swept the rest of the coins up efficiently and held her hand out for the pouch. As far as she was concerned, their business was concluded. Keren, however, did not agree. She found herself caught yet again between following orders that were right enough and doing what she knew was right for her. This time, remembering Evandor's encouragement, she decided to speak.

"And they know that, ma'am. They already know I know nothing. Today was just petty revenge, and they were willing to get someone caught just to insult me and threaten you. What happens tomorrow? They don't seem very organized or experienced. If they don't think I know what to look and listen for, they're more likely to let something slip."

Yenna met her eyes for a long, appraising moment. "Wait here."

Keren watched the priestess leave. It was several minutes before she returned, her face set and hard. "You must appreciate, Crusader Rhinn, that we don't share this lightly."

"I understand. I appreciate your faith and your trust."

Yenna turned toward the statue of the goddess and took a measured breath. Though she'd just spoken her reluctant decision to bring Keren into her confidence, she almost seemed to be looking for a sign to tell her she shouldn't. "When your assailant remarked about stones, he wasn't just being crude. He was alluding to the artifact we're seeking."

Keren watched the statue now, too. Iomedae's marble hands remained upon her sword hilt. Her carven expression was unchanged. "What is it?"

"Lady forgive us, it's a Bloodstone of Arazni."

For a moment, Keren forgot how to breathe.

9

CREATURE DISCOMFORTS

ZAE

Zae was surprised to see that the day had worn well into afternoon by the time she, Renwick, and several others emerged from the workshop. "Why the pretense with the cellar and the abandoned storefront?" Zae asked. "Why not an active tea shop?"

"No patrons means fewer accidental injuries. And we like the air of mystery," Renwick answered. "And the rent is cheap."

Rowan had appointed himself Zae's tour guide, and he led the brief jaunt to the Clockwork Cathedral building. Between herself, the halfling, and the dwarf, Zae enjoyed the novelty of being among people all near to her own height. It suddenly occurred to her that this was what humans must feel every day, and she wished she could somehow tell them all not to take it for granted.

The building was enormous, and Zae could instantly see why it was often described as a mechanical centipede with a clock tower stuck on its back. It seemed perfectly symmetrical, and so huge and so intricate at the same time—gothic arches, heavy iron plates, interlocking gears—that it seemed unlikely mortal hands could have, or *would* have, constructed it. The mythical Assembler, builder of the cathedral, was said by some to be a construct himself. Zae found herself inclined to believe it.

"Is there a reason why we don't hold classes here?" Zae asked as they ascended the steps to the vast double doors.

Renwick snorted. "We do, when we need the equipment here, but there are several reasons to do the bulk of our work off-site.

You'll see them for yourself soon enough. This building's not exactly what you'd call hospitable to living things. No, er, comforts."

"He means there's no privy," Rowan supplied.

"Among other things. No food preparation, no running water, no comfortable seats. No heating. It was built with machines in mind, not people. And then there are the gears."

A silence began to stretch out, during which Zae looked between her companions. "The gears?"

"Easiest to explain if you see for yourself first," Renwick said. "Rowan, it's her first day. Don't get her into any trouble you can't get her out of." They reached the first open corridor and the rest of the cognate turned down it, their receding footfalls echoing loudly in Zae's ears.

Rowan turned to her with a grin. "Let's have an adventure. Here—this way."

At least a dozen corridors sprouted to either side of the wide hall, making up the legs of the "centipede" shape of the cathedral. Slightly offset from each other, they were more like the legs of a walking centipede than a resting one. The main hall itself was decorated sparsely with display cases that highlighted student projects and innovations. No paintings or tapestries hung on the walls to absorb the reverberations of their footfalls and voices. Between each set of legs, the main hall was segmented by high pointed arches, buttressed with ornate curls of wrought iron. At the apex of each arch was a large black gear.

Zae felt as if she should be wearing a festive gown instead of practical leathers amid the somber grandeur. For a moment, she wanted nothing more than to hold a fancy ball in the grand hall. The acoustics would be spectacular.

Each side corridor was also segmented with bold iron arches, adding to the centipede illusion. The corridors were lined with doors, and when Rowan picked a corridor and made for the handle of the second door on the left, Zae couldn't tell if he'd chosen it deliberately or out of sheer randomness; there was nothing that, to her eye, served to visibly distinguish one from the next.

Inside was a workroom. All white, it had a high ceiling that gave the space a large and airy feel, despite a lack of windows. About a dozen workers sat on high stools at long tables. Some sketched with parchment and charcoal pencils, while others soldered and still others assembled parts. It looked more like a factory than a class.

A halfling in a white smock lifted a hand in greeting when he saw the pair of them at the door. "Come in, come in! We're working on our group project: a self-propelled ballista bolt. Today we've got two groups working on assembly of our prototype, and one group drawing schematics for a launcher."

"Isn't there already a launching device for ballista bolts?" Rowan asked from the doorway. "It's called a ballista?"

The instructor waved his hand dismissively. "What cognate are you from?"

"Alive and Ticking," Rowan answered.

"Ha! You dear souls from the Bandage Brigade clearly don't know anything about weaponry. Ballistae are heavy, ungainly things. What happens if you need to launch a bolt and you don't have a ballista nearby? No, our launcher will simply hold the bolt in one place so that it doesn't slide off course while it launches itself. A folding device, able to withstand the force the bolt will exert when it fires. It'll revolutionize warfare as we know it!"

Rowan said some faintly encouraging words of parting and retreated to the corridor. "It's an academy first and foremost," he reminded Zae. "We're encouraged to find new ways of doing things." Still, he didn't look as though he had much faith in the ballista-less ballistae. "Those were the Bronze Bombers you saw in there. Obviously, they're dedicated to projectile weaponry."

"He called us the Bandage Brigade?" Zae asked.

"That's what most of the other cognates call us. We also serve as the first aid squad for the whole of the academy. In fact, I've got a shift tomorrow night if you'd like to volunteer with me." They returned to the main hall and Rowan led the way down the center.

"And these groups work in here even though the cathedral is so inhospitable to living people?"

"Not so much inhospitable as it is completely indifferent. The large equipment is here. That's a compelling reason. But also, some cognates' work is more, ah, volatile than others. I'm sure you can imagine what would happen if your neighbors found out that you were building giant flying harpoons in your drawing room."

"Building *and* testing." Zae laughed. Canine surgery in the kitchen had gone over so well, the gnome could only imagine Keren's reaction to giant harpoons. "So the cathedral is safe and relatively explosion-proof?"

"Yes. Anyway, here we are at the Siren's Song cognate. Mechanically produced music is their interest. I won't open the door because they're very friendly—and trust me, you don't want to linger—but they're another example of a group that couldn't stay too long in one place without certain . . . isolating qualities."

"Well, you can't just dangle it in front of me like that!" Zae reached for the door handle herself; Rowan stepped back, covered his ears, and didn't try to stop her. As soon as the door was merely cracked ajar, the *plink-plink-plink* of music boxes assaulted Zae's ears. She had never thought to weaponize a music box, but if she were ever to need to, the current out-of-tune jangling of discordant melodies in competition with each other would have been the optimal way to attack. Rowan started to say something, but Zae shook her head; she couldn't hear him over the cacophony. He staggered forward and pushed the door shut with his weight.

"Soundproofing," he said. "It certainly works, doesn't it?"

Zae's ears rang. The sudden silence of the corridor felt as much like overbearing pressure on her eardrums as it did relief. Without another word, they returned to the main hall.

More staggered corridors, with no sense of what might be happening behind the many serene-looking doors. "Do all the cognates work here, at least part time? Are there assigned rooms?"

"Most of them at least dabble here, but some are better suited to special environments. There's a water cognate that meets down in the Puddles—you'd be surprised the aptitude the gillmen have for engineering—and they build strictly water-useful devices, so there's no point for them to meet this far inland."

Zae pondered that as they walked. "These corridors all run straight off this central centipede-body?"

"Only for a ways. Then most of them turn, some of them branch cul-de-sacs and dead ends, and a scant few of them lead into each other where it shouldn't seem to be possible. Oh—" he pulled at her arm. "Look!" A sound that she had mistaken for her own heartbeat pounding her ears, after the music room, turned out to be the footfalls of a rotund metal construct about the size of a housecat. This, like the message-construct that had delivered her acceptance letter, was exactly the sort of thing Appleslayer would see as a toy built just for his amusement. In her mind's eye she could see the dog tossing the construct in the air and skidding across the marble floor after it.

"They're cleaners and errand-runners. Like messenger pigeons, except that they remove debris instead of creating it."

Zae's fingers twitched. "How interesting! And they're fully automated?"

Rowan laughed and pulled her by the hand. "No taking apart the Thumpers. We call them that because of the noise they make when they walk. I don't even know if they have another name. Come quick, now. You'll want to see this."

The halfling took off at a sprint and Zae ran after him, nearly colliding when Rowan came to a halt. She turned to follow his gaze and found that the side corridor was completely shut off by a large iron grate. Or—not a grate. A *gear*. "Is this what I came quick to see?"

Rowan made a playful face at her. "We're a few moments early, but that's better than being late. You *never* want to be late in this building."

Zae put that advice away for later. The giant gear was moving, beginning to rotate aside at a stately pace, with far more grace and less noise than Zae would have expected. She watched it disappear into a channel in the side of the doorway and then reappear at the top of the arch.

Then people, six of them at Zae's quick count, shambled out from the arch. "What . . . ?"

"If a gear seals off a corridor, it can be sealed off for minutes or for days. There's no teleporting, no dimensional doors, no long-distance cries for help. The building is explosion-proof, both physically and magically. When a gear is down, there's no alternate way in or out, and you have no supplies but what you bring with you. Learning the timing cycle of the gears is what graduates a novice to become an advanced student."

"So why did *they* get stuck?" She gestured toward the band of students. Perhaps it was because of their haggard appearance, but none of them looked young or novice-like. Then again, Zae herself was proof novices could start their training at any age.

"Lots of reasons. On a deadline for a project, lost track of time, contest to see who can hold out the longest, or simply didn't listen when they were stood right here and given this very warning. It's not quite as dire for healers—a lot of us can conjure food and water—but we still shouldn't get cocky."

The engineers were pale and gaunt. They wore filthy white smocks, and it looked as if it had been days since their last shower or meal. Their eyes were sunken and surrounded by dark circles, and they glanced about with quick, paranoid glances like dogs coming out of hiding after a thunderstorm.

Zae's mind set to work. "Can't we leave a box of supplies in each lab . . . ?"

From the way Rowan shook his head before she'd even finished asking the question, she could see that such things had been tried before. "You've got a good heart, Zae of Brigh, but the Thumpers don't care. Plenty have tried to trick them and sneak supplies in one way or another, but the Thumpers seem to know what's meant for sustenance or luxury. They remove anything a construct would find unnecessary."

"It seems particularly cruel to take exactly the sort of person who *would* get immersed in something and forget to look up, give them everything they need to feed their obsession, and then punish them for getting too immersed to look up."

"Not cruel," Rowan said. "Indifferent."

At first she'd thought the exhausted engineers were all walking together in a tight knot, but as they neared Zae could see that two of the students were supporting a third, his arms across their shoulders and feet barely moving of their own accord.

"Do you need help?" she called. They all turned to her at the sound of her voice, then exchanged furtive glances with their stony eyes. "Do you need help?" she called again, taking a couple steps away from Rowan, ignoring his plucking at her sleeve. "We're healers! Hello?"

One of them, the one supporting the left side of his limp colleague, curved his cracked lips in an angry sneer. "Of course you are. Aren't you fortunate."

"Stay away, you scavengers," another one spat. White flecks foamed at the corners of his lips. "Starving us out, then stealing our ideas when our backs are turned, eh? I promise you, disturb our work and it'll be the last thing you ever do."

Zae rarely found herself at a loss for words, but just then she wasn't sure what to say. If she had been home in Lastwall, she would have treated the man for malnutrition and dehydration, and probably checked for a fever. To be accused of self-interest, even by someone who was obviously raving, stung more than she would have expected it to. At the same time, she couldn't force upon him healing that he didn't want. Could she?

He shuffled off with the rest of his group, and Rowan closed his hand around her arm to stay her.

"Shouldn't we give them water *now*?" She had found her voice, and it came out of her with an accusing tone she hadn't entirely intended. "I thought you said we were partly here to help the other cognates. Why aren't we going after them?"

"I did say that. But there's a certain degree of self-sufficiency and awareness this place requires of us. People who don't have it don't succeed here. The building itself culls them out. And those who do have it and survive being tested, well . . . sometimes they're bitter at those of us who have some of those tests a little easier."

Down the way, a quiet rasp of metal along a smooth track signaled that another corridor was closing. Zae wanted to go and watch it, but at the same time, she didn't.

"So," Rowan said. "The gears. It's important to learn the timing of the gears."

"So," she repeated, and cleared her throat. "Yes. The gears."

"Quite."

"All of them do this?"

"Oh, yes."

"And no privies, or kitchens, or windows?"

The halfling dipped his head in a slow nod. "Not so much as a cushion to be found. Don't come here alone until you've learned at least this main hallway, and don't ever venture alone into areas you haven't learned."

She turned her eyes slowly ceilingward, where the giant iron gears that moments ago had been a source of grand ambiance now nestled among the peaks and columns of the vaulted ceiling like guillotines poised to strike.

"Don't wander. Got it."

10

CRUSADERS AND CRUSADES

KEREN

Back at the Tempering Hall, in a large wood-floored studio, Keren and Evandor sparred. First with sword and shield, and then with swords alone. Keren was only slightly surprised to find herself an even match with the knight; she had dedicated herself to her sword skills, and could see that they had both learned to fight from the same masters—her father, and the other instructors at the War College in Lastwall. Evandor already knew that this was where she excelled and that magic was where she was untrained, but he had wanted to put her through her paces all the same. After the incident at the bridge and her meeting with Yenna, Keren was wound up enough to be grateful for the opportunity to expend some energy.

After, when Keren's skin and hair were wet with the sweat of exertion, Evandor wore only a faint sheen of it across his brow. He accepted water from a squire. "A good showing. Lest you think it, I didn't go lightly on you."

Keren hadn't seen anyone enter, but now that she looked around her, she saw that they had attracted a fair crowd around the edges. Two efficient young squires offered water to Keren also. They helped her out of her armor while the onlookers dispersed.

Attired in her loose cream-colored tunic and plain breeches, she suddenly felt quite small, as if she were standing before Evandor in her nightdress. The way he stood back and appraised her wasn't helping. She fidgeted with her sleeve, caught herself doing it, and shifted to parade rest instead.

"Your combat ability is beyond question, Rhinn. All the more reason those skills shouldn't be neglected while you're here. We don't want you to rust with disuse. No matter your path, your sword will still be essential. So. Let's talk about that path. On the floor, if you will. Flat on your back."

"Sir?" Keren found herself keenly aware of the distance between her hand and her sword.

"Good. You questioned it. I wasn't sure you would. We're going to take a page from Sula's book by giving you a change of perspective."

Warily, Keren lowered herself to the floorboards. Even more warily, she stretched out on her back with her arms at her sides.

Evandor paced around her with contemplative, slow strides.

"Before you learn," he said, "you'll need to unlearn. Your conflict isn't with your superiors, but with yourself. Look within yourself and tell me about your doubts."

"My doubts?"

"You've come to Absalom to find Iomedae's presence, but connecting with her isn't about going different places, it's about finding her within. You want the kind of connection your companion has with her god, but this isn't jealousy over her abilities. It's deeper. It isn't about how you compare to others, it's about what's within you."

What *was* within her, Keren wondered. Her father had distrusted magic; she had always assumed it was a path closed to her. She had respected her father, been proud of how others respected him, but that had led her to a desperation to please him, and a constant feeling that no matter how much she did, it would never be enough. Her brother had possessed the strength to act on what was within him, had followed the paths that Julian Rhinn forbade, and all it seemed to have gotten him was isolation from his family and a horrible death.

"Am I doing enough," she said out loud. Not as a question, but as an answer. "I always feel I'm not doing enough. I could be doing more. Doing better. Being better."

"What else?"

The dam had cracked; words could flow more easily now. Keren closed her eyes. "People say that when you feel a divine presence, you'll know. But when you ask them what it feels like, they say it's different for everyone. They can't tell you what it's like. I've never known what was real and what was my imagination."

"Have you prayed to Iomedae for that little extra edge in battle, and received it?"

This, at least, was familiar ground to Keren. "Many times. But I've never really known whether she's heard me, or whether the edge was mine and the praying just helped me focus."

"Does it matter whether she paints the brush stroke or guides your hand, if the result is the same?" His footfalls continued around her, loud when his boots passed her head.

"I don't know the answer to that. I think to some people, it matters a great deal. Look at all the things mortals say their gods have endorsed, when they haven't. How do I know if she's guiding my hand, or if I'm using her name like a shield and doing what I want to do anyway?"

"I suspect you do know, but you've been trained to doubt yourself. Your father trained me to be much the same."

Keren closed her eyes. She'd never spoken this candidly with anyone who had studied under Julian Rhinn. "All right. That's a fair point."

"More doubts."

"I worry that someday Zae will leave. Gnomes crave novelty, and what am I? A creature of law and routine."

"Do you love Zae?"

"Yes."

"Does Zae love you?"

"Yes."

"How certain are you?"

"Completely certain."

His footsteps halted. "Can you describe what being in love feels like?"

A moment too late, Keren saw where he had led her. She sighed and answered all the same. "It's different for everyone and when you feel it you'll know it."

Evandor started walking again. "There's a difference between being aware on an abstract level that people may not interpret a god's designs the same way, and deciding that since one commander gave you an order you didn't like, you're not going to follow orders anymore. The latter is how you fear people will see you."

"It is."

"As long as you hold fear and doubt in your head, you'll never be able to hear over their whispers. When you embrace your strengths and listen, you may be surprised by how close she's always been."

Keren thought about that, silent and still. Now that she was aware of them, she could hear the whispers of doubt for what they were. That didn't mean she knew how to silence them, but hopefully that would come.

"So. Sit up, if you would."

She opened her eyes, got her bearings, and pushed herself up with her hands until she was seated.

"Crusader Rhinn, this is what I've observed about you today: You're a good fighter. You're righteous. You have passion, but you keep your head. You're to be an agent of Iomedae, keeping her justice, but I need to trust that once you're filled with the power of that office, you won't decide to become an agent of Keren Rhinn instead. The biggest failing I see in inquisitors is a tendency to give in to their own power. Understand?"

Keren had never contemplated having enough power to even make such a thing a possibility. "I understand."

"I give you leave to shed the conflict between orders and instinct. You answer only to Iomedae now. This doesn't put you above the hierarchy of the church or your order—your superiors are still superior—but you are no longer a foot soldier in their army. You are not a defender, but a true crusader, to go forth and uphold Iomedae's edicts by any means that serve her ends while honoring what she stands for."

He held out a hand; she took it and let him pull her to her feet. "I can do that," she said.

"I suspect you can, at that." Evandor straightened. "Now. Have you ever cast a spell?"

"Never. I wouldn't know how."

"Performing divine magic isn't much different from calling on Iomedae in battle with those short prayers. Some swords are wielded with one hand and some require two; they might have different shapes, but they're all a blade and a place to put your grip. Yes? It's something you can already do and something you already understand."

Keren nodded again. "Thank you. That helps."

"Here. This is for you."

She held out her hand and he filled it with a small statuette of Iomedae's golden sunburst-and-sword symbol, on a thick leather thong. "This is your holy symbol," he said. "It will be your focus. Wear it someplace conspicuous, like around your neck or on your wrist, and never be without it."

She turned it over in her hands. It was carved, not cast, but she felt nothing particularly holy about it. "What distinguishes this from the statuettes we saw at the God's Market?"

"Spend some time with it, and maybe I'll ask you to answer that question for me someday. Tell me, when you make your small prayers in battle, how do you visualize what you ask for?"

The answer was something she'd never put into words, so it took her a moment to respond. "I think on the specific thing I'm trying to do, and how I need to execute it. I envision it like . . . like asking Iomedae to fortify a bridge before I cross it."

"Well put," he answered, surprising her; she thought she'd been clear as mud. "When you channel through the symbol, you're doing just that, but you're requesting that she create the destination at the other end of the bridge, as well."

"All right." That made a sparse dusting of sense, but Keren couldn't imagine how to frame it in her head to make it happen. "Why did you have me lie on the floor?"

He smiled, and a fleeting curve of his lips matched the warmth of his eyes. "In dog training, that position is a submissive one. It calms a frenzied dog and shows it that you have dominance over it. With people it's not so pronounced, but it brings a feeling of vulnerability. Of letting the walls down, if you will. Being safe in that vulnerable state helped you express vulnerable things."

"And you kept walking so that I would feel safe."

"Yes. So that even when I was silent, you would know where I was."

Few people in the world had ever been so concerned with Keren's own perception of her safety. Fewer could be trusted to make her vulnerable in order to show her that she was safe. Emotion swelled in her chest, and she could only nod.

"Now, we move onward, Crusader Rhinn. We're going to teach you to cast a spell—a very basic one for detecting magic. Be patient with yourself. This will be difficult, and will likely take some time to master, but know that it's within your grasp."

Keren collected Appleslayer and walked home. She wasn't sure what was headache, what was strain from trying to perform magic, and what was her imagination. She hadn't been able to cast the spell, and the whole process had been disorienting, but Evandor had seemed to think she was doing well regardless.

She found Zae in their kitchen and hugged her tightly in greeting. Her gnome looked a bit wild about the eyes, but otherwise none the worse for wear. Appleslayer, also pleased to see Zae, sniffed her all over and licked her face when she ruffled his ears. Inspection done, he turned his attention to the water bowl Zae had put out for him.

Water was put out for Keren too, in a manner of speaking. That is to say, it was already steeping in a tea service made of a deep red clay, fired but not glazed, with slender cups to match. "Here. I found these in the cupboard." Zae brought the tray out to the couch and poured for two. "You look like I feel. If you feel like I feel, then this will help."

Keren curled her hands around her teacup and inhaled the steam. It was strong, with faint notes of fruit and honey. "Thank you. How was your first day?"

"My mind is full and my finger is stiff," Zae answered. "How was your day?"

Keren blew across the surface of the tea, then sipped. "My mind is also full." She paused. "And my finger is . . . not stiff? Is that code for something?"

"I'll tell you about it later. Your day first!"

"Productive, I think? I don't entirely have words for my training yet, but I did learn what we're all wrapped up in."

"The artifact?" Zae handed over a bowl of thick barley stew. "Here. I didn't know when you'd be back, so I already ate." Keren set it on the table while the gnome settled in beside her. She realized she hadn't kissed Zae hello, and did so now, while she put her thoughts in order.

"The artifact. It won't mean much without context, and it's kind of a long, complicated story."

"I'm listening," Zae prompted. "Once upon a time . . . ?"

Keren settled back. It wasn't how she'd intended to start, but it made the telling easier and she went along with it, grateful for the detachment it offered. "Once upon a time, which for our purposes means about a thousand years ago, the god Aroden had a handmaiden. She was a demigod, and her name was Arazni. She was the patron of the Knights of Ozem."

"I thought Iomedae was the patron of your order, and isn't Arazni—"

"Now, yes. But this is a story about back when Arazni was our patron and Iomedae was mortal. She was a member of the order—the leader of it, in fact—but she wasn't a god yet."

"Okay. Go on." Zae had a cube of cheese in her hand, but was too rapt to remember it. Appleslayer padded into the front room, flopped himself down across Keren's feet, and nudged his nose at Zae's knee. She gave him the cheese.

"So." Keren wet her lips. They weren't yet to the hard part of the story, but foreknowledge of the words was already knotting her stomach. "So, it came to pass that Taldor launched what we call the Shining Crusade, uniting with the Knights of Ozem and the dwarves of Kraggodan to fight the Whispering Tyrant, the lich-king ruler of Ustalav."

"That's the guy you were patrolling against, back in Lastwall?" Zae asked. "The one who's slumbering but not actually dead, even now?"

Keren nodded. "Even now. That tells you how powerful he is. Well, at the time of the Shining Crusade, they didn't know he was that powerful, but they figured it out soon enough. Overwhelmed, the Knights of Ozem—"

"Led by mortal Iomedae?"

"Led by mortal Iomedae, the Knights of Ozem called Arazni to their aid. But the Tyrant was stronger than the Knights realized. He was not only stronger than the three combined forces, but he was stronger than Arazni, too. You'd think once a god, or even a demigod, joined the fight, it would be over fairly quickly. Maybe not in a few minutes, but certainly by the end of the day. No.

For five years, she helped them fight. And eventually the Tyrant captured her."

"He killed her?"

"Not at first." Keren uncurled one hand from her cup and then the other, stretching her fingers to unclench them, as if she could calm herself with will alone. "He tortured her first. Accounts differ on how long he tortured her, or exactly what he did. Then he killed her."

Zae looked up from her tea. "He killed a god."

"Demigod, technically. But yes."

"No wonder Vigil is so, well, *vigilant* about making sure he stays asleep."

Keren had made that same statement more than once. "Exactly. But he wasn't put down right away. The crusade went on. A few years later, at the Battle of Three Sorrows, the Tyrant threw her broken body out at her knights, to demoralize and distract them."

Zae winced. "I can't even imagine how I'd feel if someone took Brigh apart the way Apple took apart that construct." She reached down and rubbed the dog's head.

"I can't imagine it either. It's one of those things you learn about as a small child, and either it gives you nightmares for years and makes you vow to keep the Tyrant from ever getting that strong a foothold in the world again, or it makes you move and take up some other vocation entirely, very far away."

"And as the daughter of someone who'd made that vow and wasn't going anywhere . . ."

"Two someones who'd made that vow. Yes." It was out before she could stop herself. Keren never spoke about her mother, not to Zae or anyone else. Avoidance of the topic was another thing she had inherited from her father.

"Keren—" Zae offered her hand, for comfort.

Keren shook her head. There would be time for comfort later, curled up together in the dark. She thought about her training session earlier, about how being on her back had made her vulnerable and open. Maybe that was part of why pillow talk felt so intimate.

This was not a story she could tell while vulnerable.

"Arazni's knights laid her body to rest in state in Vigil, where their influence was strongest. Then they went on in their crusade against evil, in her name. Sixty-some years later, though, the Knights of Ozem again underestimated the strength of their enemy. By this time, they were fighting the evil necromancer Geb, who ruled over an undead country of the same name. Geb—the ruler, not the country—raised the Knights of Ozem he slew, called them graveknights, and ordered them to steal Arazni's corpse from its resting place. They brought her back to Geb, who reanimated her as a lich to be his plaything. He called her his Harlot Queen."

Zae's eyes shone wetly. She brushed a sleeve across her face and shook her head. "Liquid empathy. Sorry. As if that poor woman hadn't been through enough. Tortured by a creepy dead king, killed, stolen, brought back to be used by another creepy dead king. I've never been to Geb, partly because I'm small and tasty, but I've traveled through Nex . . ."

"And Nex has a long, bad history with its neighbor," Keren finished for her.

"Right. That's why I knew the name. Even now, Arazni rules Geb, while Geb himself—well, if stories are true, Geb-the-ruler spends all his eternal unlife obsessing about whether Nex will encroach on his borders again. But anyway. Arazni."

Keren drank her tea, which had gone cool. Zae refreshed the cup for her. Its warmth felt like the heat of life, and she clung to it. "Arazni. Yes. Once upon a time there was a lich queen named Arazni, who retained nothing of her former self. Over centuries, Geb had stripped away her goodness and humanity, turned her against her former life, and brought her to accept her new station. But Arazni, as a lich, had a weakness. Her internal organs were no longer internal. They had been removed during the . . ." She fumbled for the word.

"The liching process?" Zae supplied.

"I think I was going for 'ritual,' but yes. They had been removed in the liching process and stored in canopic jars. The Bloodstones of Arazni, they're called. One for each of her four vital organs. They say that the jars continually drip with her blood."

"Well, that's pleasant."

"Very. Anyway, now the Knights of Ozem come back into the story." Keren drank, wetting her throat, and took a moment to inhale the steam.

"Did they know Arazni was there? Did they try to rescue her?"

"Oh, yes. And yes. We've never given up, not really. But don't forget, the first knights to invade Geb were raised as graveknights for their trouble—her own elite army of corrupted, undead servants, made from the bodies of knights of her former order. Their souls aren't in their organs, like with Arazni, but in their armor. As long as the armor is intact, it will regenerate them again and again. They're made from people like me, to destroy people like me."

Zae stared. That liquid empathy she had mentioned was welling up again, and it threatened to spill down her cheeks. It touched Keren so much that she had to look away. "By the Bronze, Keren . . . And they teach this to you as *children*? How do they expect you to ever sleep?"

"When you grow up with these truths," she said quietly, "you find them woven into the very fiber of who you are. They form your heart, making you loyal to your cause. They form your spine, making you brave for your cause. They form your hands and feet, making you an instrument of your cause. It's so ingrained that, after a time, you stop thinking about the story because it's in your bones. You don't have to think about it for it to be with you in every moment."

Zae squeezed her arm. "And you surround yourself with other people who also live it, so you don't need you to explain it."

"Yes. So. The horror is there, but it feeds the conviction. Someday, we'll figure out how to get her back. We'll rescue her and put her to rest. We just haven't figured out how yet. Geb is too strong, and she's stuck under his thrall, so she doesn't want to go. Anyway, the point of all this is, the Knights of Ozem didn't manage to save her, but they managed to retrieve her canopic jars—the Bloodstones of Arazni—and they keep them hidden for a time when they might be used to revive her."

Zae stared. "Oh, I know where this is going, don't I?"

"I suspect you do."

"Someone's stolen one of these things, and the opposing side that's looking for them . . ."

"Answers to Arazni, yes."

Zae sat back, putting thoughts together. "I don't know what I find more strange: you knights of valor sneaking into the land of the undead to steal really old bodily organs, or someone wanting one enough to fight you for it. Do they do anything?"

"For you or me? Not very much. There's a blessing, I think, different blessings depending on which organ. Because she served Aroden, they contain a trace of his divine magic as well as her own. But if Arazni got them back, people believe she'd be as powerful as she was before. Among other things, that means she would have the power to slaughter all the knights of her former order and raise them as undead under her control, desecrating them and giving herself a powerful undead army." Keren reached out and ruffled Apple's ears. "For obvious reasons, that can't be allowed to happen."

"You have my full support and aid. If you had to be a lich, it would probably strain our relationship."

This was the sort of whimsical pragmatism that had attracted Keren to the gnome in the first place, and it had never worn off.

"Only probably?" She drew Zae into her arms and they spent the rest of the evening in cozy, vulnerable silence.

11

DRAFTED INTO DRAFTING

ZAE

Zae went about her usual morning routine, different only in that she poured two mugs of tea instead of preparing two and pouring one. Keren, who always rose later, had wanted the extra morning time to tell Zae about the pickpocket who'd gone to lengths to press a pouch upon her at the Starstone Cathedral the day before. It was alarming but, in light of the nature of the artifact and the complex relationship which Keren's order had with it, not surprising. When Zae showed Keren her finger, even though it had been healed over and there wasn't much to see, Keren sighed and declared them even.

"I'm glad Yenna trusted you, but what does this mean in terms of what we need to look out for? More undead people in alleys?"

"Most of Arazni's people aren't undead. Sometimes the living try to curry favor so that they can be well placed in Gebbite society when they die. Taking a mission like this, to secure one of her organs, would certainly be worth a lot of favor. Others are nationalists; regular people whose ancestors happened to have settled in Geb, and whose families have never moved."

"Anything becomes normal if you live with it long enough," Zae agreed. "Or if you're born to it."

They shared a moment of tender silence. Zae brushed brown hair back from Keren's temple, drinking in the strong lines of her cheek and jaw.

"But you asked how we can help." Keren leaned in to the touch for a moment before straightening. "Yenna said there are a lot of different rumors buzzing around, about where the Bloodstone is and what it's been stolen for."

"For instance?"

"For instance, that the necromancers of the Whispering Way want it, as leverage against Geb. There's also talk of it being used to power some new construct in the Clockwork Cathedral."

"Oh," Zae said. "I did see one group that was more secretive than most of the others. In fact, I've already promised to go back for a medic shift tonight. I can peek around then. Are we sure, though, that one of Arazni's people didn't steal it?"

"We're sure. They'd have taken it right back to her. They wouldn't still be milling around town with it."

"And there's no divining for it, I imagine, or they'd have done that already?"

Keren nodded. "Yenna couldn't say whether it's Arazni who's blocking our efforts, to keep us from finding the Bloodstone, or whether it's a property that was imbued into them when they were created, or if it's a protection Iomedae added later to help us keep them hidden. Even Arazni can only detect them when they're used—which means that the thief must have some sort of shielded container that keeps her from feeling the stone. No one else can detect them by magical means at all."

"Arazni . . . feels them?"

"They're still her internal organs. If the jars are out of whatever protections keep them hidden, supposedly she can feel them twinge, then send a graveknight to retrieve them."

"Wait. One of those nightmare things might be here?"

"Was here. Yes. I'm as pleased about that as you might expect. One showed up, which was how the order knew the Bloodstone was here. They drove it off, at great cost, but if the stone is uncovered again it'll be back. And on that cheery note . . ." Keren scraped her chair back. "It looks like breakfast is about to boil over."

Zae kissed her knight, they broke fast together—porridge with fruit and preserves stirred in—and Zae wandered off to pray to Brigh and prepare her spells for the day.

Yesterday, she had needed to heal herself and potentially others. Today, she added mending and other artifice spells, since she wasn't sure what sort of work Renwick would have her doing. Considering Keren's new information, she put a few others on the list as well.

Content with her choices, she closed her eyes and focused in prayer, thumb ticking the spells off on the teeth of her gear pendant, each in its turn. When she was finished, all was quiet. She peeked in on Keren, who seemed to be concentrating deeply, seated on the bed with her sword across her lap and something small held lightly in her hands.

Zae dressed quietly, kissed Appleslayer on the head, and left a hasty note on the table for Keren. Carefully, she eased open the front door, only to have her stealthy exit blocked by Apple, whining at being left behind.

"Aw, sweetie dog," she whispered, cradling his face in her hands and rubbing behind his ears. His muzzle parted, pink tongue lolling out, and his tail started up a hesitant but happy wag. "You'll go with Keren again today. You'll learn all sorts of fun dog stuff. Okay?"

Appleslayer huffed, a particularly expressive canine sigh, and licked Zae's nose. He sat back on his haunches and yawned, watching her leave. She still felt guilty, but she was certain that on some level the dog understood her. She knew he'd have fun playing with his trainer and learning tricks, so she didn't feel *that* guilty; not for long.

Zae was among the first to arrive at the tea shop cellar. Renwick, already halfway through a chipped cup of steaming tea, gestured toward the samovar and then invited Zae to join him. He had a stack of gears on the table in front of him, but apparently these didn't count as active work and could share a table with a couple of beverages. When she returned with a full mug, she saw that they were her gears from the previous day. At least, her initial was marked on them in grease pencil, and she hadn't yet met anyone else with a Z name in the cognate.

"How's your finger?" he asked her.

Zae's trepidation at being judged had eclipsed her memory, even though she'd told Keren about her injury just this morning, so it took a moment to realize what he meant. "Oh—back to working order, thank you. Glivia's looking forward to studying it. Are those my work?"

He lifted the topmost spur gear from the stack, turning it in the light. "And good work they are. You're a natural at it. Ever done wooden gears?"

"Of course."

"Cut whole or with inlaid teeth?"

"Both."

"Let's see some, then."

Zae fumbled around in her satchel and pulled out a velvet pouch. These were her ceremonial gears, because they were her best work and too precious to put into a device and never see again. She spilled them out onto the table and sorted them flat.

Some were simple, some were ornate. She had spur gears, worm gear sets, and planetary gears. Some of them, wooden and metal alike, were filigreed or engraved, or had intricate inlays of other materials.

Renwick's low whistle was better than praise. "You could make a living off these in some parts of the world."

"I have, from time to time. Not a terribly successful living, since I never want to sell the pretty ones."

The dwarf answered with a booming laugh. "I think you're sufficiently advanced to join the main student body. It's clear you don't need remedial instruction. We'll be over at the cathedral today, using some of the larger drills and presses. So, drink up, but don't drink too much."

Ruby was the next to arrive, her bird fluttering off her shoulder to fly a circuit of the room. It landed on her saw contraption from the day before, preening its pinfeathers and waiting for her to catch up. She spared a warm smile for Zae on her way to the samovar for tea.

The rest of the cognate gradually trickled in, arriving in the cellar and moving immediately toward the stack of cups and mugs on the sideboard. Zae listened for footfalls on the floorboards above, but heard none; each new arrival was a surprise, suggesting that the rickety cellar was at least as well reinforced as the cathedral workrooms themselves.

Rowan was one of the last to arrive, and he bounded down the stairs as if they were on fire. "Zae, Renwick, you'll never guess what happened. I got offered a commission from the city government. They want me to make them a device! Is it all right if I use cognate resources? It's kind of a rush job, and—"

Renwick held up one thick hand. Rowan stopped talking, pressing his lips together tightly. The halfling vibrated with the effort to keep still.

"Slower this time," Renwick requested, "and with breathing."

Rowan took a couple of slow breaths, glancing at the cognate's leader as if seeking his approval for them. Renwick nodded, and the halfling started again.

"I got a commission from the city government. This district councilor summoned me to a meeting and said they need a prototype for a weighted net that's magic-resistant, and something to carry it with to make it manageable despite the weightedness. It's so the city guard can detain wizards and sorcerers humanely, because it's hard to capture a fleeing caster without harming them. I reminded the councilor that I'm a healer, and she said they want healers building it to make sure it's humane and won't hurt the targets. 'The best way to heal someone is to not hurt them in the first place,' she said. I think that might have to become my own personal motto now."

Renwick tugged at his beard. "Interesting. Do you know how you're going to do it?"

"Not exactly."

"I know a smith who has a quantity of a noqual alloy on hand. He mentioned it to me last night over a pint. It's expensive, but it's got anti-magic properties. If your client is the city of Absalom . . ."

"Whoa," Glivia breathed. "Noqual's a skymetal. Do you want help? I've never worked with skymetal."

"I've got an advance to buy supplies. I get another payment when I show them my plans, and the final once the work is done," Rowan said. "What if I can hand in the plans after class? Where's your friend? It would be great if we could start drawing wire tonight. Zae's coming with me to do rounds. Who else wants to help? It'll be faster as a group, and I'll share the pay."

Zae was touched to be automatically volunteered without having to ask. It increased her sense of belonging even more. Noqual was rare enough to be nearly mythical in most parts of the world, since it only appeared when it fell literally from the sky in meteoric form, and she was as eager to try working with it—even with metal that only contained a bit of it—as the rest of her peers.

"All right. Here's what we'll do. Today's assignment will go ahead as planned, but Rowan and Zae, you'll use the net as your subject, and Ruby and Glivia, you'll take the net-carrying device. If we get plans that work, then tomorrow we'll start fabrication and construction. No rushing, people—these components won't be cheap. Let's do it right the first time."

Yesterday Zae had gone over to the cathedral with just a small group, but now they all trailed down the street in twos and threes. They gathered at the top of the stairs, clumping up into a single knot of students, and made their way inside together. Halfway down the main hall, Zae got an uncomfortable tingle down her spine. She stopped, extending her senses, and turned toward Renwick to see if he had felt it, too. He gestured with his chin; the massive iron gear was churning down into place across the main entryway. The others continued on, not seeming to notice or care that they were all now trapped.

Though the hollow feeling in the pit of Zae's stomach counted as a new experience, it wasn't a welcome one. It would be okay, though. She could make food and conjure water, and she was sure several of the others could, too, and . . .

"It's just a short cycle." Renwick's light touch on her elbow brought her back to herself. He prompted her to walk, leading her farther down the corridor. "It'll be out of the way in three hours, and we'll still be deep in our exercises then. You won't even notice."

Zae looked at the others, some of whom were still passing them at a comfortable stride. "They all know the cycle?"

"Nah. It's not like it's the same every day. You've got to observe a long time before you get a sense of the pattern. Learning the whole Cathedral is the test that separates the advanced students from the novices."

She remembered Rowan mentioning that, as well. "Then they place a great deal of trust in you."

Renwick scanned over the familiar faces. "Most of them. You'll note a few absences. They'll come along later, or they won't."

As always, it seemed the corridor at which her companions turned was chosen at random. Zae couldn't help but notice that it was next to the hall the suspicious, unwell engineers had come out of the day before. Once she got to the workroom, she could see why Renwick had chosen it.

Where the other corridors she'd seen so far were lined with doors to small classrooms, or classroom-sized workrooms, this corridor's rooms were lacking some interior walls. The space was more like a single long room than a suite of workshops. And the machines! There was a large stationary sawing machine that looked like a pillar, or a giant tree. Drills and presses with crank handles were bolted to the floor.

Renwick's booming bassoon voice gathered all the students back to him. "For this assignment, you will conceive of a new device, and you will design two different versions of it. Sometimes, a thing must be simple and straightforward; it must do its job, and not attract the eye. But sometimes, a thing must demonstrate great artistry and beauty. A true artificer can take any device and strip it down to its most necessary components, or embellish it until it is fit for display in a palace. So. Draft your idea. Those of you with specific assignments know who you are. The rest of you, it must be something you haven't made before. Design it once, with the greatest efficiency you can muster, and again for greatness of aesthetic. Both must be identically functional. You will find all the supplies you need on the shelves at the far end of the room."

Zae bounced on her toes. This was an incredibly advanced assignment, and that excited her. She had been worried that she would be spending months learning the theories behind things she already knew how to do, performing boring exercises with no worldly applications. Tasks like this were a true challenge, one that would stretch the mind and abilities of any engineer. Yes, she was most assuredly in the right place.

"Are you ready?" Rowan had slipped up right beside Zae without her noticing. Together they walked toward the drafting tables and picked two side by side. Rowan lifted the hinged tabletop of his, manipulated something inside it, and when he put the lid down the writing surface was lit from underneath. Zae tried to mimic his actions, and saw a round metal tin inside her table, about the size of her closed fist.

When she removed the lid, cool light shone forth. She lowered her tabletop. "That's brilliant. Is that a continuous light spell?"

Rowan grinned at her. "It's the simple things, right? You didn't answer me, by the way."

Under the table was a pullout drawer that contained parchment, writing implements, and some simple straight-edges and templates for circles and curves.

"Sorry." Zae selected a sheet of parchment and perused the drawing tools. "I'm ready, but distracted."

"Overwhelmed?"

"A little. And a little surprised by how no one seems to care that we're stuck in here."

"Making you a little claustrophobic? It does that. Here." Rowan tapped Zae's blank parchment. "Just focus and don't think about it. It'll be open before you know it."

Zae looked to her empty page, and then to Rowan's, as if she might draw more inspiration from his than from her own. "So, net. That means making wire. It has to be thin enough to be woven, but thick enough to keep from breaking or being broken easily."

"I was thinking of weaving three strands and seeing how strong it is, and going from there. If that's not enough, then a braid of three strand-of-threes."

Zae nodded and began sketching. "We'll have to try it out and see how anti-magic it is. It depends on the strength of the alloy, I guess."

The halfling beamed. "I know! I can't wait to see it. I've heard it's green. Gemstone green, not metal green or mold green. Do you think the wire will be green? Or will it be boring silver? It's probably mostly steel and just a little skymetal. I'll have to see."

"Will we still go on rounds tonight?"

"Yes! I'll take these drafts up after class and then go with Renwick to get the metal and then meet you back here? We're all gathering at the local pub after. Bring your special someone, if you have one. Oooh. You sketch really well."

Zae recalled Renwick admonishing the halfling to breathe, and grinned. "So, this is the single wire and this is the three-strand, and this is a net pattern that provides good coverage, and the weight can be distributed like this, so that it's extra heavy all around the edges but it'll still flare out when you throw it."

"That's really good, but do you think the weave is too open?"

Zae hastily scribbled a key down at the edge of the page, showing scale. "Not anymore!"

Next she started on her ornate design. This one was made of rings of wire instead, with some of them coated in different colors, on a backing of cloth to set it all off brightly.

"Won't the cloth weigh it down too much?" Rowan asked, peeking over from his own paper.

"More than the weights will? Probably not. And it solves the sticking-a-finger-through problem, right?"

"I forgot about the weights."

"We could just use a heavier metal, like make the last few rounds out of lead? That would distribute the extra weight evenly."

"But if the whole circumference is that heavy, it'll just plop straight down instead of unfurling. Here. What if . . ."

Zae decided that "what if" were her new favorite words. They were the shortest possible way to combine *I value your opinion* and *let's figure this out together.*

12

NEW TRICKS

KEREN

Keren brought Appleslayer to Sula Charish after her morning prayers. She found the houndmaster on horseback, and Evandor sparring with her from the ground. As before, every one of Sula's movements looked choreographed and efficient. That was the difference between a training exercise and a real fight, Keren thought. Real fights were messy and unplanned. But training had its purpose, too. The more you trained your muscles to recognize a given move and respond to it a certain way, the easier it was to react that way instinctively in battle.

Omari and two boys in similar loose white clothing watched from the sidelines, so Keren brought Apple over to join them.

"Who's training whom?" Keren asked in greeting.

Omari favored her with a warm smile and a half-bow of his head. "The houndmaster is training the horse. It has to learn that to be the instrument of its master, it must overcome its instincts to shy away from the clash of steel. A good lesson for us all."

Keren wasn't sure if he was still talking about the horse, or if he was speaking in some abstract metaphor that she didn't quite grasp. Rather than fumble for a response, she turned to Apple, patting his head. The dog watched with rapt attention, occasionally straining forward against thin air, as if he wanted to join in the playtime but knew he shouldn't. At the same time, Keren was proud of him for correctly assessing that there was no actual threat to any of the participants. The loll of his tongue and the perk of his ears showed that his posture was eager, not aggressive.

Evandor put up his sword to signal that the session was done. Sula ran the horse one more circuit around the room, then dismounted and handed it off to a waiting groomer. Appleslayer's tail started to twitch, then wag fiercely, as she approached, but he stayed seated at Keren's side until she called for him.

"It's good for him to have the scent of horses around."

"What will you be working on today?" Keren asked.

"We're working on keeping focused and brave despite the moods and fears of those around you. He's more comfortable fighting free than with a rider, but that might not always be an option for him. And he's very attached to you and his rider. Having to press on despite an upset is something no one wants to think about, but it's a valuable thing to learn."

"And what will I be working on today?" Keren asked, turning to Evandor.

"Things you'll probably find equally challenging. Are you ready?"

"I'm ready." Keren made herself sound more confident than she felt.

Evandor and Sula clasped hands for a moment, and Evandor led Keren off to their own training room.

"I notice Sula's fans are back today," Keren said. "For someone who doesn't want to train here, Omari's around a lot."

"She'll be shooing them along before she starts work with your hound. She's the only person Omari's found who can best him barehanded. It's only been the last week or so that he's had this renewed interest, but we don't mind it. The sparring practice is helpful all around."

The smaller room he led her to was more for sitting and less for sparring. Its chairs—about two dozen of them, arranged classroom-style—weren't luxurious, but they were well made and large enough to accommodate bodies in armor. Keren expected the chairs to face a lectern or even a worktable, but instead they faced a bookcase as long as the front wall of the room would allow, and at least as tall as she was. Books and assorted objects decorated the shelves, which were neither sparse nor overstuffed. She spotted a seashell, a candle, a ball of twine, and a toy soldier at a glance.

Evandor sat beside Keren in the front row. "You won't need your armor today, as such, but I also don't want to condition you into thinking that you can only work spells without it. Today we'll be working on the detection spell again. Various items in the bookcase are spelled with different auras. Once you've managed to cast the spell, I'll tell you what I want aura I want you to find for me, and you'll point out an object that bears that aura. From here. You'll come to hate these shelves and everything on them very soon, but in time the detection will come naturally."

Keren had affixed her holy symbol to her wrist. Now she closed her hand around it, tracing its shape with her thumb. "I'll try not to waste the goddess's time. She must have bigger things to attend to."

Evandor eyed her pointedly. "Do you think Iomedae, who once fought among us and led our order, considers training a waste of time?"

Keren lowered her gaze. "No, sir." She allowed herself a deep breath, straightened her spine, and said, "I'm ready. Let's begin."

"Good. So. Detecting magic. You remember what I told you, about holding the prayer in your mind?"

Keren nodded. "I'm just not sure how to focus through the symbol."

"Don't worry about the symbol. The symbol takes care of itself. Focus on what's inside you. Think of the small prayers. Think of the bridge. Make yourself the bridge from this seat to that shelf. Your anchor on the other side is an object with magic in its aura. Ask her to connect you to it."

Keren closed her eyes, breathing and focusing. She reached for that place inside her where she'd reached for Iomedae so many times in battle. She tried to feel confident. It wouldn't be her imagination telling her that something on the shelves was magical. It would be real, and powerful, and good.

If she could get it to work.

No, it wasn't an it. It was a *her*. And even if she knew Keren was learning, was practicing—*especially* if she knew that—she wouldn't take it easy on her and let her have it just because she'd tried. order was going to make sure she had proper form. Justice was going to make her earn it. Honor was going to make her appreciate it.

First she had to open herself to it, and that was a little like falling in love—a feeling she could capture, but that no one could teach her. Now she understood why Evandor had wanted her to feel vulnerable and safe. Being a soldier was about strength and discipline, but being a holy conduit was about vulnerability and trust. To let a god work through her, she first had to let that god in.

She felt something. A glimmer of something external but familiar, filling and guiding her.

It frightened her. It startled her, even though it had been exactly what she'd been trying for. The spark went out; the moment was lost.

Keren opened her eyes.

"Good. Very close," Evandor said. "Now, again."

Keren hated the shelves by the end of the day. She kept getting close but then losing it, like trying to reach a teacup in a too-high cupboard. Her fingertips could touch it, but when they tried to close on it, they only managed to push it just out of reach.

Evandor, of course, spun it toward the positive. "Now you know what you're reaching for. Don't try to pull at it. Touch it, and then stretch yourself just a little farther."

If Keren knew how to do that, she'd have done so already. Frustration was making her short-tempered, and her temper was getting in the way of her concentration.

"I don't suppose we could do something else for a while? Get at it some other way?"

The knight shook his head. "This is the foundation on which all the rest is built. Reaching your focus through, knowing what the divine touch feels like, grasping it and making the bridge secure. Are you envisioning the bridge?"

"I was envisioning a teacup, actually."

"Try changing how you visualize it. A different metaphor might suit you better. Try the bridge. Or a fish: you throw out the line, be prepared to hold it fast when it catches."

Keren tried a bridge. And a fish. And a dozen other things. Finally, when Evandor called a halt for the day, she felt wrung out. She *was* the fish, beached on the bridge, desperate to reach the teacup.

"It isn't meant to be easy," Evandor reminded her. "You've made good progress."

She thanked him, even though inwardly she had already decided he was just being kind.

After a break, they discussed magical theory. Despite his earlier insistence that she master the detection first, he outlined others— spells to boost abilities in combat, or stabilize the fallen and keep them from bleeding out. On the theory of them all, she was sound. She understood what to ask for. She just didn't seem to know how to get her question heard.

"Enough for today. You have an appointment, yes?"

"Yes. I'm supposed to meet up with Zae, and introduce her to Houndmaster Charish," she said, rubbing her temples.

"Come, then. Let's see what kind of day the slayer of apples has had."

Zae was at the main entrance, chatting happily with a few trainees when they approached. Keren felt envy creep up the back of her spine like an insect and swatted it away. She could make polite chatter with strangers just as easily as Zae could, so it wasn't that. It wasn't worry that the gnome might say something inappropriate or offend with a random question, though that happened sometimes. It was the joy of novelty, and knowing she wasn't novel to Zae anymore.

"Keren!" Zae broke off from her conversation, smiled in a way that filled her with warmth, and offered both her hands for a squeeze. Keren had noticed Evandor and Sula using the same gesture and suspected it meant the same thing: a polite substitute for when a lover's greeting or farewell was intended but not appropriate. It was a simple thing, but it lifted Keren's spirits immensely. Zae made the introductions to the trainees, who responded politely and then continued on their way, and Keren introduced Evandor.

"Sword Knight Evandor Malik, my trainer; Sister Zae, cleric of Brigh and rider of Appleslayer."

"An honor, Sister Zae. Your steed will be pleased to see you. Right this way."

The big white dog perked up at once, aware of his rider's presence, but didn't rise to go to her until Sula gave him permission. At her word, he bounded toward the gnome, a blur of motion. Keren wasn't sure whether to stand behind Zae to brace her against impact or try to intercept Appleslayer and slow him down. Neither was necessary. He came skidding to a halt at Zae's feet, nuzzled her and licked her hand. His plumed tail beat at the air, stirring up a low-lying tempest of dust, white fur, and stray bits of hay.

Sula gave them a moment, then strode over to join them. Zae greeted her warmly. "Has he been saddled up all day?"

"No, we gave him a rest and a meal, and some playtime with the other dogs." She grinned at Appleslayer, his tongue lolling out while Zae scratched his ears. "It's a rough life, I can tell."

Zae laughed, and the last vestiges of Keren's frustration fell away upon hearing it. Her gnome was beautiful, and a source of light everywhere she went.

"Would you mind riding him around for me a little?" the houndmaster asked. "I'd like to show you what we're working on, and I'd like him to practice it with you."

"I'm happy to!" Zae climbed up into the saddle, and the dog pranced a bit once she was on his back. She had her canvas satchel with its strap slung across her chest; Sula offered to put it somewhere safe for her, but Zae declined. "I'm always wearing it when I ride him. What do you need us to do?"

The trainer explained the maneuver to Zae, who nodded. With Sula's guidance, they trotted a couple of warm-up circuits around the ring. Sula took a wooden sword off a nearby weapons rack and charged them with a feral cry, ignoring Apple and swinging at Zae with a strike intended to pass over her head and miss. Apple's gait faltered, but he recovered and heeded Zae's command to continue on.

The dog's first instinct was to protect his rider. He knew how to handle attacks aimed at him, but a sword swung over his head, out of his line of sight, put him on edge. Keren recalled the horse she'd seen training that morning, and could see how the idea was similar. A fighting dog could use his own judgment in combat, but a mount needed to trust his rider, follow direction, and predictably get his rider to the requisite position, no matter what was going on around him.

Zae didn't ride Apple in combat, but she could. If caught unawares while she was already in the saddle, she would have to.

"He's doing well," Evandor noted, at Keren's side. "Soon she'll move on to throwing fear and other emotions at him, once he's mastered this."

Keren imagined how strained things could get for all concerned, if Zae's mount was hit by a fear spell and started running away with their healer aboard. She didn't think Apple had ever been in that sort of position, and while she didn't like thinking about it, she liked knowing that he would be prepared.

They repeated the exercise several times. Once, Appleslayer dodged a wide circle around Sula and her sword. A few times he faltered, startled. But a few times he kept his gait and direction true.

When Sula signaled a halt and Zae confirmed the command, Apple slowed to a happy prance, coming to a stop by the trio of humans. Zae looked flushed, her hair windblown around her delicate face. "That was fun," she said, breathless. "Can we do it again?"

13

MEDIC, HEAL THYSELF

ZAE

I wasn't sure if you'd show . . . or, actually, if you'd charge right in without waiting for me." Rowan unfolded himself from the shadows beside the door.

"You know I saw you, right?" Zae jogged up the front steps to meet him. She had ridden Apple harder than she was used to, during his training session. It had been exciting, but now her thighs carried the echo of it.

"Maybe. Are you trained to spot people hiding in shadows?"

"Maybe! Are you trained to hide in shadows?"

"Maybe. Well, not the trained part, but the shadow part."

"Wait, really?"

Rowan shrugged. "I ended up out on the street at an early age. I learned what I had to, wherever I could."

"Were your parents dead?" Zae thought of Keren's father.

"Only in a manner of speaking."

He didn't offer anything more, so Zae didn't ask. As they passed through the imposing main arch, her mind churned with all the potential next questions she wasn't asking.

Rowan gave her a sideways glance, and then laughed. "Go on, then."

"Go on, what?"

"You're turning purple. Go on, creature of curiosity. What do you want to know?"

Zae was absolutely sure she wasn't turning colors, but try as she might, she wasn't able to take even mild offense at the accusation.

"You're a sneaking type and a healing type. Don't get me wrong, I think it's an extremely practical combination. I'm just curious how you went from sneaking around on the street to being in a healing cognate."

He laughed again. "I'm clergy, if you want to call it that, but I'd rather make healing devices than do healing. Have you seen what potions cost? I'd like every adventurer who sets out alone, and every backstreet orphan, to be able to heal themselves, whether they can use magic or not."

"Wow. That's—"

"Insane?"

"I was going to say noble, actually. Hey! Wait up . . ."

Rowan had turned down the first corridor on the right. Zae glanced left to see that the opposite archway was blocked by its iron gear, and skipped a few steps to catch up. He didn't wait for her, but he didn't rush ahead of her, either.

"Okay," he said once he'd slowed to a leisurely walk. "Now we just roam around, listening for moaning or explosions or calls for help. There probably won't be any, especially if people are injured behind closed doors, but it's good to have healers around just in case. So, how about you? What made you decide to heal stuff?"

Zae shrugged. "My family . . . group . . . unit . . . thing was a traveling caravan of clockwork and construct makers. I got the tinkering urge from them. The calling to heal, from Brigh, came after I saw enough family lose blood, limbs, and bits to the creative process."

"So you grew up on the road?"

"Yes. And you grew up . . . ?"

"On the streets, like I said, here in Absalom. When I parted ways with my parents, I lived down near the docks for a while, hiding from the slave traders and learning to be a thief. After a close call too many, I ended up throwing myself on Desna's mercy. The dream goddess took me in, and I learned healing arts so that I could earn my keep and repay the kindness. Wait. Did you hear that?"

From far down the corridor came the sound of a door squeaking on its hinges. It was followed by a weak whimper. Rowan and Zae exchanged a glance. The gnome hitched her satchel more securely on her shoulder and took off after her companion.

It turned out to be nothing but a Thumper cleaning up scraps of metal and piles of sawdust. Hinges opened on its top, providing a bin for disposal and producing the squeaking sound they had heard. She smiled brightly at it and patted it on the head to cover her disappointment. Again, she imagined the fun Appleslayer would have playing with one of these, after the thorough mess he'd made of the construct that delivered her acceptance. She wondered if she could set him on one accidentally-on-purpose in order to have an excuse to take it apart and put it back together.

They continued their patrol of the building, corridor by corridor. The gear that had rotated out of the way on Zae's first visit was still at the top of its arc, poised like a raised portcullis. All was silent within, and spotless without, but in her mind's eye she could still see the exhausted, paranoid cognate staggering out when the gear moved aside and granted them their freedom.

"Let's go down this way," Zae said.

Rowan's brow furrowed. "Why? What's down here? Do you hear something?"

"I just have a weird feeling. This is where those students stumbled out yesterday. Maybe someone was too exhausted to leave. We should check." She started off toward the arch and Rowan followed without objection.

One room of the vacant wing had been set up as living quarters, with bedrolls still open on the floor, while the rest were labs and workshops. None contained the detritus Zae would have expected, from the appearance of the wing's refugees. "Have the Thumpers already cleaned up? There isn't even a smell in here."

"The Thumpers can go in and out of individual rooms even if the doors are locked."

"Wait, they can bypass the gears?"

"No, I didn't say that. Nothing can bypass the gears. But there are usually some constructs that get stuck in the hallways when the gears seal them off, and they keep doing their thing. And look . . ." He knelt by one of the doors. When he traced the outline, she could see it: a smaller door set into the larger one, without any apparent handle or lock. "A normal door doesn't stop them."

Now Zae wanted to dissect a Thumper even more. "Something in them gets recognized by a lock at a certain proximity? Clever."

"And thorough. That makes me think that the lack of hospitality toward the living in this place isn't an oversight, it's part of the grand design. You can't lock your food and water in and expect it to be there when you get back."

All the rooms were empty of students, but that only facilitated Zae's search and fired up her curiosity. She tried the latch on the last door at the end of the hall, but it didn't move at her touch. "Locked. Who gets the keys to these doors?"

"I don't know. I presume the cognate leaders have them. Let's move on."

"Well, wait. The Thumpers can get into the rooms, but would they remove a person? Would they call for help? What if someone's in here?" Zae knew the odds of this were unlikely, but the people who'd left this hall had been so secretive and suspicious, and so far there had been nothing to see that bore any need of it. True, they'd had a full day since then to remove everything, but that only made it more likely that whatever they were working on was all behind this one door.

"Fine. Hold on . . ." Rowan drew a small leather roll from a hidden pocket and opened it to reveal a set of lockpicks.

While he got to work on the keyhole, Zae found she almost felt guilty for having preyed on his better nature so easily. She didn't for a moment think that there might be an injured person inside this room; she just really wanted to peek into it *because* it was locked. That was a sentiment a halfling might understand, but she didn't want to take the chance that his adherence to the Clockwork Cathedral's rules might cloud his judgment.

She watched, standing back out of his way, while he worked his deft touch on the lock, and she managed not to rush forward when the tumblers clicked their release.

"Whoa . . . Looks like they're building some kind of big construct in here." Zae's instincts had been right; the door swung open on a sight that matched the rumors she'd agreed to investigate for Keren's order. A step at a time, as if in awe of the massive machine, Zae moved forward into the workroom.

"We've checked for people. Now we should go," Rowan said, but didn't stop her.

He hovered in the doorway, ready to leave, but the moment Zae said, "Wow, look at this!" the halfling was right by her side.

The mechanical head alone was taller than Zae's entire three-foot-three frame; she knew this with certainty because its dented, unpolished chin rested on the floor and its vacant eye sockets gazed out over her forehead.

"People make a lot of constructs here," Rowan said. He sounded unimpressed, but his wide eyes showed all the curiosity she felt. He rapped on the bronze with his knuckles, canting his head to listen to its hollow echoes. "Not much inside it yet. Finishing the shell before the insides is a bold choice, and by bold I mean foolish. I hope all the guts fit."

At the thick marble-topped worktable nearest the giant head, schematics scrawled on parchment had been left behind in haste. Zae hopped up on a chair to have a look. "For as secretive as they acted, they don't seem to be discouraging curiosity," Zae said.

"Right. That locked door? That said 'come right in and poke around,'" Rowan quipped. "Don't touch the pages. They might be warded or trapped. What can you see without moving them?"

"Just typical construct stuff," Zae said, but it wasn't the truth. Studying them as closely as she could without touching them, she saw a chest cavity and a power source, and that source looked very much like a cylinder. Or a jar. And beside the drawing, the specifications of the jar. To her disappointment, there was nothing magical about it or its contents; the jar was only a housing for simple alchemical reactions—unless that was just what its builders wanted any wandering eyes to think. While Zae tried to make sense of the notes, Rowan took a tour around the perimeter of the room, and then around the giant metal head. "There isn't any magic coming from the pages," she reported.

"There wouldn't have to be. Devices can be of all shapes and sizes, and most of us have other tricks, too. Renwick is an alchemist—you should see the things he's come up with. But here? Let's see . . . The paper itself could be treated, or something that's light-sensitive could come out of a hole in the table beneath it if it's moved . . ."

Zae considered this. "I'm used to only thinking like an engineer when I'm actively engineer. I can see that I'm going to have to get used to thinking like one all the time."

Rowan gave a little boy's smug lift of his shoulders, which again made Zae wonder if he could be as young as he sometimes seemed. He leaned back against the table and crossed his arms. "I don't know if it'll do you any good. I mean, would an engineer notice the hidden panel in this table?"

There were two options available to Zae: she could concede that Rowan was better than she was at finding hidden things. Or, she could feign nonchalance as she had when he'd startled her at the front door—she was too proud to admit that she hadn't actually seen him in the shadows. Ultimately, her curiosity won out over her interest in playing games.

"Hidden panel? Where?"

Rowan led her around to the back side of the table, and specifically to a spot that looked, to her untrained eye, exactly like the rest of the side edge of the tabletop. The work surface was about six inches of solid marble, as far as she could tell.

"How do you even know?" she asked.

"The sound is different in this room than the others, and by turning my head while you spoke, I could feel a shift in the acoustics."

Zae was aware of staring at him as if he'd grown a second head, but she couldn't stop herself from doing it, all the same. "You, sir, are messing with me."

He laughed. "Honestly? I used a spell to search for hidden things while you were checking out our giant friend's insides."

Zae smirked. "Okay. So, the panel. Are we going to open it, or are you waiting for me to say please?"

Rowan beamed, winked, and flourished one of his slender picks. "I thought you'd never ask. So, what do you think we'll find?" He finessed the sharp tip along an invisible seam in the marble. Even knowing where it was, Zae could only see the variations of natural veining that hid the opening. "Money? Secret plans?"

"Maybe whatever they plan to put into that thing as a power source." Zae was thinking of the Bloodstone, but she picked her words carefully. "Could be diamonds, or other rare things that are too precious to leave scattered around."

"Care to wager on that?"

Zae pursed her lips. "Sure. I bet you half the diamonds we find that it'll be diamonds."

"And they say *I'm* trouble." Rowan turned back to the hidden panel as if his profile could hide his grin. He worked at it slowly, testing the seams, tapping lightly and listening, and doing all sorts of careful things that looked impressive but hopefully had purpose, too. "Ready?"

"Ready."

Rowan straightened, brushing his hands on his thighs and shaking out his wrists. "Okay. You never want to be at eye level with something like this when you open it, because you never know what might come out. You can try your hardest to check for traps, but you never know if there are really no traps, or if you just haven't found them." He inserted the pick into one side edge, twisted it slowly, and used it as a pry bar to slide one side of the panel outward.

He gasped, a sharp almost-pitched rush of breath, as if his vocal cords hadn't quite had time to move out of the way of his breathing. "I'm all right," he said, and Zae was set to laugh, and to ask him how big her share of the diamonds was.

Then he turned, and Zae saw how apt her analogy had been. A dart was lodged deep into his leather vest, roughly over his heart. Like his vocal cords, he hadn't quite had time to move out of the way, either.

She was at his side in an instant, ready to treat the wound. Shock slowed Rowan's movements, but he batted at Zae's hands, pushing her away each time she tried to reach for the buttons on his vest. "Come here," she demanded. "Would you stop wriggling? Are you a halfling or a fish?"

"No, no, I'll see to it. Stop. Please stop!"

There were tears in his eyes, stuck in his long black lashes, and his voice was raw and full of panic. She raised her hands and stopped. An entreaty to Brigh told her there was no poison on the projectile; he wasn't suddenly hallucinating and seeing her as a multi-tentacled thing, or awash with chemically induced paranoia.

He just didn't want her to open his shirt, and that was a thing she could respect.

"I'm sorry, Rowan. You're a healer, too. Can you handle it? Can I offer you a potion?"

"I can handle it." He blinked and the tears fell. "I'm sorry, too. I'm just . . . touchy about being stripped."

"That's a completely reasonable thing to be touchy about. Personally, I'm touchy about people standing around with sharp things stuck through them. Think we can respect both those things at the same time?" Zae turned to give him her back, staring off resolutely past the open compartment. She'd lost her thrill for whatever the contents might be. "For whatever it's worth, whatever you've got in your shirt is nothing I haven't seen before."

Behind Zae, buttons opened with little pops, a quiet gasp caught in the halfling's throat, and then she heard the awl-punch sound of a sharp-tipped instrument pulling out of leather. "That may be. I still appreciate you respecting my space."

Without the halfling's appearance to temper it, his voice seemed even more dulcet, despite his pain. "Do you sing?" She asked suddenly.

"Ha. Let's just say you wouldn't want me to. Why do you ask?"

"To keep you talking and assure myself you're doing okay back there. Listening to you without seeing you, I was just thinking that you've got such a melodious voice."

"A girl's voice, you mean."

A girl's voice? Zae worked her way backward through the past few moments, and several things fell into place. His voice. The long lashes. Not wanting her to open his vest. Rowan had been born female, and now he was male. She was glad she'd backed off. Whatever his chest looked like, he was right: it wasn't her place to look at it without permission.

"Well, not quite," she said, before her silence could be taken the wrong way. "I just meant I liked your voice."

She thought about how she'd taken men's chests for granted in the past, and had never actually thought of them as nudity. Was that fair of her? On one hand, it was a healer's prerogative to see the wound she was treating, but then again, seeing a wound didn't change *how* she treated it. She had always taken her viewing of a patient's wound as her right, and couldn't remember a time when she had asked before pushing clothing out of the way. If someone was unconscious, then yes, circumstances might demand not waiting around for permission, but with minor injuries and conscious patients, was exposing them always the best course? She'd never thought about it, but now she was looking forward to meditating on it with her morning prayers.

"You can turn now."

Zae did, to find the halfling shrugging back into his vest. There was a hole through the leather that was wide enough to remain. "How bad was it? The dart, I mean."

He handed it to her. It was well made but simple, and bore grooves that suggested the design of its launching apparatus.

"No poison, not too much blood. More a 'stay out' gesture than anything meant to be deadly. Pulling it out felt about like a spider bite, but it's all better. That's the good news."

Zae clutched the dart; her stomach dropped. "What's the bad news?"

Rowan gestured toward the open compartment in the table. "You lose. I don't have to give you any diamonds."

14

A Girl's Second-Best Friend

Zae

The cubbyhole failed to produce diamonds, but it was not empty.

"Books!"

Rowan eased the first object out of its hiding place. It was a hardbound old book, with gold and black faded on its leather spine. He opened the cover and Zae did her best to read the spidery script over his shoulder.

"*A Treatise on Procedures and Processes to Magically Kindle Life in the Inanimate*," he read from the front page, then flipped through it. "Sounds a bit dull, really."

"Look at this glyph." Zae traced around the embossed stamp with her fingertip.

"It means the book is property of the Forae Logos—the grand library of Absalom, affiliated with the Scriveners' Guild. None of the books there can be taken off the premises. This was stolen, not checked out."

Zae reached for the next book, bound in yellow where the one atop it was brown. "*On the Controlling of Mind and Matter*. And a different glyph."

"That's the stamp of the Arcanamirium, the academy of magic. These are definitely being used to research this construct."

She glanced out toward the hallway. "We're sure that this building is shielded from magic? No one's going to suddenly detect these books and swoop down on us?"

"Completely shielded. I can't promise that the engineers won't know their cubby was disturbed, but if you mean are angry librarians going to swarm in here and peck our eyes out, the answer's no."

They went through the rest of the books and found more of the same. Rowan identified the glyphs as property of the libraries of several institutions and academies around Absalom, then carefully returned all the books, positioning them just as he'd found them. Zae watched with growing respect as he eased the panel back into place, using picks at both sides to make minute adjustments and bring it perfectly flush with its surroundings. She would not have been able to cover her tracks as smoothly.

"Onward?" she offered.

"Yes. I don't want you thinking I get myself punctured on every shift, just to have something to heal! Come this way." He led her out, pausing to relock the door.

"That's a relief, because I might well have started thinking that if you hadn't said anything. How long before we get to make wire?"

"Just a little longer." They emerged to the main hall. "When the fourth gear on the right goes down, our shift is done. And then we have until the first on the left goes down and then up before we have to leave."

"You sound like you know your way around pretty well."

"I know the front gate and those two. I'm nowhere near being able to navigate the rest of this place. It's not like it's on a single repeating cycle. That would be far too easy."

"Then how—" she started, but he'd already gone off ahead of her, and she skipped a step to catch him. "How can you possibly learn it?"

Rowan only winked and darted off again, challenging her to keep up.

Here and there, a trip down a corridor would reveal a cluster of students using a giant metal-cutter, or a furnace, or some other large piece of equipment that would be unwieldy to replicate elsewhere. It was mostly quiet, and fully injury-free. Rowan himself remained the only casualty of the night.

When they returned to the main hall and found the fourth gear swinging down into place, Rowan rubbed his hands together. "Good. A successful shift! Now on to the wire. Have you made much wire?"

Zae followed his lead, into the first corridor—the one with the gear he said would go down and then up before they had to leave. "Tons and tons of wire. Are you sure we can't put a bell on this thing to tell us when it's moving?" She looked up at the gear as they passed under the archway.

Rowan shook his head. "Trust me. We'll be fine. Come on in here." The workroom he led Zae into was unquestionably set up for their purposes. Crank-powered machines that looked like laundry mangles were bolted to the floor, gleaming with polish and attention. They were at many heights and of many sizes, and along the walls were worktables with vise clamps and drawers filled with all the necessary tools. A small furnace was offset in a corner, and a woman knelt in front of it.

"Hi, Ruby," Rowan said.

She straightened with a serene smile that seemed almost out of place in front of an open hatch of roaring flames. "Hello, Rowan. Zae. I was early, so I thought I'd get the fire going. This will be fun!"

"Perfect. Thanks!" Rowan joined her, consulting the temperature gauge on the side of the furnace.

Making wire was a straightforward but time-consuming process, quite similar to making noodles. That was exactly what wire was, Zae decided: metal noodles.

Zae set out tools while Ruby waited for the furnace and Rowan conjured water into the quenching bucket. When all was ready, he took out a fully laden pouch from somewhere in his clothes and opened it, revealing greenish white pellets.

"They look like rabbit food," Zae observed.

"That would be one expensive rabbit, when it was done."
Rowan poured a small handful into a crucible and eased it into the
furnace. Zae and Ruby stood out of the way of the heat and watched
the metal shimmer and melt. Rowan poured it into peg-shaped
molds. When quenched and firm enough to handle with tongs,
each of those pegs—no longer than one of Zae's fingers—would
be worked into a slender wire at least twenty feet long.

Fidialory, the gnome with the purple hair, wandered in with
Glivia, the dwarf, at some point. Zae fell into the hypnotic rhythm
of working with wire. She fed the softened metal through ever
smaller apertures in the machine with the crank, and then moved
to a draw plate clamped to a table, which had even smaller ever-
decreasing holes. Each time she drew the metal through, it would
get thinner and longer. If it toughened up and started giving her
trouble, she had a solution for that. Others coiled the wire and
put it back in the fire for a few moments, but Zae had a trinket
to do the same. It was painted ceramic, shaped like a dragon, and
it heated whatever metal was put in its mouth to a molten red
glow. She set it out by her workstation, to ease the queue for the
small kiln. Once the wire was reheated, she would quench the coil
in water, and it was back to the draw plates and pliers to pull the
metal through. Again, and again, and again. She had a similar
trinket to chill metal, shaped and painted like a snowflake. She had
gotten them both at some point during her travels, bartered for
her delicate, ornate gears.

A little tired, a little hungry, and happy to work off the
excitement of the first portion of the evening, Zae embraced the
rhythms of the work. She was herself a part in a machine—a wire-
making machine—entrained in efficient rhythm with her fellow
components.

By the time they were done, the finished coils of wire were
stacked together into what looked like a metal hay bale larger than
Zae.

"Tomorrow we weave?" she asked Rowan.

"Tomorrow we weave! And in the meantime, we drink. You're meeting us at the tavern, yes?"

Zae hesitated. "I'd like to, but Keren's probably waiting for me."

"Bring the Keren," was Rowan's response. "Kerens are welcome!"

Zae laughed. "All right. I'll go home and clean up, and meet you in a bit." She gathered her satchel, then paused at the workroom door. "How are you going to keep all this secure? It's not like you can move it yourself."

"It's not like anyone's going to take it." Rowan gave Zae a pointed look, even though it wasn't as if they'd stolen anything from the room they'd snuck into.

"Not in a stealing way, I mean, but how will they know it's been claimed? If I wandered through and saw a big heap of greenish wire, what would stop me from just using some?"

Glivia cleared her throat. From her pocket, she pulled a scrap of black leather. "Prototype glove for throwing and transporting the net," she explained. "We haven't had a chance to test it as much as I'd like, but I think it works pretty well. We can take the wire to the tea shop for safekeeping, and then bring it back in the morning."

15

Duck and Castle
Keren

Under the kitchen table, Appleslayer shifted with a whuff. Keren extended her bare foot, absently rubbing his soft flank. When he whuffed again and sat up at alert, tail wagging, she roused herself from her woolgathering and rose to swing the kettle back over the fire. Zae was home.

A few moments later, the gnome's key clicked over in the lock and the door pushed open. "Did you miss me?" Zae asked, peering inside.

"We both did," Keren answered, opening her arms. Zae went right to her embrace and hugged her tightly, then knelt beneath the table to rub the dog behind his ears.

"You look exhausted," she told Appleslayer. Getting to her feet, she said, "You both do. I know why Apple's tired. I'm sorry I didn't get a chance to ask you about your day earlier!"

Keren rolled one shoulder in a tired shrug. "You first. How was your field medic shift?"

Zae came around behind Keren and started rubbing her shoulders, seeking out and destroying knots of pressure with expert revolutions of her thumbs. "It was a quiet night. Not much to treat. I did get a chance to search the workshop of those shifty engineers. They're building a construct, but all they've got hidden are contraband library books in a secret cabinet. The power source is a cylinder that could be jar-shaped."

"Our jar?"

"Hard to say at this point. I'll keep peeking in as things progress."

"And the books?"

"They were from all the various magical libraries around town. They're not supposed to be checked out, so technically they're stolen property. That's why they were hidden." Zae felt Keren's neck tense under her fingers. "But we can't turn them in. Not if we want them to keep working so that we can figure out what their power source is." She felt the tension fade again.

Zae gave her shoulders a squeeze, then turned toward the hearth and pulled the kettle off the fire, handling it carefully with folded cloths. "Refresh your cup?" she offered, and Keren nodded, sliding the earthenware mug to the edge of the table. Zae poured carefully, then made tea for herself. "So, tell me about your lessons."

Keren had been dreading this, and as a result, hadn't been able to decide how to say it aloud. If words gave power to thought and intent, would saying she had failed make it more real—or more permanent? She considered her words for a few long moments, discarding options that sounded too self-deprecating, too hopeless, or too frustrated.

"You make it look easy."

Zae canted her head. Keren wasn't sure if Zae had learned the gesture from Appleslayer or Apple had learned it from Zae. "Pouring tea?" she asked.

"Channeling divine magic from your god," Keren said.

That silenced Zae for a good few moments. Her lips moved, her lip ring clicked her teeth, but no sounds came out. Finally, the gnome took a long sip of her tea. Her goggles, still on her forehead, clouded over with the steam. Keren watched the mist wash across and fade, and decided that her conviction was not going to evaporate so easily.

"Your connection with Brigh," Keren said. "What's it like?"

"Ah." Zae gestured toward the parlor with a tilt of her head, and Keren scraped her chair back to follow. Appleslayer padded along too, and when they had settled comfortably together on the plush loveseat, he curled up over Keren's feet.

"My connection with Brigh," Zae said slowly, fingering the gear on its pendant at her throat, "is hard to describe because I'm so used to it. I wish there were a way to share the feeling of it with you instead."

Keren eased the forgotten goggles off Zae's head, set them aside, and ran her fingers through the dusky blue waves and curls. "Evandor is very patient. He understands what I want to learn, and he tells me that it's within my reach. He says I have the potential for magic. Divine magic. But it's like he wants me to use a muscle I've never had to use before and I don't know how to find it."

"Like wiggling your ears," Zae suggested. Keren watched Zae's nearer ear, pierced with its line of bronze rings from lobe to tip, but the gnome didn't demonstrate. "See? I don't know how to either."

"Like that," Keren agreed. She sipped her tea, then rested the mug on the arm of the loveseat in a slow, controlled motion. Calm, she told herself. Not frustrated. Not hopeless. Just calm. "I know volumes of information *about* Iomedae, but it's not as if I know *her*, or know how to contact her. Have you ever seen Brigh?"

"Has she appeared to me? No. Not like you mean. But I can think back to times when I've felt a presence and known she was with me, and then I can try to tap into that feeling and recreate it. Have you ever felt Iomedae's presence? When you took your oath, or when you were sworn into the order, or . . . when you stepped into the Seventh Church?"

"The back of my neck tingled and I felt lightheaded," Keren admitted. "But I don't think that was her. I think that was just me being overwhelmed by my own thoughts. How do you know the difference?"

"Hm. Do you have something to focus on yet?"

"You mean a holy symbol? Like your gear, or the birthmark on your hand?" Keren unfolded Zae's small fingers and traced the darker blotches on her palm that almost resembled a set of gears. "Yes." She pulled up her sleeve with her free hand, showing the miniature sword that dangled from her wrist like a charm on a bracelet.

"This mark is my focus. The gear pendant is just more fun to fidget with." Zae closed her hand around Keren's, and around the small sword. "But we're talking about you now. Your focus is essential. You can't do divine magic without it. It's like the difference between knowing where Brigh's house is, and having a key to her gate."

"Her gate, not her house?"

Zae shook her head. "I'd never presume to enter her house. But if I have the key to her gate, then I can knock on her door. Or she can leave packages on her step for me to retrieve."

"But without it . . . "

"Without it, I can hope she's looking out her window at the exact moment I'm waving from the street. And that's all. Magic-wise, I mean."

Keren let that swim around in her head for a few long moments. "So even though you're dedicated to her, and you channel her power through you, it isn't a very direct connection."

"It's called a focus because it focuses two things: your attention and will, and your god's attention to . . . You know what? Maybe a key isn't the best comparison. Let's call it a whistle. People are praying at gods all the time, right? The gods have an infinite attention span and an infinite number of things to pay attention to. They want to favor their followers, so they give you a whistle so that you can cut through that other noise and get their attention. And it's not for things you want or need them to do—it doesn't work like that. Or at least, it shouldn't. It's for things you can do to glorify them."

Keren recalled Evandor's assurance that training and learning were glorifying to Iomedae. She related this, adding, "I just don't know how to whistle yet?"

"Exactly. And part of it is the mindset. If I heal someone in Brigh's name, it's not because I want them healed. It's because I see an opportunity for her power to help someone, and I'm offering to be the conduit through which that happens. If I smite the undead in Brigh's name, it's not because I want to kill some skeletons, it's because they're an abomination and I'm offering to be the conduit through which she can purge them. If *I* don't think these things I want to do are worthy of her, that's self-fulfilling—I'm not going to be whistling loudly enough for her to hear. Does that make more sense?"

Now Keren nodded slowly. "A lot more, actually. So it's not me asking Iomedae for a favor, it's me offering her a favor—a conduit through which to express her nature."

"Exactly."

"So your focus . . . it's not like a wand that lets you use her power as much as you want, for any reason you want. It's the key that lets *her* in, not the key that lets you in."

"That's a much better way of looking at it, yes. But if you've never used a key before, you're probably not going to put it in the lock the right way on the first try. You have to understand the shapes and ridges and what they say about where the tumblers are, before you understand why the key needs to be oriented the way it does."

Keren didn't feel like she understood much of anything. She felt as if she were spinning in place, unsure which direction was forward anymore. She said as much.

"When was the last time you learned—and I mean mastered—a new skill?" Zae asked, breaking her from her spiraling thoughts.

Keren thought about it. She'd trained Appleslayer about a year before, and that had been the first time she'd trained a dog for a rider. But that hadn't been a new skill, just a new application of an old one. Before that . . .

"About five years ago, I tutored one of my father's students in military history. In return, he gifted me with a flute and taught me how to play it." She hadn't thought about that in a very long time, and had only remembered it just in that moment, but now the memory flooded her.

"What were those first few lessons like?"

Keren grimaced. "I see what you're doing, Pixie. Point taken."

Zae shifted in Keren's arms, turning to face her. Her eyes were a shade of pale lavender that Keren had never seen a human possess, and they always betrayed the gnome's age and wisdom. "When you only do what you've already mastered, you forget how to respond to your own imperfection; you forget that it's okay to fail."

Keren turned away from that knowing gaze. "Says the collector of new experiences."

"And why do you think I seek out novelty so vigilantly?"

Keren's lips turned in a smirk despite herself. "Because you're a gnome?"

Zae poked Keren in the side, right in the one spot where she was ticklish. "That's the easy answer and you know it."

"I do understand what you're trying to say. Making mistakes gracefully is a skill you deliberately keep up on, and one that I'm going to have to relearn. I know I'm not expected to be perfect at things I've never tried, and I have to figure out how to allow myself to fail and not take it hard." Keren understood this in principle, but in action . . . all her life, the value of perfectionism had been impressed upon her by her father, by screaming drill sergeants, and by her combat officers. The price of getting something wrong the first time, as Keren had learned, far outweighed the benefit of having a learning experience. On patrol or on the battlefield, there was no lenience.

"Well, you can parrot it, at least. Believe it or not, that's a start." Zae sat back and stretched like a lazy cat. "My cognate is being social at their local tavern. I'd meant to collect you and wander over. Will you come? You can pretend to be checking out my new acquaintances and figuring out who the spies are, and in the meantime, maybe get your mind off things for a while?"

The last thing Keren wanted right now was to be social with a troupe of strangers, but she did want to get out of her own head for a while, and she *was* curious to meet Zae's new classmates. "All right. But not for too long. I need to get up early tomorrow, with you." She rose with a sigh to retrieve her mail shirt and sword.

It was dark in the bedroom and she hadn't bothered to light a candle, so she shrugged into her chainmail tunic in the faint moonlight. Paleness reflected outside the bedroom window. Keren thought she glimpsed a raccoon's eyes out of the corner of her vision and looked again. It was gone, but she had an odd feeling, similar to when she prayed the small-prayers. If Iomedae was telling her something, or even if there was an outside chance she might be, Keren needed to listen. She turned to leave the room, but instead of passing through the doorway she ducked inside it and waited.

"Did you fall asleep in there?" Zae called.

"Give me a minute. Something's odd."

Zae could see better in the dark, but Keren didn't want an extra presence to make whatever she'd seen run to ground again. There. A rustle of branches, a gleam of moonlight against steel. The presence in the yard wasn't a raccoon, unless raccoons were man-sized and crawled on their knees.

Keren let out a yell before she could quite help herself. The man's cover broken, he took off, and Keren sprinted toward the front door. Her instructions not to engage flitted through her awareness as she darted off into the night, trying to buckle her sword belt at a run, but she discarded the orders without guilt. She was halfway down the street before she realized she hadn't told Zae where she was going, but she heard the presence of gnome and dog behind her and gaining quickly. Satisfied with that, she turned her full attention back to the chase.

The man sped around the corner, into the end row house's garden. Keren approached carefully, but in her mail she wasn't silent. If anything, her own mail shirt was a disadvantage, keeping her from hearing the jingling of his.

A short sword gleamed out from around the corner just as she turned. Keren deflected it with the mesh of metal rings on her forearm, glad for the armor after all. She lunged for the man and nearly had him, but he dodged her and took another swing. She barely drew her sword in time to block his blade, but his strike was a feint; he reversed the sword and smashed the butt of it into her temple. While she wove on her feet, centering herself, he turned and ran. She gave chase to a dead-end alley where she drew up, panting. Battle rage had her in its grip now. She had the spy cornered and she approached him with her sword raised, but he smiled broadly at her with broken teeth, as if he still had the advantage. He lunged for her, holding her close enough to smell his fetid breath. Too late, she recalled Yenna's warning about these agents: that they were unafraid to die. The man was shifting his tongue, poking at something in his mouth, and Keren wheeled away, turning and crouching. She pulled up her chain sleeve to her elbow and buried her face in her forearm, in the damp cloth of her tunic. Already, her eyes were burning. She tried not to breathe, exhaling air slowly. Slower. Slower. Dreading the moment when she would need to breathe in again.

Behind her, a bark and growl, and Zae's voice. "Are you all right? Just lift your hand if you're all right. There's a cloud of green mist, but it's fading. Don't lift your head yet."

Keren nodded, remembered the instructions she'd just been given, and raised her free hand.

"He's very dead," Zae continued. "Poison cloud is almost gone. You should be able to breathe through your sleeve now."

Cautiously, Keren inhaled against the cloth. She smelled nothing but her own skin. Her eyes still burned and she was reluctant to lift her head, but she heard Appleslayer's feet pad up. A cork popped and a cool glass vial pressed against her palm. "Drink up."

The potion tasted like Zae's healing potions always did. Keren found herself braced for the worst, the first jarring taste of it, and by the time it resolved itself into something fruitlike and pleasant, it was gone. She peeked her eyes open, one and then the other, and lifted her head for a breath of actual air.

"Well." She offered the vial back to Zae. "That wasn't fun."

The gnome slipped her hand into Keren's and gave it a squeeze. "Come on. We need a real drink even more now."

The night had turned cool against Keren's face, with a pleasant breeze that ruffled Zae's curls and brought the occasional hint of the sea. The Duck and Castle wasn't far from Lumpy Orange Crescent, as Zae had taken to calling their street. Now Keren couldn't think of it as anything else.

The muted jingling of chain accompanied Keren's every step. She found the noise and weight of the chainmail tunic strangely comforting now. Perhaps it made her easy to track, but it warned her followers, if any had returned after the chase, that her patience with their scrutiny had an end.

The tavern was easy to spot when they turned onto the high street, even before Keren saw its hanging sign. Its windows were aglow with flickering yellow light, suggesting the warmth of fire and company within. As they neared the open door, they were greeted with the reedy plucking of lute strings and the cozy din of voices. Stew was simmering on a fire somewhere, adding a savory base to the wheaty scent of ale. Only now did Keren realize she'd forgotten to eat all day.

Taverns were taverns. This one looked like a tavern in Lastwall, like the tavern in Bladswell where she and Zae had once spent a memorable night, and like every other tavern at which Keren had ever raised a pint. Warped wooden tables that had seen many a spill, a hearth on one end of the large open room, and a bar across from the front door, spanning the entire far wall. Stairs in the back beside the hearth presumably led up to rooms available for rent, and a swinging door behind the bar presumably led to kitchens and the entrance to a cellar.

It was the diversity of the crowd that surprised her. Perhaps she'd expected more gnomes, since Zae was the only mechanist she'd ever known. Perhaps she'd expected a mostly human crowd, since that was what she had grown up with back in Vigil. But here, humans and dwarves, a few signs of elven lineage, and some rarer races were all represented, and in a full complement of skin tones, besides. The minstrel who played by the fire was a woman with a thin face and lush, dark hair. She had a voice as gentle as silk, and the song she played was one Keren had never heard. There was something old-fashioned, almost archaic, about its structure. For the second time that evening, Keren thought of the wooden flute tucked away somewhere in her home in Vigil.

Keren steered her way toward the bar, fished a few silver weights from her coin purse, and held up two fingers. Taverns always had their specialties, so while ordering blind was in some ways a greater risk, in some ways it was also safer. Better to get the fresh ale than the one cask of sad, vinegary wine that sat in the cellar just in case some hapless traveler should ask for it someday. Not that she expected a bustling tavern in Absalom to have such issues, but there was no real benefit to breaking a habit born of common sense.

A small brown blur darted out from the crowd and tackled Zae. Keren's heart pounded for a moment, but the gnome's happy laugh brought her back down from alert. It was a halfling, shorter even than Zae, with hair that was windblown like a child's.

"Of course I came," the gnome was saying. "I said I would! And this is Appleslayer, my dog. And—where'd she go?—Keren! Keren, this is Rowan. He's in my cognate."

The moment she and the small whirlwind exchanged pleasantries, Keren knew the calm was over. Rowan led them on a circuit of the common room, introducing them both to everyone—including people whom it seemed Zae hadn't even met yet. The students were friendly and not too boisterous, but that was easily the result of being just far enough into their cups. And at that thought, she realized she was still holding two mugs, and took a long drink from one. It was dark brown, nutty in flavor, and quite pleasant.

Rowan ushered them to a weathered table and pulled out Zae's chair for her with a flourish, then did the same for Keren, adding an absurdly low bow. Keren returned a low curtsy, which felt equally ridiculous in her mail shirt and close-fitting breeches. The minstrel playing by the hearth had switched to a jauntier tune, one of merrymaking rather than melancholy. Keren gave the half-full mug to Zae, whose head for ale was slight at the best of times, and kept the full one for herself. Zae caught the maneuver and squeezed Keren's knee under the table in thanks.

On Keren's other side was a weathered old dwarf who introduced himself as Renwick. His silvery beard still held a hint of the ginger of his youth, and was intricately braided and ornamented with colored beads. Keren complimented him on them.

"When I was a young potion seller, I braided my beard each morning to reflect the brews I had on hand to sell that day. My customers came to learn the code, and could eye my stock from a glance," he explained. It was the sort of sensible efficiency that appealed to Keren, and she showed her appreciation of it by signaling the serving boy and buying the dwarf another round.

"The woman playing the lute . . . she's excellent."

"Her name is Pendris," Rowan cut in, "and she's my girlfriend." His cheeks flushed an adorable pink when he said it. Apparently Pendris had good ears, because she rolled her eyes at Rowan from across the room without missing a note. The halfling giggled. Keren hadn't known many halflings; she suspected they could hold more ale than Zae, but still she wondered how drunk he was. After the flying hug Rowan had given Zae, Keren was ashamed of exactly how relieved she was to learn that the halfling was romantically attached. Still, Rowan had cozied up to Zae rather quickly, and she hadn't thought to ask how attentive he had been during Zae's snooping.

Keren nodded toward the musician. "Is she a student, too?"

"No, she's a performer full time. She plays here, and up at the Barking Swan, and all over the city. Sometimes she plays at posh parties, and once in a while she can sneak me in as her assistant. She pretends to need music, and I turn pages for her."

Keren's instinct was to suspect a con job or a pickpocketing team, especially since all she knew about Rowan was that he'd helped Zae snoop around the Clockwork Cathedral earlier that same evening. Her skepticism must have showed in her face. "Oh, no. Nothing like that!" he swore. "I just enjoy sipping fancy wine and daydreaming about living like gentry. If anything untoward were to happen, she'd never be invited back."

Admirable rationality seemed to be a common trait in engineers and artificers, if Keren's experience with a whole three of them could be considered any guide. "How long have you known each other?" she asked.

Before Rowan could answer, Zae spluttered, spitting ale. By the time Keren could make sense of things, an ale-soaked toad had hopped out of the gnome's mug and was floundering, confused, on the table. Zae wiped her face with her sleeve, then calmly scooped the creature up in both hands—which moved through thin air. It was an incredibly lifelike illusion. The gnome giggled and glanced around.

The only one intently avoiding looking in their direction was a gangly young man across the room. Keren asked for an introduction, so Rowan signaled the lad, whose name turned out to be Jesper, to join them. When he excused himself after exchanging a few pleasantries, he landed flat on his face behind Keren's chair. Rowan pulled his foot back in under the table and fluttered his lashes at the sprawled young man. Keren extended a hand to him, he clasped it, and she helped him to his feet.

"Sorry about all that," Renwick said from Keren's other side. She turned and found him wearing a look of genuine concern "It's tradition to haze the new student. No disrespect intended."

"None taken," she assured him. "I was raised at the War College in Vigil. Barracks pranks were the order of the day."

"So, how does a knight from Vigil end up traveling with a tinkering gnome?" Renwick asked, as though they hadn't been interrupted.

Without looking, Keren slid her fingers between the gnome's and squeezed warmly. "She availed upon me to reach something from a high shelf in the market one day. And I kept her." It was the shortened version, but true all the same.

A smattering of applause broke out, and Keren's cheeks burned crimson.

"Thank you all!" It was the bard, Pendris, who rose, set down her lute, and strolled over to join them at the table.

"What are you drinking?" Keren asked her, rising, to cover her embarrassment—and her relief that the applause hadn't been a teasing response to her show of sentimentality. She offered her chair.

"A Blue Lady, please." Pendris took the seat with a half-bow of thanks. "They know how to make it."

Keren drained her tankard on the way to the bar, where she ordered another round of drinks. The concoction that was passed across the counter was, indeed, as blue as advertised. When Keren queried as to its contents, she was informed that it was hard cider flavored with thick blueberry liqueur, which added even more sweetness and gave it the lovely cobalt color.

She brought the drinks back to the table. Pendris started to thank her, but something caught her eye and she straightened a bit. Keren turned, following her gaze.

A familiar figure in monk's robes had just strolled in. He wove his way with a dancer's grace through the growing crowds. Keren grunted in surprise.

"Do you know him?" Pendris asked.

"Not well, but we've met. You?" She tried to avert her gaze, but he spotted the pair of them looking his way and waved with a self-assured smile.

"I see him in various taverns around the city. He never drinks, but he's trying to commission a bard to write the tale of his ascension, like it's all but assured, and it feels like he's picked me for the task, lucky me. It can't be a coincidence that he shows up no matter where I perform. I've thought about taking him up on the commission just for the money, but he's so confident that he refuses to pay in advance."

Keren laughed out loud. By the time she'd recovered her composure, the monk had reached their table.

"Lady bard with the Azlanti eyes; Master Renwick of the gears; Evandor's lovely student," he said, bowing in greeting, and helped himself to an empty chair. Appleslayer sniffed at his trousers, then settled back down under the table on Keren's feet.

Zae, drawn by curiosity about the newcomer, drifted nearer. "Hello, I don't believe we've met. I'm Zae."

"Omari." He sketched a half-bow from his seat.

"Ruby, Rowan," Pendris finished the introductions.

Keren hadn't noticed Ruby joining them, but then wondered how she could have missed her. She had an inviting smile and large, round eyes.

"Omari is an aspirant to the Test of the Starstone," Keren explained to Zae. "He intends to become a god."

"And he's a former student of the Clockwork Cathedral," Renwick added.

That surprised Keren. Omari laughed at her expression. "It's true, it's true. While I have little interest in magic, I've attended nearly every major school or academy in Absalom at one time or another, even if only briefly. I serve Irori, god of perfection, who considers it important to be proficient in a range of important skills."

"Meaning he stays until he feels he knows enough, and then he moves on," Renwick said. Omari bowed his head, not denying it.

Gears turned between Zae's ears. Keren could almost hear them spinning up. "You're really trying to become a god? That's fascinating! Do you get to choose what you want to be a god of, or is it picked for you?"

Omari's laugh was as smooth as the whisper of feathers. "I don't actually know," he said. "I'll be going in with a few choices just in case, and I'll just have to hope that the Starstone finds me worthy of one of them."

"Do you worry that your god might be upset with you if you ascend? Would that be like saying that he's not enough for you?" Keren asked.

"Of course not. My ascension will be a testament to the god of perfection. When I ascend, it will be an honor to him that I have purified and trained myself in his image, in his path. I like to imagine he'll greet me as a brother."

Keren looked for a hint of irony or humor, but there was none. Omari's deep violet eyes were wide and shining. He truly believed that he was his deity's equal, and that everyone else just didn't realize it yet.

"What are you doing to prepare?" Zae asked.

Omari considered the question like he was rolling it around on his tongue, deciding whether it was worth answering. "I keep myself to a very specific diet, of course. I've gone to fortune-tellers, real ones with the gift for sight, for advice. And I've studied other aspirants. When most people make preparations, it's out of pure superstition. Mine, on the other hand, are the product of enlightenment. I eat no flesh, I drink nothing impure, I fight without weapons, I wear no metal, and I avoid the arcane. These things are all tools of mortality, and no one can transcend mortality with mortal tools."

Keren recalled the legends saying that Cayden Cailean, god of wine and freedom, had taken the test so drunk that even he couldn't remember how he passed it. Omari's rigid purity was nothing more than the same superstition that he took his superior stance against. Not in the mood for debate, she kept her silence.

"When will you take the test?" Zae asked.

"We could walk down to the chasm right now and you could watch me cross it," he asserted, then held up a single finger. "But I'm waiting for a number of specific factors to align. I'll go to my test when fortune shines brightest on my attempt. I hope you'll all come and witness it."

Carefully trying to match Omari's water-over-rocks smoothness, Keren said, "That would be quite the inspiring sight."

The monk stood and bowed deeply to Keren. "You honor me. I'm already looking forward to our next chat, should I see you again before I ascend." He drifted off toward the bar. She kept watching until she saw that he received water and simple bread. He seemed to be known to the servers, and was now chatting pleasantly with the thin young man who had brought the ale.

"What did he mean before, about your eyes?" Keren asked Pendris.

"Oh, that? We have the same shade of violet eyes. It's a rare color in humans, and some people think it signals Azlanti heritage, especially when it's paired with dark hair and a certain skin tone. Azlant was an ancient human empire, and some people treat it as sort of a status thing." She tilted her head pointedly toward the bar.

"So he thinks he's part Azlanti?"

"Oh, yes. He's convinced of it. And he thinks I am, as well. It's why he imagines some kind of rapport between us. At least he doesn't think we're related or something. Then he'd think he had a far bigger claim on my time."

"But at least he'd flirt with you less," Rowan muttered.

Keren sought the bard's eyes. They were not dark brown, as she'd first assumed, but deep purple, like an overripe grape. "Do you think Omari could succeed?"

"To be sure, it does take a certain demeanor to want to be a god, and very seldom is that demeanor humble and meek. Seldom are they quite that confident either, though." Pendris shook her head. "I think if they understood what immortality really means, fewer would aspire to it. The old songs are full of mortals who weren't careful what they wished for. I don't know if Omari could succeed. I just hope for his sake that he loves himself as much as he thinks he does."

Keren lifted her mug to toast to that sentiment. "And I hope for our sake that the Starstone doesn't."

Though she'd only intended to stay long enough to be friendly, Keren was surprised when she heard the bells for last call and realized how much time had passed in good company. She could hold her alcohol particularly well—an attribute she had always credited to her upbringing among soldiers—so the end of the night found her happy, sober, and alert enough to escort her tipsy gnome along the darkened streets. She spotted no followers; perhaps their shadows had retreated for the night.

16

THE BANDAGE BRIGADE

ZAE

Zae arrived at the tea shop shortly after dawn the next morning, eager to assist with weaving the enhanced net before class. Renwick, Rowan, and an older, bald-headed human named Andan were there before her, and more students straggled in soon after. Renwick demonstrated the knots and the pattern, starting them out, and they took turns at it. One worked the shuttle and gauge to construct the net itself, while the others braided wire three strands thick, trying to keep well ahead of the person doing the weaving so that they wouldn't run out of material. Renwick retreated to a seat near the samovar and hummed under his breath, in time with the planing and whittling of a wooden curve for a project of his own.

As they had the previous morning, they all marched over to the Clockwork Cathedral together once the cognate had assembled.

In the long workroom with the large saws and stationary crank-driven drills, Zae's supplies were just as she'd left them the previous day. Glivia and Ruby hunched over the prototype glove, discussing what had worked and what hadn't when they'd brought the wire back over in a single awkward brick with the net-in-progress draped around it. Zae and Rowan took turns braiding and weaving. Renwick wandered by a few times to examine their work.

Things went by in a haze, until Renwick called out a warning about an hour before the gear was due to close. A couple of students slipped out—presumably to find a privy while they still could.

Round by round, the net grew. The tripled strands weren't too stiff to weave, but they were strong. Soon enough, the diameter eclipsed Zae's height. Instead of clamping the center of the net and revolving it around a fixed point, they had to fix it to the floor and walk around it to weave each new row.

The weighted border provided an interesting challenge, but that was where the glove came into play. Glivia tried it on, adjusted the resizing straps, and modeled it. "It fits either hand, and you adjust the sizes with these sliding buckles here. There's a plate of the skymetal alloy in the palm, on the back of the hand because that'll be the palm if you wear it on the opposite hand, and in smaller plates in the fingertips, all connected through the material so that they recognize each other. When the glove detects another piece of the same alloy that isn't connected, it triggers a spell on the wearer that lets them carry three times what they could normally carry. Eventually it'll reset more than twice a day, and it'll let you trigger it without the alloy, but it's a functional start. Want to try?"

Rowan held his hand out. Glivia slipped the glove off her hand and fit it onto Rowan's. "Okay, now pick up one of the weights."

The halfling grinned, rubbed his hands together, and reached out toward the stack of lead shot. Each ball had been painted with some of the noqual alloy, a cheaper solution than making weights out of the expensive stuff.

His hand made contact and his expression changed to one of wonder. "This works! Here, someone hold the net steady. I'll have these clipped on in no time."

Zae returned to her drawings; she would still have to make the simple and fancy nets she'd drafted the day before, but now that the main project was done she was free to do so with cheaper metals and on a much more demonstration-friendly scale. She lifted her desktop and removed the cover from her perpetual light jar.

Without warning, the entire workroom listed hard to the left.

Or at least, it felt like it had. The tremor came before the sound, but when the sound came it filled her ears and overflowed, leaving her unable to hear anything else. She couldn't be sure what was real. There was smoke, and Rowan had thrown himself over her. They were under her desk, and bits of metal were pelting the table with a percussive rain that Zae could feel more than hear. She lifted her head, grateful to still be wearing her goggles. The great sawing machine looked like a massive tree that had been struck by lightning. All that was left of it was its stump, surrounded by a debris field of singed and scattered things. Rowan got up gingerly, brushed himself off, and offered his hand to help Zae to her feet. All around the room, groaning and cursing students were taking stock of the damage. Thankfully, none of it seemed too serious.

"You all right?" Zae asked him.

He nodded. "You?"

"Intact, I think. Thank you for squishing me. That was fast thinking."

"Don't mention it." Rowan looked a little glazed from shock, but so did everyone else. Zae grabbed her satchel and staggered out to the corridor, then the main hall, where she saw smoke billowing out from several other corridors, too. A few early stragglers like herself were also making their way to the main thoroughfare. "Do you need healing?" Zae called. Her voice still sounded tinny and distant in her own ears.

She ducked back into the workroom. "It wasn't just us! Anybody we can spare, please help the other wings." Contented to see a few others starting toward her, she left and made her way carefully on shaking legs toward the next corridor down.

The wing with the locked door and the giant construct. She had gone there without thinking. Most of the laboratories were open and empty, but one door was shut and had a wedge pried under it to keep it that way. After only a moment's hesitation at the reception she'd gotten from them the day before, she pulled at the rough block of damp wood, but it had been hammered in too well, and because it was wet, it had expanded once in place. It wouldn't budge.

A sinking feeling settled like a counterweight in the pit of Zae's stomach. She sat down in the doorway and set both feet against the wedge, her back braced by the doorframe, and pushed her whole weight against it, but she wasn't enough to move it. If there'd been an explosion and people were still alive inside, there might not be time for her to go and find help; she'd have to make do with what she had.

What she had was a half bottle of acid, which she sometimes used to etch designs in metal. She uncorked it, holding her breath, and dribbled a bit on the wedge. Smoke trickled upward, dispersing into the air, while the liquid ate through the wood. Zae corked the bottle carefully and put it back. Then she pulled at the door and kept tugging until the wedge gave way.

She opened the door a crack, using it to shield herself from the room.

Thick smoke trickled out of the opening, bearing the charred scent of burnt wiring and crisped flesh. Zae pulled the door open fully and slipped inside.

While Alive and Ticking seemed to have suffered no actual casualties, the same was not true of whoever this cognate was. There were eight bodies in the room, all crumpled into individual little heaps and covered with debris. She turned over the nearest one, but it was too late for him. A large explosion in a small confined room, magically muffled and isolated, had created a concussive force and given it nowhere to go. In her head, something clicked into place. Whoever had rigged all the machines had to have done so to cover their actions here.

She checked over all the bodies, in hopes that one of them had survived. They all disappointed her in that regard, so instead she picked the most intact of the bunch. Kneeling beside him, she brushed away the debris and dust to rest her palm against his cheek. "Lady Brigh, one more whisper of life, I beg you." She closed her eyes to concentrate and pushed magic into the corpse, a golden heat like sun-warmed bronze. When she felt the face shift, she opened her eyes. He was still dead, but now his lips moved soundlessly.

"Hello?" she whispered to him, "I'm sorry I couldn't save you. Please, let me help your death be a testament to your work. Tell me, were you slain by a person?"

His lips were turning a fascinating shade of pastel blue, and in the midst of their random movements they formed a word and put sound behind it. "Yessss . . ."

"Were you slain by someone you knew?"

"No . . ."

"Was anything taken from your workroom?"

The lips worked for a moment, as if the corpse was thinking, or winding up its gears enough to push more air past dead vocal cords. "Tuuuris."

"Turis." Zae sounded the word out for herself, tasting it. It tasted like burnt metal, and ash, and blood. It wasn't from any language she knew, but she'd have been the first to admit that she didn't know them all. Yet. She hadn't thought to cast any sort of language comprehension on herself first.

The dead lips were stilling. She raced to think of something else to ask, but couldn't come up with anything useful. "Thank you, friend. Rest well."

Zae rejoined her cognate. The fraternity of healers had taken stock of their own, then spread throughout the Clockwork Cathedral to help heal the others. Sometimes it was as simple a matter as providing water or rudimentary bandages. Ruby insisted on leading the large-scale effort; since one of her witch's hexes allowed her to heal the small wounds of as many people as needed healing, she could cure the minor injuries and then send the severely wounded to anyone available to help them further, allowing the priests among them to save their spells and potions for the people who needed them most.

"It only works once per day on any given person, but it works on an unlimited number of people in a day," she explained to Zae. The gnome created water in a large jug and Ruby helped her pour it out into small drinking vessels—improvised from clean, empty salve jars. The jars had the benefit of sealing tight so they could be carried without spills. They loaded up as many of the water jars as would fit on a rolling cart and started down the corridors, calling out for survivors. In each wing there were some lightly wounded tinkers who limped out, dazed from shock, to take water and healing and beg help for their worse-injured colleagues inside. At each stop, Zae asked them which cognate they were part of, with the idea that they might need to provide some sort of accounting to the mysterious, unseen administrators of the academy.

Down one corridor, they found a few stragglers who emerged in complex goggles and with air-filtering masks over their noses and mouths.

"We're from Alive and Ticking. Is anyone badly injured in your workshop?"

"We'll be fine," one of them said. "Only three of us here, and we weren't near the machine when it blew, just updating our notes. You should check on the Steel Singers down the way." He gestured toward the far end of the corridor with a tilt of his head. "A few of them stumbled past us, but there might be more inside."

Ruby thanked them, gave them water, and pushed the cart on down the corridor, following the tinker's advice. A burnt electrical scent now dominated the cathedral.

The Steel Singers had fared poorly. Musical constructs had been connected to their machine—a central generator—and now the cognate's hard work lay in mangled scraps of charred metal, some still giving off steam. A low moan was still coming from one of the automatons, as if it had been caught mid-note by the blast and was still waiting for the rest of the quartet to rejoin it in song.

In the rubble, one engineer in goggles sat holding the stump of her arm. Another, bare-faced, wailed while he prodded gingerly around a thick curl of wire spring embedded in his eye.

"Oh, gods. Don't touch it!" Ruby called, rushing toward the student with the injured eye. Zae left her to it and made for the handless woman, already pulling a sturdy length of stretchy rope from her satchel to serve as a tourniquet.

"It's all right," she said, covering the woman's remaining hand with hers. "We've got you now. Do you know where it went?"

The woman shook her head, eyes downcast. It didn't mean no, but instead signaled a particular sort of hopelessness that Zae had seen in patients before. Then she lifted her gaze, wincing, toward the generator.

"Was it crushed in the machine?"

A shallow nod answered her. "All right. You're in the best place for it, you know. There's got to be a group in here making artificial limbs. They'll give you tools built right into your fingers, and different attachments for different tasks . . ." Part of Zae's banter was a proven way of distracting patients from their injuries by keeping their attention on her voice while she worked the worst of a wound. But the more she spoke, the more Zae almost wanted the enhancements she described for herself. She thought of the metal bar embedded in her pinky, for the kindly dwarf's side project, and envisioned replacing her whole littlest finger with a multitool covered in realistic flesh.

But now wasn't the time to draw schematics in her mind's eye, now was the time to heal a traumatized student. A bottle of potion from Zae's satchel, scented of orange peel and colored to match, served to clean the wound so that she could see it clearly, while numbing the area.

By now the blood had slowed and the analgesic had taken effect. Zae drew in a breath to pray, but a hand on her shoulder halted her.

It was Ruby. "Please, you've got limited resources. Allow me."

Zae's first instinct was to argue. She'd started this patient, and she would see her through. But when she did a quick mental tally of the spells she had left for the day, she relented. "Thank you. Anything I can do for . . ."

"If you wouldn't mind cleaning him up . . . ?" Even as Ruby knelt by her side and took the patient's arm, Zae glanced over toward the other patient. The eye was bandaged and the patient seemed either restful or actually asleep, but was still crusted in metal dust and drying blood.

"Of course." Zae crossed to the other patient, her orange peel potion bottle still in hand. With clean cloths, she gently washed the student's face.

"How did you come to healing?" Ruby asked her.

"I grew up in a troupe of traveling engineers and artificers," Zae said. "There were always accidents that needed healing. I sort of came into both skills at once. How about you?"

"A similar sort of thing. I grew up in the family tradition, but I was always fascinated by my mother's familiar. I knew I would inherit it when she died, so I was motivated to learn how to keep it in good health."

"I'm sorry for your loss. How long ago did your mother die?"

Ruby tilted her head, tapping her finger in a silent count. "Three years. It was clean and painless, and now she's with my father again. Are you ready? We should probably move on."

17

WAYLAID

ZAE

Zae had agreed to meet Keren back at home after they were both done for the day, but she was too shaken and restless to be alone with her thoughts. She approached the grand doorway of the Tempering Hall, pushed her way inside, and followed her memory to the hall where Appleslayer trained. If Houndmaster Charish was surprised to see her, it didn't show. She welcomed her in and let Zae observe, then invited her to ride Apple the way she had the day before.

This was how Keren and her trainer came upon them. Zae, on Apple's back at a gallop, wielding a wooden sword, while Sula charged at them. Whatever the threat to Zae, Apple had to listen to his rider, not his instincts, unless she gave him free rein.

It was, in many ways, precisely the opposite of Keren's training, in which she had to learn to trust her own instincts but still be willing to give Iomedae the reins when it was time for the goddess to work through her.

Perhaps she wouldn't share that observation with Keren quite yet. There were more important things to talk about first.

On the way home, speaking quietly from dog-back, Zae described the explosion at the Clockwork Cathedral. Keren's lips tightened to a grim line as she listened. "All right," she said when Zae had finished. "What does it look like to you?"

Zae had been pondering this all day. "I can't be sure it means anything, but . . . assuming it's not coincidence, the workroom that was wedged closed was the same one Rowan and I peeked around in."

"The one with the hidden panel. The one building a construct powered by something in a jar."

"The very same. Do you think it's worth telling your church about?"

"I don't know. I doubt there's anything they'd do about it besides tell you to be careful and alert, and you seem to have that covered. It's not as if we can prove the jar was ever there."

"Mm. And if the whole thing was staged to steal a Turis, whatever that is, then it's nothing to do with us or the Bloodstone at all."

They reached Lumpy Orange Crescent and skirted the fountain in a careful, alert manner. Zae dismounted and went inside first. Just within the doorway, she extended her senses to check for disturbances or traps. Keren did her own physical circuit once Zae pronounced it clear.

"I'm sorry I didn't have dinner ready. Plans got waylaid."

"It's okay, Pixie." Keren knelt to hug her close. Hugs were awkward with Keren's armor, but still worth it. "Let's do something else. It's been a tense, horrible few days, we're in a new city, and we haven't even explored it yet. I think we can be careful and alert and still take a little time for ourselves, like we should have been able to do our first day here."

"I . . ." Zae blinked. "I wasn't expecting that. After everything today, is it respectful to go out and play?"

Keren squeezed her hand. There was an earnestness in her eyes that was open, vulnerable, and not entirely familiar. This was something that Keren needed for herself, but didn't know how to ask for. "I can't focus on anything when I'm this weighed-down. I know you can't either. Just for a night, let's enjoy the novelty of not being exploded, poisoned, or ambushed for a change."

Zae still smelled smoke in her hair, and when she closed her eyes she still felt the way the room had jolted. Replacing those milling thoughts with more pleasant ones sounded like a necessary thing for both of them. "I like the way you think."

Zae helped Keren out of her armor, then washed up and changed into a simple pale blue dress with a white underskirt. She waited with her ever-present satchel over her shoulder and soft leather shoes on her feet. She wore thick leathers for working—a single stray spark could be deadly to fabric and anyone in it—so it was novelty enough just feeling layers of soft skirts brush against her legs and swish around her ankles.

Keren had also changed, into tailored leather trousers, her formal boots, and a brown suede tunic with gold embroidery at the neck and sleeves. She jingled when she emerged from the bedroom, suggesting chain and another layer of shirting underneath the loose tunic.

"You look beautiful." Zae folded both her hands over her heart.

Keren should have been used to the compliment by now, since Zae said it to her almost as often as she thought it, but the knight floundered for something to say. "So do you! When's the last time you dressed up?"

"There was the— No. Or . . . Hmm." Zae shook her head. "I don't actually remember. I can hear your mail under there. Are you going armed?"

"Probably should," Keren said with a grimace.

"No, don't apologize. It's comforting. Safe and alert, right?"

"Right."

Keren locked the door behind them while Zae got up into Appleslayer's saddle. "Where are we headed?" the gnome asked.

"The Ivy District. I thought maybe we'd take in a concert and a diversion."

The boundaries between some of Absalom's districts were subtle or even indistinct, but Zae knew the moment they crossed into the Ivy District. Even the air smelled different, of leaves and perfume. Gone was any hint of the sea.

The sun was on its descent, and the hanging plants that lined the narrow cobbled street filtered it into dappled light. Zae stopped and breathed deeply. She thought it might have been the deepest breath she'd taken since her arrival in the city. Even Appleslayer walked with a lighter step.

The main road curved around a large, open-air park, punctuated by groves of trees and lakes that reflected the orange hues of approaching dusk. At some point Keren directed them to turn. A short block of residences opened out onto such a lush and well-groomed market that it was hard to believe it occupied the same piece of land as the shifty bazaar in the Coins. Sellers' portable carts overflowed with freshly cut flowers and others still alive in decorative pots. Other vendors offered perfumes, teas, fruits and vegetables, pottery and carvings, and even the materials of scribes and clothiers: vellum and inks, and fine cloth and dyes. Permanent shops ringed the market, offering books, pastries, and artisans to tailor or sew the cloth sold just paces from their doors.

"I could live here," Zae proclaimed. That earned her a gentle brush of fingertips against her cheek and into her hair.

"You've still got your goggles on," Keren teased, tugging lightly at the strap.

Zae laughed. "I'm so used to perching them up there, I completely forgot. Hopefully they make the outfit?"

"Absolutely."

They eventually wandered toward the food sellers and purchased a bag of fresh greenhouse berries and two pastries filled with venison and mushroom in a savory herbed gravy, and a wrapped parcel of just meat for Appleslayer. A bottle of sparkling wine finished out the impromptu picnic, and a park bench at the edge of the market proved the perfect place to eat. A trio of violinists was just setting up nearby, so they dined and listened to string music, while the sunset painted the treetops and a breeze gently stirred their hair.

"This is perfect," Zae said. "Thank you so much. I had no idea this city had so much serenity in it."

Keren leaned in and kissed her. "I wanted to give you something new and different. I know it's your favorite thing."

The gnome felt her cheeks flush. "You get dropped into the middle of a giant mess that could turn into a holy war, and you're thinking about me?"

Keren laced their hands. Their matching rings glinted. "I'm always thinking about you."

Zae scooted closer, into the circle of Keren's arm. Appleslayer leaned against their legs and slid down to a graceless sprawl, basking in the afterglow of his meal.

Before Zae knew it, it was almost fully dark and the musicians were packing up. She got up and gave them a few coins for a lovely performance, and stretched. "That was wonderful."

"Oh, we're not done." Keren rose, dusting off her tunic, and grinned. Zae, intrigued, slipped her hand back into Keren's as they set off at a relaxed stroll, Appleslayer at her side.

"How did you learn about this place?"

"I asked around," Keren answered. "It should be just up . . . here. This one."

She turned up the walk to one of the meticulously groomed houses, double-checked the discreet plaque beside the door, and knocked. In moments her knock was answered; a beautiful woman with a narrow face and ears that suggested elven heritage opened the door wider and invited them in.

Pale wooden floors and orchid-stenciled walls dominated the front parlor. These were the sorts of floors you had when you wanted to show off how perfectly dirt-free your existence was. Zae, self-conscious, dug a hammered brass saucer out of her satchel. She bent and applied it to Appleslayer's paws one at a time, cleaning them with the simple spell triggered when his paw pads touched the surface. The dog, as if trained to this, turned after every paw to accommodate her.

Keren waited patiently, making small talk with the woman who'd let them in. Corn-silk hair framed her face and spilled in a straight fall down her back. She was dressed in white-and-pink silk. When Zae was finished, she introduced herself as Alturiel and led them further into the house. Zae tried to catch Keren's eye with a questioning look, but Keren's only response was a faint smile.

Their first stop was a comfortable, carpeted room with a cushion on the floor. "If you'd like, your companion can rest here a while. We provide water and grooming."

Appleslayer looked content and relaxed. The dog sensed no threat, so he'd be willing to part from them for a while, especially if brushing was involved. She suspected Alturiel had no idea exactly how much Apple could shed, or what she was getting herself into, but at Keren's nod of agreement, she said, "That would be very nice. Thank you."

With Apple settled, Alturiel led them farther into the house and down a flight of stairs. Humidity rose as they descended, and Zae soon saw the source: a sunken bath carved into the floor, filling the room with the mineral scent of hot springs. Potted flowers thrived here, fed by the dampness and magical light.

"There's a cabinet for your clothing here. Powdered soaps are in jars at the poolside. Help yourself to water or wine, by the soaps, but I don't recommend drinking from the pool itself. And here are towels, and just ring the bell if you need anything, or when you're ready." She bowed her head pleasantly and started back up the stairs.

"Keren . . . you got us a private hot spring?"

Keren toyed with the ends of her hair. "And an oil massage for two, with the attendants of our choice for after, if you'd like."

"How are we—"

"Affording this? With the money we didn't spend buying meals on the sea voyage we didn't take to get here." She pulled her tunic off over her head, and then bent over to wriggle her mail shirt off.

"We never did get to finish celebrating," Zae said.

Keren peeled off her final layer of clothing and strolled nude toward the square stone pool.

Zae, heart beating fast, got to work on her laces.

"Why didn't Vigil ever have gorgeous breezes like this?" Zae asked as they made their way home. It was a calm night, clear and cool enough to hint that the change of seasons was on the way. She felt drunk with relaxation and happiness, a glow due more to intimacy than to wine.

"You had a long day." Keren tousled Zae's hair with her fingertips. Appleslayer padded alongside them.

"Class, the . . . incident, at the Clockwork Cathedral . . . that was all still today, wasn't it? No wonder I'm ready to drop."

Keren squeezed her hand once in warning, then let go, hand moving toward the hilt of her sword. They had strolled into a narrow street at the start of the Merchants' Quarter, and silhouettes moved atop the buildings.

Unease sat heavily in Zae's stomach, but there was nothing to do but continue onward and stay alert. With every stride, Zae expected a group of attackers to appear from the shadows with a growl and a flash of steel. She considered her options, ticking through her remaining spells, and settled for quietly murmuring a prayer to Brigh to bring favor onto herself and her companions.

The attack came not as a sword or spell, but as a high-pitched swish like the flutter of bats' wings growing ever louder, and a heavy, shining web that emerged from the night sky and descended to tangle them in its cold wings. It was upon them before they could make sense of it, much less move out of its way. Zae knew that it had been flung onto them by the silhouettes atop the nearby rooftops, and didn't question how she knew or why it was happening. Panic overtook her even though she fought it. Instinct was to tear at it, as she was doing, or slash at it, as Keren tried to do, but they only ended up tangled further. Before Zae could be sure entirely what had happened, both of them were bound up in strong mesh and tumbled together on the ground. Appleslayer, only feet away, was barking and baring his teeth at a woman in leather, snapping his jaws warningly. For now, the woman was poised defensively and shooing him away, but one of her companions was approaching with his sword bared. Zae tried to direct a surge of energy at the man with the sword, but nothing happened.

Zae had come to love her silly white dog very much, and her worst nightmare was of seeing him cut down before her eyes. She'd had quite enough of that sort of helplessness for one lifetime.

"Apple, no!" Zae yelled. "Run, Apple!"

The dog whined. He paused for an indecisive moment, then ran. Zae was so relieved to see him sprint off into the night that she almost didn't mind the dull blow to the back of her head that followed.

18

THE TURIS

ZAE

Zae awoke, head pounding, to find she was sleeping on a hard stone floor. A few sparse shafts of light filtered in around the edges of a doorway, but that was more than enough for a gnome to see by. She could tell that she was under the weighted net, which held her prone, close to the floor. Even if her head hadn't been threatening to split apart, she wouldn't have had the clearance to sit upright. A handful of feet away, Keren was similarly bundled under her own net. Her armor and sword were gone, and her hands were tied with rope behind her back. Only when Zae shifted her shoulders did she realize she was similarly bound, at her wrists and—as another shift of sore limbs told her—ankles as well. Her mouth was strangely dry, and it was a few more moments before she was aware enough to realize her lips were held apart by a gag.

Unable to call to Keren with words, she instead made a questioning hum. After watching for what felt like a long time, she saw dark hair shift and recognized the way Keren always moved when she was surfacing from slumber.

Well, things could be worse, then. Zae was alive and seemed unharmed, and Keren likewise. Without the use of her hands to roll herself over it was hard to be absolutely certain where she was, but she could see well enough in the low light to recognize the greenish color of the metal—the metal *she* had helped to braid and weave.

A flush of bitterness at the betrayal rose in her like bile. Who? Was Rowan her enemy after all? Or one of the other creators?

No—anger and panic weren't helpful in a situation like this. She had to observe, remember to breathe, and wait for opportunities if she wanted to make it through.

She thought about Appleslayer. To the best of her knowledge, he had run home. She wasn't sure how far away home was, or whether their captors had gone there looking for them first. But it wasn't helpful to think about that, either. Whatever happened back at the house, there was little she could do about it from here. But it was all right to think about Apple in general. He was such a smart dog, and she had enjoyed the chance to participate in his training herself. She wondered if Sula could speak with animals and interpret his barks into the common tongue. That prospect amused Zae greatly; she would have to find some way to speak with Apple, sometime, and find out whether he was happy living with her, and what his life had been like before she'd rescued him. She wondered what his name had been before he was a slayer of apples.

There. Calm again. This time when Keren shifted, coming awake now, Zae felt relief instead of worry. And then, because she could, she raised her head and looked around.

Keren was under a second net. It looked more traditional, made out of thick, varnished rope. A third net seemed to hold a third captive, but this one was unconscious. If she concentrated, she could see clothing move with the slow and even breathing of deep, drugged slumber.

The room didn't look like an actual dungeon or jail, but rather a makeshift one. It was the sort of stone room Zae would have expected to find in a warehouse or a keep, filled with perishables that someone wanted to keep cool. The door was wooden, bound with iron. From the way light made its way through the cracks, she could see the shadow of the bar that latched it shut from the other side. A series of open horizontal slits up near the ceiling, probably barely large enough to fit a gnome's hand, ventilated the cool room and gave the warmer air—since warm air rose—a way to escape. The small openings may have been viable escape routes for air, but they were not an option for gnomes or humans.

Zae shifted her wrists, checking for leeway in the bindings. She could feel the braiding and knew that she was in rope, not steel. That was something, anyway.

When she curled her fingers, trying to scrunch them under one of the coarse loops, she felt a sharp jab of pain. She'd forgotten all about her injury with the milling machine; it had been eclipsed by the explosion and all the injuries she had helped to heal. It hadn't taken much effort to keep her finger straight through all of that, so only now did she recall the shard she had left in at the other tinker's request. She was reluctant to disturb it now, but it was almost certain to be the only tool she had on her. Maybe Brigh had even caused the accident in the first place so that Zae would have the piece of metal available to her now.

Not that it was readily available. She had healed the skin over it. Even if it wasn't far beneath the surface, it would take some getting to. She could feel the outline of it with the fingers of her other hand. Working behind her back would make an even greater challenge, but if Brigh had provided then it was up to Zae to take the opportunity she'd been given; it wasn't as if she had anything else to do with her time now.

Her fingernails weren't sharp enough to pierce the skin of her pinky, so she would have to work the metal up from the bottom. Shifting the shard inside her finger felt strange, sort of tingly in an unpleasant way, but was proof that she was able to move it. After some experimentation, she decided that a single hard push was what it would take to break the surface. She took a deep breath, recalling young Darrin in her treatment room back in Lastwall. She would do it on the count of three. One . . . two . . .

And push.

Zae couldn't recall ever having passed out from pain before. She blamed the earlier blow to the back of her head for weakening her sensibilities, but a detached part of her was taking notes on the experience. *Queasy . . . I see. Interesting. And can you recall today's date, your own name, and what you ate for breakfast? Good, good. Still held captive, no change there. Do you feel excitement? Hopelessness?*

Captivity led her to think of the metal shard in her finger, which led her to—very gingerly—feel across her fingertip for it. Ah, there it was. Jostling it brought a welcome shock of pain that helped her regain her senses, even as it made tears sting her eyes. Just the tiny tip of it was sticking out, but it was enough for her to grasp onto with her short nails and pull it out the rest of the way. She did it all at once, and the searing through her nerves left her gasping. She muttered insensible apologies to the tinker, Glivia, whose experiment she had just ruined. She may even have cried out, but she couldn't have sworn to it. Nothing in the room stirred in response.

Zae pressed her pinky tightly to the small of her back, applying what pressure she could by twisting it in the fabric of her dress. She would have to get loose in order to heal it with magic, so she hoped that she wouldn't have to heal it with magic in order to get loose. Fingers bled a lot—it was just their nature to do so—but it didn't feel as if she'd nicked anything vital in there.

Fortunately, the metal was sharp. Twisting it, closing her eyes and biting her lip in concentration, she found a single strand of the braided rope, wedged in the shard, and pulled. The pop of snapping threads was loud to her ears, as was her heartbeat.

It would work. Slowly, tediously, but it would. She felt for another single strand and manipulated it with a surgeon's careful touch. And then on to the next. Zae was so focused on finding and snapping each strand that when the door opened and light flooded the room, she was sure for a moment that they had heard her rope threads breaking. She went still, barely daring to breathe.

Heavy boots clomped across the floor directly past Zae's face, without stopping. They halted at the third body, where a large person bent down and peeled back the weighted net. The captor's voice was rough and deep. "Up you go, Turis. Time for another chat."

Turis was a person! He had been stolen from the Clockwork Cathedral, and the rest of his cognate slaughtered to cover up his kidnapping. The gears in Zae's head felt grainy, but she forced them to work. This meant their captors were the same people who had been trailing them, the same people who had sabotaged the machines.

Rowan's net, which they had been assembling when the machines were sabotaged, had been made for the same people who had sabotaged the machines.

No. Zae desperately wanted to believe that Rowan had no part in this. Maybe he hadn't known who he was really making the net for. Maybe the net had been stolen in the chaos that followed the explosion. Maybe the sabotage hadn't happened to get to the plans for the giant construct, but to have a way to steal Rowan's net. There were a hundred implausible things about that possibility, but Zae clung to it anyway.

Turis staggered, too groggy to stand unaided, but their captor was not impressed. Zae watched through nearly closed eyes as the tinker was hauled up over the captor's shoulder and carried from the room. Before the door closed behind them, Zae could see at least one other captor in the room beyond.

"Harnsen Turis!" This was a new voice, muffled by the partition but higher of pitch and with knife-sharp diction. She heard the soft slap of flesh on flesh; most likely, Turis was being roused with a few pats on the cheek. A few incoherent moans and mumbles followed. "That's a good lad. Come on back to us, Turis. Would you like a drink of this? Oh, you would, very much, I see. Well, tell us what we need to know."

"I've told you everything I—"

"Yes, yes, you've told us much. You're being very cooperative. Just a little more, now. You have something that belongs to our queen, and she very much wants it back. You and your friends in the other room will surely be rewarded if those things which were stolen from her find their way back to her possession with your help."

That was it, then: it was indeed Arazni's people who had captured them.

"What are they using to power the construct, Turis?"

"Electrical energy, harnessed and captured in a jar. I know—I know how mad it sounds. But it works. It's been done before."

"I think you're using divine energy, and I want to know where you're keeping it."

"I'm only the chronicler. I work with the cognates to document their inventions, but I don't do the actual planning or the work. I don't know where they keep anything!"

The questioning and accusing went on, and Zae noticed that when she was busy listening she wasn't busy breaking rope. With effort, she partially tuned the conversation out. She kept an awareness only for sounds of pain or coercion, but there were none. The main focus of her attention was the rope bound around her wrists. One by one, she snapped the little threads that made up the larger braids. It was tedious, but she could do nothing else until her hands were free. Pop, went one. Then another. Soon she was playing games with herself, to see if she could break them in specific rhythms or within a given time count. During all this time, Keren barely shifted. Knowing now how clearly sounds carried between the rooms, she was hesitant to make noise for Keren's attention again.

"We grow weary of you and your books, old man. Either you're somehow evading our truth spell, or you're skilled at dodging it with half-statements. We should have expected no less, since scriveners like yourself are merely scribblers of lies. Perhaps you've told so many false tales that you've come to believe them." The accent, now that Zae could hear a substantial bit of it at a stretch, seemed slightly guttural and foreign. The speaker sounded alive, but the woman who had pretended to be Kala the priestess had also sounded alive.

Turis muttered something. He sounded weak and hoarse now, and Zae wondered how much time had passed while she'd been meditatively snapping rope strands. She unwound her finger from her shirt and found it no longer actively bleeding. That was good, at least.

A chair scraped against the floor in the other room, and the pitch of Turis's voice raised to a keening, pleading tone. With concentration, Zae could discern that he was begging for something to drink. Thus it was no surprise that, after the pleading stopped and was replaced by effusive thanks, the scribe was glassy-eyed and weaving on his feet when the door opened and the captors escorted him back to his net. He was all too eager to stretch out with his cheek to the cool floor, muttering to himself as the webbing was replaced over him.

Without more than a glance toward Zae, Arazni's servants halted by Keren. One kept her shoulders pinned to the ground while the other pulled the weighted edge of the net up with a grunt of effort. Then they yanked her to her bound feet and took her away. Zae's heart pounded in her throat. Keren didn't struggle; she had taken a page from Turis's interrogation, Zae was relieved to see. Her fancy tunic and her chainmail were gone, leaving her in her long undershirt and leather trousers. The white cloth made her glow like a beacon for a moment, and then the door closed and returned the cell to its semi-darkness. Zae was left to her thoughts and her bindings; both felt equally frayed, and she wasn't certain which would snap first.

19

SUBJECTIVE TRUTHS

KEREN

The interrogation room held a chair, an oddly shaped stool, and a small round table upon which a thick pillar candle burned brightly. There were no windows along the rough plaster walls, and the few furnishings did little to fill the space. Keren managed to notice all of this while her captors led her to the odd stool and sat her upon it, affixing her ankles to the junction of a leg and the horizontal rung. A sharp wedge rose upward across the seat, not quite centered, and she was settled on it so that the ridge protruded across the spot where her bottom met the top of her thighs. No matter how she tried to adjust herself, it dug uncomfortably. For now it was a small annoyance through the leather pants she wore, but she knew it would turn painful in short order. One of the stool's legs was unbalanced from the other two, so that every time she shifted her weight, the seat would rock and betray her unease.

Her captor had wide-set eyes in a face that was pockmarked and rimed with dirt. The rest of his skin held an odd texture; after a few moments of trying not to stare, she realized his chest and arms, and even his bald head, were crisscrossed with scars overlaying other scars. She wondered if he was undead, like Tezryn who had met them in the park.

"You'll forgive my haggard appearance, my lady." He sketched a mocking bow as the other captor loosened her gag. "You haven't given us much chance for rest."

"I'm sor—" The sarcasm stuck in her throat and she winced, reminded of the truth spell she had heard them mention earlier. She could feel its compulsion on her, as if a blanket of honesty had settled around her shoulders.

"Sore? Yes. You will be. We know the Knights of Ozem sent you to Absalom to hunt the Bloodstone. Our associate confronted you about it and you killed her." The voice came from behind her; she had no idea who might be back there, or indeed how many of them. It was meant to put her off balance, just like the uncomfortable stool. It was also just as annoying.

"No. I came to Absalom to train. Your associates tried to kill me because I didn't know about the Bloodstone. I only defended my life."

"But apparently you know about the Bloodstone now."

Frustration boiled at the base of Keren's spine. She took a slow breath, refusing to let it show. "Yes, I know now. When I got to the Seventh Church with all that was left of their priestess, they were kind enough to tell me what I'd nearly been killed over. It's still not why I came to Absalom."

"You killed Tezryn."

"Because she was going to kill me!"

The *tsk* the man made behind his teeth sounded like the chitter of a bug. He leaned in close, holding a blade that vanished into her peripheral vision where she couldn't follow it. "She was only going to question you. Arazni gets the honor of killing you. But you struck her down, and now I have to mark you up to avenge her. Tezryn was my ticket, you see. 'Do what I ask, Del, and I'll guarantee a good word for you to Her Majesty. I'll get you and your family exalted when you die.' But now there's no Tezryn to vouch for me. Now I have only an eternity as a shambling, drooling clod ahead of me, unless I gain favor some other way . . . like by bringing Her Majesty one of Ozem's own. And for that, you get to stay alive and squirming a while longer."

The blade was sharp enough that Keren only felt cold against her face until after he had straightened and paced away a few steps. Then she felt the sting that meant he'd done more than threaten the skin of her cheek. Keren said nothing. At least now she knew he was living. She wasn't sure what good that knowledge might do her, but it was something to slip up her sleeve in the hope that she might be able to make use of it as a weapon later.

"So. I've done you a courtesy and told you why you're here. I don't owe you that. I could just take it out in your blood. Now it's your turn to be forthcoming. Shall we resume? You sent your squire to the Clockwork Cathedral to spy on a particular workroom. Why? What information led you to believe that they had the Bloodstone?"

"She—" . . . *isn't my squire*, Keren had started to say, but stopped herself. She couldn't lie, but she didn't have to be forthcoming about the truth. Best not to direct his questions down that path. If they thought Zae held less value to her, so much the better. If they thought they could use her affection for Zae against her, to coerce her, they already would have. The power of omission was another weapon for her mental armory. "She's studying there, of her own volition, just the way I'm studying at the Tempering Hall."

"She entered the cathedral late at night and investigated a particular workroom—on your orders, no doubt. What information led you to believe that they had the Bloodstone?"

A chill ran down Keren's spine. "You caused the explosions—you slaughtered the engineers in that workroom—because someone associated with me poked around in there?"

Her questioner's grimy face barely showed a reaction. "You are here to hunt the Bloodstone, the pair of you, and you hunted there. What information led you to believe they had the Bloodstone?"

Keren said nothing. That those injuries, the destruction, and the deaths were the result of Zae's curiosity and Yenna Quoros's encouragement weighed heavily on her conscience. There was no justice in it; she hoped Iomedae forgave her.

Del was not content with her silence, and prompted her again. This time it was a caress of sharp steel along her jaw. It stung for a few moments; warm wetness dripped down her neck, and she wasn't sure if it was sweat or blood. "Perhaps some whisper you heard at the God's Market, before our brother got himself dragged off in chains for you?"

"That was your—" The young man who'd played the role of caught thief had said his brother put him up to it, but she had assumed that had only been part of his act.

"My own little brother, wanting his piece of immortality. Well, he got it. Managed to martyr himself and take a Graycloak with him to the afterlife. I pray the queen rewards him for his deeds. Meanwhile, I will ask you again: what information led you to believe that the workers in that room had the Bloodstone? Someone at the God's Market?"

"Evandor took me to the God's Market to put Iomedae's ascension into context." The cut on her face started stinging again when she moved her mouth to speak, but she was braced for it and gave him no reaction.

"How clever of him to have given you a secondary goal, so that your denial of the truth is not quite a lie. The timing of all of this is just a coincidence, is what you'll tell me next? Maybe those merchants you spoke with will share a different story."

Keren fidgeted, shifting her wrists in their bindings behind her back. Staying balanced on the stool and pretending that the cuts on her face weren't drawing her entire focus to two stinging lines—these tasks stole away more of her concentration than she would have expected them to. She knew her best course was to not even try to speak in suppositions, and she would have to be very careful if she tried to skew the truth, but did he have the power he said he did? Could he threaten the safety of others if he believed her to be less than forthcoming?

The incident at the Clockwork Cathedral had been dramatic, but it was overdone and not the work of tactical thinkers. He'd put his own brother up to approaching her at the God's Market. And all for a chance to be raised to a better social position after death. She didn't have to wonder whether his behavior was rational. She knew it wasn't.

But Keren also knew that overdone, irrational violence wasn't beyond him. It was true that Veena was protective of Keren; if she knew that Arazni's agents were swarming to Absalom, she wouldn't have wanted a group of them to overtake Keren and Zae on their travels. But it was also true that Veena knew of the situation in Absalom and had sent them here deliberately. That made it hard for even Keren to believe that Veena had done so for any other purpose than to have Keren assist with the search for the Bloodstone. Still, that didn't mean it had been Keren's intent. She could use another reason as a supposition and have it still ring as truth.

She let the words pour out. "The timing is a coincidence. You're overestimating my importance in all of this. Look, I'm sure the precentor knew about the Bloodstone, and that's why she teleported us; she probably thought it would be unsafe for a lone Knight of Ozem on the roads. But this is just my guess, in hindsight. She kept her reasons to herself."

"More likely, they wanted you here to investigate."

"We're only here for training!"

"All right. We'll leave off with that for now. It was kind of them to send more Knights of Ozem along. The Harlot Queen does have an affinity for your flavor of holy servant, doesn't she?"

Keren's response was barely a flinch, but her questioner's wide eyes spotted it as if he'd been watching for it.

"Does that bother you, my lady, that Aroden's former handmaiden, the original patron of your very order, now exists to serve and pleasure the king of Geb?"

He paused, waiting for her to rise to the bait and give her protest voice, but she said nothing.

"I've never met my queen. I'm hoping I'll get the chance to travel along and present you to her in person, but I assure you my loyalties are with Geb and I'm very well versed in my faith. Her Majesty has fully embraced her role. Can you imagine having the full glory of being a demigod of justice, getting lured to your death by your own servants, and then being brought back to life as a king's whore?" He trailed his blade down the side of her throat, tracing around her collar. He let it bite in, but only where the bleeding out would be slow. "Oh, it might take you a few centuries to fully forget your former self. A few centuries of your lord and master whispering through your bones that your knights, your people, called you to your doom. And then imagine this: as if to spit upon your memory, your knights steal your very organs—all that remains of your living body, your humanity. Not enough to kill you once, no. Now they want you to suffer for eternity and never again be whole."

Keren breathed slowly. In for the count of five, out for five. She refused to respond to him. What angered her most was the title, the Harlot Queen. Arazni was not a whore or a harlot. She was a slave. A whore held the power; a whore chose what to do with her own body. A harlot was just a woman who enjoyed pleasure and wasn't ashamed of it. No, what upset her the most was that Arazni had not been given that choice. Her body had been raised and then claimed as property and used without her consent. She had been demeaned and degraded so that some undead husk of a king could make himself feel important.

She knew there was no point to trying to educate her captor on the finer subtleties of consent. Instead, she held her silence and dug fingernail crescents into her palms behind her back.

Her interrogator lifted his gaze above her head, then looked directly at her and smiled. She'd forgotten about the man behind her; he must have given his companion some sign indicating her anger, and now he would mock her all the more for it. If only she could strike them down with power, like Zae might. She tried to open herself to holy light, to offer her body as a beacon. She felt a brief lightness in her chest, but couldn't be sure it was anything other than her imagination. Nothing happened.

"If you struggle, you'll fall over. If you fall to the floor, I will continue . . . and leave you as you land."

With effort, Keren relaxed her shoulders and let her hands rest limply. Her interrogator wasn't a novice, and wasn't fooled, but he nodded anyway. "As obedient as your patron—well, your former patron. Though, Iomedae kneeling at Geb's feet . . . Now there's a thought. I can only imagine the pleasure he'd take from breaking her. Who would step up to the Starstone then? Would it be you, lady knight? Would you be next in the cycle?"

Keren's vision misted over, but she refused to blink her eyes and let him see the tears fall. They were frustration and rage building up in her and overflowing through her eyes, but he would think them sadness, or fear, and read in them his victory. He leaned closer to her, practically nose to nose, but just out of reach. A little closer, and she could bash his forehead with her own. As it was, to do so would be to fall to the floor as easy prey. And from his triumphant grin, he knew it.

His breath smelled like ash. "You will die for Her Majesty's pleasure. You're beyond avoiding that fate now. She'll bestow favor on me for bringing her a Knight of Ozem. If you're respectful, perhaps she'll choose to raise you. What a grand graveknight you would make."

And now she saw it: He knew that she had no answers for him, and had probably known for a while now. He was toying with her, taunting her for no greater purpose than his own enjoyment. Don't give him the pleasure of a response, she told herself, repeating it silently like a mantra.

He stood back, exchanged glances with his colleague behind her, and started again. "Why did the Knights of Ozem send you to Absalom?"

At least he asked the wrong questions.

"To train at the Tempering Hall."

Del growled with frustration, raising his fist but pulling his punch just before her cheekbone. She had tensed for the blow, and when she relaxed from the feint was when the real punch came, sending a burst of heat across her cut cheek and a shower of white sparks across her vision. From some detached, fuzzy place, she thought only that it was going to make an ugly bruise.

"Easy," the man behind her said. "We're too close to lose your head now. Remember everything we stand to gain if she's intact. Status, power, a way out of this city and a new life in Geb . . ."

A quick knock at the door startled her, and another accomplice peeked his head in. "Del, there's been a development."

Her interrogator huddled by the door with the newcomer and exchanged muttered words beyond Keren's hearing. She strained at the ropes on her wrists again, but couldn't get them to budge.

She sat straight and still as they reentered the room. The new arrival took a melon-sized crystal orb from a stained leather bag and set it beside the pillar candle, grunting with the effort of handling the heavy solid sphere gently.

"This is a scrying ball, your knightlyship. Very valuable. Our master sent it here, just for you." Del gestured her attention to it with a flourish of his knife hand. "Apparently, your compatriots are facing down a graveknight. I'm sure you'd love to go to them and help, but that's not going to be an option. To prepare you for your role in the life to come, we've been ordered to let you sit and watch them die." She could see faint shapes in the ball, and as she watched they resolved into clearer focus.

She could pick out Evandor, in his gleaming armor, and Yenna with her light-colored robes and dark skin, and even the dwarf guard from the church entrance. And a fearsomely tall creature clad in a horned helm and black armor that seemed to bring its own shadows with it. That would be the graveknight, and knowing that it had once been a living knight of her own order made it an even more terrifying sight. Arazni would have the power do this to Keren herself, and all her order, with the Bloodstones restored to her.

The strong guard, still behind her, said, "Go on. I'll handle things here." Del nodded to him and left with the man at the door.

Keren expected the guard behind her to come around and taunt her to her face, but he stayed where he was. He leaned in toward Keren's ear, so close that she could feel his breath. "Ever seen one of those before?"

She shook her head as slightly as she could. She didn't relish the thought of bringing her skin in contact with his.

"In for a treat, then. Just watch."

Wielding a greatsword with both gauntleted hands, the dark knight laid about himself in all directions, cutting down one paladin mid-cast and shearing the arm off another. He tore through the soldiers' armor like paper.

"Ha. Now they're seeing it. Anything holy is weaker against him. Should be stronger, you'd think, right? But it isn't."

While Keren had faith in Yenna's abilities, and knew that they had successfully defended the city from this graveknight once already and knew how to drive it off, she could feel the guard's narrative filling her with doubt, and with anger. She was angry at him for making her doubt, and angry at herself for doubting so easily. The common thread through all her training sessions was that she could recognize her doubts and control them. She had to control them now.

Yenna took a step back and switched from calling down holy light to heal the others. Keren knew Yenna to be capable. She tried use what she knew to push out what she was hearing.

"They desecrate the very ground, you know. All you holy folk, you get complacent, thinking your power's stronger than anything anyone else's got. But him, he's stronger than any of you."

The graveknight turned his attention to Sula, Sula who moved like water and could run Appleslayer all day without breaking a sweat. He swung, turning her blade aside with enough force to break her arm. Before she could recover he swung again, and great spouts of blood followed as he pulled his blade free. Evandor charged the shadowy assailant, but the graveknight barely seemed to notice the weapon connecting with his armor. Swords and arrows were less than insects to him.

Keren could see Yenna gesturing toward Sula and guessed that she was attempting to heal, but her spells didn't seem to help. Now she was shouting, beseeching Sula to retreat toward her, but the stubborn fighter refused, instead switching her sword to her good arm.

Sula, Evandor, and the three other defenders suddenly staggered back as one.

"Did we lose you?" The guard kicked one of the legs of Keren's unbalanced stool, jolting her. "Come on, focus now! You're missing the good parts."

Rivulets of bilious green streamed along the ground, acid etching a delta of trails into the stone street. Their point of origin was a pile of corroded leather on the ground where Sula had been standing.

It took Keren a few moments to realize what she was seeing. The guard chuckled when it stiffened her spine with dread.

The graveknight turned on Evandor, breathing deeply as if feeding on—no, as if savoring—the man's grief. Evandor screamed at the horned knight. She couldn't hear him, but she could see him gesturing.

"Wouldn't you like that kind of power? Imagine it . . ." There was a reverent tone to the guard's voice. "You'd be nearly invincible. Take a whole army to bring you down, and even that wouldn't be permanent. Unless they knew how to destroy your armor, you'd just resurrect from it and keep on killing."

"Is this why you took us captive?" Keren meant the question, so the truth spell didn't stop her, but she tried to make it sound more flippant than she felt. "So that you wouldn't have to watch the fight alone?"

Keren thought of the little prayers she had worked on with Evandor in her training session, and grasped for one now. Whatever power or slight edge they generally gave her, it was currently beyond her grasp. She envisioned the destination of the bridge, as Evandor had taught her, but the man still gave his discouraging commentary on the scene playing out in the crystal, taunting her for praying; for thinking she could affect the course of battle from afar. But he didn't move to stop her, so she kept her gaze firmly on the scrying ball while her lips moved in silent prayers.

O Iomedae, goddess of justice, please give these men what's coming to them for this—and please let me be your hand when you do.

20

STONE AND CLAY

ZAE

Zae listened silently to Keren's interrogation, using her own anger and fear to redouble her efforts at the rope that bound her hands. She nearly had it now; with each new strand that she broke, she could feel the structure falter. She tested it, twisting her wrist, but couldn't quite get her hand free. Just a couple more. Just a couple . . .

And there. It was a tight fit and probably took some skin along with it, but she shifted the base of her thumb out of the frayed rope and the rest of her hand slid easily through. Stretching her arms after the long confinement brought pain, but pain of a welcome sort. She made quick work of the gag and the rope at her ankles, then squirmed to the edge of the net and pushed up onto her hands and knees, raising it with her back. That brought one weighted segment off the ground; it took all her strength and cunning to wriggle herself free from it.

She rested a moment, catching her breath. The interrogation continued, and it seemed no one was the wiser to her partial escape. Still on hands and knees, she crawled to Turis's net and struggled to peel back a corner.

He was human, sharp-boned, and barely conscious. With the net partially out of the way, Zae rested a hand on his cheek, calling upon Brigh for aid. Warmth spread across her palm from her birthmark, and almost instantly the scholar began to stir.

"Shhh. Welcome back, and be careful. We can hear them, so they can likely hear us if we make too much noise," she whispered.

Turis frowned. When she freed his hands, he was able to push himself up and sit. Zae untied the rope binding his ankles next, giving him a few moments to gather his wits. By the time she was done, he had composed himself somewhat.

"Thank you. Harnsen Turis at your service. You're that healer from the corridor, aren't you? I apologize for Daarek. He gets a little excitable at the end of a shut-in."

"A little excitable" didn't quite cover the unprompted verbal attack on Zae and Rowan, but she let it go. "Yes, that's right. My name is Zae. That's Keren in there, getting questioned. They don't seem to be hurting her, at least, but I'm worried for her. Are you all right? Is there any other healing I can do for you?"

Turis rubbed the bridge of his nose. "I feel relatively whole, just fatigued. It's been a long . . . I don't even know how long it's been."

She hadn't thought about it, but Zae realized now that she didn't know how long it had been either; it had been dark when they'd left the church, she'd been thumped on the head and wasn't sure how long she'd been unconscious, and there were no windows here. "I'm very sorry about your cognate," she said instead. "The workers who were in the room with you—none of them survived."

He lowered his head, sighed, and then deliberately straightened again.

Zae worked at peeling back the net so that she could reach his bound hands. "So, what were you trying to do in there?"

"They—it's not my cognate, I'm just the chronicler—they were going to use a jar of electrical magic to power a construct. It's been done before, but there were a few proprietary modifications—purely experimental improvements—which I really can't talk about with the prototype unfinished."

"What will happen to the project now?"

"It might be reassigned elsewhere within the cognate, perhaps, but that's just—ah!"

Zae had freed his hands, and now sat back on her heels, watching him push the net off the rest of the way. Like Keren's, it was just a normal net. Only she had gotten a special anti-magic one.

Turis patted his pockets absently. A nervous tick. He had probably been searched and disarmed as thoroughly as Zae and Keren had. He withdrew a dented pocket watch and frowned at it. "It's morning," he observed sourly. "I'm going back to sleep."

Zae blinked. It made sense, since their capture had happened late in the evening, and she didn't know how long she'd been out cold after that. But it also meant . . . "Wait. If it's a new day, then I can pray for new spells!"

Zae scrambled to her feet and rested her hand against the wall, beside the door. It was very likely made of solid stone, in which case she had a spell she could prepare in order to defeat it.

She would need clay, and clay at its most basic was just wet powdered rocks. She searched on hands and knees for the stress points between the flagstones, and managed to brush together about half a thimble's worth of stone dust. She conjured a trickle of water and molded it in her hands until it was a sticky gray ball. Not the best, but it would do. Now, with one last ear toward Keren on the other side of the door, she turned her focus inward and prayed. A shortened meditation for now, but it would serve. Brigh would see her intent and her predicament, she was certain of it.

When she was done, the clay in Zae's open palm had gone slightly hard and powdery, but was still malleable enough. She centered it on her gear-shaped birthmark and closed her other hand over it. Focusing on the clay, she prayed to Brigh for Keren's safety and a swift escape, and offered herself as a conduit for punishing their captors, who had sabotaged the Clockwork Cathedral and killed talented crafters. She didn't know how many of those had actually worshiped Brigh, but the Bronze Lady felt affinity for all artificers and machinists, as far as Zae knew, so throwing in that bit couldn't hurt.

Prayer given, Zae turned her attention to the wall. She picked a spot beside the door, close to where the latch was sure to be, pressed the clay to the wall, and then began slowly pressing her hand *through*. With the spell and the clay, she could give shape to a limited quantity of stone, and now she chose for that stone to be a tunnel.

As if the clay was turning the stone around it as pliable as itself, gradually an indent, then a pocket, then a tube took shape. Zae hadn't worked out exactly what she was going to do when she broke through to the other side, but she was prepared to send a burst of magical fog through the hole to obscure her actions if she was noticed, or to wait and send the fog after she unlatched the door, if she managed to succeed without attracting attention.

Just a thin barrier remained now. She could feel it with her fingertips. She paused, listening. An androgynous voice murmured quietly in the other room, just barely audible if she strained her ears. Instead of trying to catch the words, she switched her focus to the cadence. The rise and fall could sometimes reveal as much intent as the words themselves, and sometimes even more. There was a taunting lilt to this speaker's cadence. Zae guessed—hoped—that this was one of their captors, speaking to Keren, and that Keren's lack of response was of her own choice. If the knight was unconscious, there was no way that Zae could carry her. Zae hadn't planned for that.

A crash shuddered through the building, freezing the blood in Zae's veins.

No, it was a door at the other side of the interrogation room. Earlier she had heard it open gently, but this time it was flung with excited force, and it was followed by a shout from a new voice. "The Bloodstone is in play!"

"What do you want me to do about it? I'm supposed to stay here and watch the graveknight with this one."

"That's what the thief wants, isn't it? For us to be all tangled up watching the graveknight and not bother coming after him. Kill the knight and come on, you son of a shambler's dog! That's what we left you those preservation spells for. What do you care if Del delivers her alive or dead?"

Zae swore under her breath. She'd run out of time for subtlety.

The gnome punched her hand through and immediately conjured fog. Vapor rose around her, thickening the air and pouring through the conduit. She couldn't get her ear to the hole while her arm was still through it, so she strained to listen while she fumbled for the door latch. It had to be right here. It had to . . .

It was. Her fingertips brushed it. But she'd miscalculated the height of the hole, the length of her arm, and the amount of reach she would have with just the bend of her wrist on the other side. It was just slightly too far and too awkward for her to get purchase.

A crash on Keren's side of the wall sent her heart leaping into her throat. She withdrew her arm, looking around wildly. There had to be something she could use to extend her reach. Anything!

She drew her hand through her hair. There was no time.

Her fingers caught on hardened leather and glass.

She still had her goggles. They had been tangled up in the mess of her hair during her struggle in the net, and no one had searched her bird's nest of wild curls.

The connection between the lenses was sturdy but not stiff. She would only have one eye-cup's worth of extra reach, but it would have to be enough. Winding the strap around her wrist so that she couldn't drop them if she lost her grasp, she navigated her arm back into the hole, with an eye cup clasped firmly in her hand. Sounds of scuffling could have been a fight, blind navigation, or just her paranoia. She couldn't focus on them now.

Once she was through the other side, with her shoulder pushed flush against the wall, she manipulated her grip on the leather and made as if to scoop up water with the eye cup. It caught on the latch and she jerked her hand upward. The door flung free and the metal bar clattered, catching nothing. She pulled her arm back and charged through.

Feet shuffled on stone, but without a visual reference Zae couldn't tell how many feet there were. For a moment she thought maybe fog hadn't been the best choice, but she had committed to it so there was no point in questioning it now.

A quick glint of light flashed in her peripheral vision and she ducked. It was a knife in a large hand, attached to a black-clad arm. She cataloged it quickly: human, taller than Keren, unfriendly. She wanted to call out to Keren, but she didn't want to give anyone else help finding her.

She saw wood, some sort of stick, on the ground just faintly in front of her feet and paused, reaching out to trace it with her hand. The cross-rung was looped with rope and the rope was attached to ankles, and at once she filled in the rest: Keren on her side, next to a wooden stool with three legs. Now that she knew what she was looking at, the vague shapes fit together more sensibly to her dampened vision.

After having removed her own bindings behind her back, the mobility to undo knots while unbound was a luxury. She didn't need her eyes for this, just her fingers and a little bit of time. As soon as ankles were free, Keren moved. She'd just woken, or she'd been playing unconscious until she divined the intent of the hands that had found her, but by now she must have recognized Zae's touch. She sat upright, offering her hands. The shape of her strong nose, vague outline of her hair, little details like these teased at Zae's eyes without fully resolving into Keren. When the knot was loosened enough for the knight to free her hands, Zae squeezed them. She was comforted to feel the same squeeze in return.

Keren released her and reached for the stool rungs. The wood rose up and out of sight. Keren was standing, readying the stool to use as a weapon or a shield, or possibly both.

Zae shuffled backward until she felt wall at her shoulder blades, ticking off the spells available to her and getting ready to cast them. Keren was whole enough to recognize her, and to stand, and that was enough to fill her with relief and strength. She prayed for courage to fill herself and Keren, then lifted the fog.

It burned away as if dawn were rising, starting at the ground and gradually clearing past Zae's line of sight. She did a quick scan around the room and saw only one pair of legs other than Keren's. Focusing on those, she prayed for their captor's weakness as she'd prayed for Keren's strength.

Keren was shorter than her captor, so her vision cleared a moment before his, but a moment was enough to give her an advantage. She swung the stool, connecting with his shoulder. He staggered back but recovered quickly and lashed out with his knife, catching Keren's sleeve. Zae cast about for something she could use. Near her was a small table with a pillar candle on it. The fog had quenched the flame, but the candle was thick enough to bludgeon with. Then she remembered how she'd almost tripped over Keren's stool and knew what she could do.

The man facing Keren was huge and muscled, with a fine fuzz of black hair over his head and jowls. He was focused on subduing Keren and didn't seem to have noticed Zae yet; she watched for a moment, creeping along the wall, and he didn't look her way.

Keren swung again and he grabbed for a stool leg. It slipped from his hand but muffled what was meant to be a hard swing into a jarring close-range thud against his jaw.

Zae was behind him now. She set the candle down, started it rolling toward him, and slipped out of the way. Keren was careful not to look at her, but Zae knew she was at least peripherally aware. Her next swing was slow enough for the man to grab the stool. Once he had a grip on it, she leaned in with her full weight, pushing him back. He tripped over the candle, Keren let go, and down he fell. Before he could get his bearings, Keren had snatched his knife away. She knelt on him and brought it down into his chest.

The candle stopped rolling with a tap against the wall. For a moment, silence was louder than any sound.

Keren straightened and looked her way. Her hair was stringy and matted, and her face and shirt were stained with blood. She eased carefully from a kneel to a slump, wincing. Zae had the prayer to Brigh already at her lips before she could reach Keren to touch her cheek. One deep gash healed, and the bruise behind it faded, color coming back to her ashen face under the layer of blood.

"Hey, Pixie. Are you okay?" Keren eased back, crouching, studying Zae at arm's length.

"Me? They didn't do anything to me. Are *you* okay?"

Keren turned away. "I tried. I tried to call to Iomedae and she didn't answer. Maybe I failed her by getting captured and she was disappointed in me. Maybe I'm just not meant for magic."

"Quit that. You can't know how a god thinks, or what a god thinks, so you can't second-guess them. Maybe you needed to be here for a reason. And you don't have your holy symbol on you. You need that, remember?"

"Yeah," Keren muttered. "I know all of that."

"At least you're safe and—"

"No one's safe now. There's a graveknight on the loose—they made me watch while it killed Sula and Barent and probably more by now. By the time we get out of here, I may not have an order left to report to." She took a deep breath and let it out roughly. Her eyes still looked haunted, but they turned hard and her strength shone through them. "Let's not let it be for nothing."

Zae sighed a sharp breath. Her skin tingled with adrenaline and relief. "Good. Let's find our stuff and get out of here."

When she turned, Keren let out a sharp curse and was instantly at her side again. "Zae, you're bleeding."

That drew her up short. "I am?"

Her dress was crusted and stiffening in the back, but Zae couldn't remember injuring herself. When Keren touched gently, feeling for a wound, Zae remembered. "Oh! That's just from my finger."

"Your finger?"

"I'll explain later. Long story. Come on, there's someone else in the other room here that we need to rescue."

21

Paper Trail

Zae

It's a maze in here," Keren complained. The building in which they'd been held captive was indeed a repurposed warehouse, as Zae had suspected, but there was little rhyme or reason to the way in which the space had been reapportioned. The interrogation room's other door led to a flight of stairs leading upward. The second floor took them through twisting hallways to a landing. Only the two of them explored. Turis had made a hasty retreat once freed from his net.

"Up or down?" Zae asked. Keren jerked her chin upward, and Zae followed her up another set of wooden stairs.

There weren't provisions enough for the warehouse's top floor to be the main lair of Arazni's agents, but there were signs of it having been an outpost. Under a roof of oilcloth nailed to bare rafters, they found a sitting room of sorts. A weather-beaten wooden door had been repurposed as a warped, splintery table, and rickety chairs were scattered around it. Their gear was piled on the table, all intermingled. Zae picked out her bits and set Keren's aside.

"Come and look," Keren called, and the floorboards creaked under Zae's slight weight as she joined Keren in the middle of the room.

The wall behind the door was a patchwork of maps, diagrams, and plans, with more of each spilling out onto the floor. Keren lifted the top sheet of parchment from a fallen stack. It was a crude pen-drawn map of Absalom with district boundaries marked in. Nothing was labeled, but a few areas had been circled in red. "The ink on this one is still fresh."

"Where?" Zae craned on tiptoe to look. Keren, distracted, lowered the page so that she could see it.

"This circle. The older circles are dry. I'm not sure where this is . . ."

"That's in the Wise Quarter. Where the libraries are."

"Hm. And this one?"

"That's the heart of the Coins—not far from where we were ambushed. And this one's in the Foreign Quarter. Do you think these circles are where the thief has used the Bloodstone? I wouldn't think they'd stop to document it before running off to chase it."

"No, they probably told whoever was up here to stay behind, and they were probably were too excited to listen to orders. It would make sense, especially if the latest attempt is what made them all scramble out of here so fast. If they could catch up with the thief . . ." Keren's lips were pale, pressed together tightly. "Help me go through these papers. There might be something else here."

Zae desperately wanted to ask Keren about her interrogation, to make sure she was all right, but she was learning that there were times when humans didn't want help; the times when help was most needed were the times when humans got the most stubborn. She had to let Keren talk about in her own time. In the meanwhile, there were snowdrifts of papers to sort through. They reminded her of the drifts of Appleslayer's fur that accumulated in the corners of the house if she didn't brush him often enough.

The top sheet was a bill of sale for food provisions. It was an interesting glimpse into obsessive cult life, especially since it suggested how many living agents Arazni had in Absalom. After all, the undead didn't need to eat.

"This is strange."

Zae looked up to find Keren studying a sheet on the wall. "It's the floor plans of this warehouse, Keren."

"Yes. It's the plans to a very simple building that they're already in, and yet it's in a position of prominence."

Zae frowned and extended her hand. "Let me see."

Magic was sunken into the page, strong enough to tingle her fingertips. She felt the strong urge to ball up the page and destroy it, but some small twinge in the back of her mind told her that wasn't a reasonable urge to have. Why would she feel compelled to destroy it instead of putting it back where they'd found it?

"There's something else here under the plans. Give me a moment." A quick murmur under her breath and ink started to fade, as if it had returned to the very fibers of the parchment. While she glanced over the writing that had emerged instead, Keren looked on, her gaze stormy.

"What's wrong?"

The knight shook her head. "Just . . . How easy that is for you."

"You'll get it, in time. Nobody masters magic in one day. Think of it like this: if you'd gotten free sooner, we wouldn't have this fresh ink on this map to track down; or we would have had to fight them all ourselves, instead of with most of them having run off."

Keren considered that instead of answering right away. "What's on that page?"

Zae clicked her ring against her teeth. Or tried to, and only now realized it was missing. They'd taken her lip ring but left her goggles? On second thought, it made sense that an organization which used poison capsules in their teeth would think to be suspicious of jewelry she could bite.

While Zae had heard the guards talking to Keren, she'd been too focused on escaping to pay attention. As long as the cadence of their voices stayed even, she'd assured herself that there had been no change in conditions. Now she wished she'd listened more closely. "It's a list of names. Do you think these are the agents in town, or . . ." Zae skimmed down the entries, then did a double-take. Ruby Tolmar. "This name. I know this name."

"That's the Ruby from your cognate? The one I met?"

Zae nodded. "I'm positive. I don't know what it means, though. Is she an operative? A spy? But the net they caught us in was Rowan's commission. I'm sure of it. I helped him make it. So did Ruby, but . . . the job was his. So maybe he's the one on the inside and he's been assigned to follow her? Should we warn her?"

"Are any of these other names familiar?"

Zae slowed down and looked again, lingering on each line. "No, just Ruby. How about you?"

A lock of hair fell in front of Keren's eyes as she leaned down over the page, but she didn't seem to notice it. Zae's fingers itched to tuck it back behind her ear. "This one sells fruit in the God's Market. I've passed his stand several times and his name's printed right across the banner." They exchanged a look.

"Spies, or suspects?" Zae repeated. "Do we warn them or pretend like we aren't onto them?"

"Maybe if we find the rest of the people on this list, we'd know . . . but it'd mean running all across town, and they're already closing in on the Bloodstone."

"Maybe not. These circles cover a lot of ground."

Keren looked unconvinced, but let it go.

Once satisfied that all her possessions were accounted for, Keren went through the process of shrugging into her chainmail shirt with practiced ease. The familiar jingle of it settling on her shoulders made her stand a bit taller. She didn't replace her good tunic over it.

"So, what's our next step?" Zae asked. "The list, or the map, or keep digging here?"

Keren grimaced. "We need to get out of here. This clearly isn't the Araznians' main headquarters—or her top agents, for that matter—but we can't afford to be here if they come back."

"You should take the list to the training hall," Zae said. "Maybe they know more. If not, there's got to be a city census record or something that can help you track these people down. I can take the map and go visit the places where the Bloodstone was used. Between my magic and Apple's nose, maybe we'll pick up a trail."

Keren stiffened. "What? I'm not leaving you."

"Are you the same Keren who was worried that we're running out of time?"

"Yes, and you're the Zae who, in the last day, cast a lot of spells and lost a lot of blood. You may not mind that your back looks like a butcher's apron, but the city guard might take an interest in that long story I look forward to hearing."

Zae looked back over her shoulder, but couldn't see the blood in question. She didn't think she'd bled *that* much in the process of pulling the metal sliver out of her finger, but it was true that she didn't know how long she'd spent stanching the wound with her dress or how much it had spread. "I'll go home and clean up first," she conceded.

"Here." Keren draped her tunic over Zae's back like a cape, fastening it with a knot of sleeves around her chest. "That'll do for now. So we'll stop by the house first, and then we—"

"Keren."

"What?" Keren asked, but her guilty expression said she knew exactly what.

Zae took Keren's hands and squeezed them. "I know you're worried about me, but we don't have time for this. We have to split up, at least temporarily. I can take care of myself. And so can you."

Keren's lips moved like she wanted to protest, but no sound came out. At last she squeezed Zae's hands back and said quietly, "I know."

"That's settled, then. You take the list to Yenna. I'll check out the circled areas. If those are places the Bloodstone's already been used, they should be relatively safe. And if I can find a clue your order's missed, maybe Yenna will start taking us more seriously. But getting those names to the church is key. We don't know if they're targets or allies to the Araznians. And if they're targets . . ."

"If they're targets," Keren finished for her, "then they might not have much time."

22

BLOOD TRAIL

ZAE

To Zae's relief, she found Appleslayer pacing outside their flat, whining, when she arrived home. He ran to her, bowled her over, and barely left her side while she changed quickly out of her bloodstained dress and into something clean and practical, then raced through her spell preparations.

The sites where the Bloodstone had been used days ago held no information that Zae could find, when she overlaid a city map with the crudely sketched one. Because of the map's small scale, the first two circled areas encompassed too much ground to be informative.

She started closest to home, riding through the Coins on Appleslayer's back. If the circle on the map was remotely precise, and she had no choice but to go on the assumption that it was, it could have marked a rickety hostel where the turnover of tenants was too high to offer any leads, or the very center of the market, or a cul-de-sac where a slave auction was just beginning. A pleasant-looking human apparently assumed she was there to buy and offered her a front-row seat. Zae swallowed her disgust and managed a polite refusal before continuing on her way.

The second site was equally unhelpful, too large to thoroughly canvass and too rowdy, with a fight just beginning in the arena. Taverns were full of eager gamblers who preferred to spend their money on bets rather than on seats to actually watch the combat; criers were dispatched to all the taverns and dice dens to indicate who had won a particular match. Zae welcomed chaos, but this was chaotic enough that the gnome began to doubt the efficiency of her plan. Maybe she should have turned the map over to the Knights of Ozem and let their numerous, experienced investigators question all the businesses within the circles.

But, no. Too much activity and the thief would go to ground.

Of the three sites from the map, the Wise Quarter, the one most freshly circled, was most promising. Assuming again that the cultist who had made the mark was operating with any sort of accuracy, the circled destination could only be the Forae Logos—the vast library which served as home to the Scriveners' Guild and was considered one of the largest libraries in the world.

Like all the important buildings Zae had ever seen, the library was daunting and beautiful in equal measure. She found herself thinking of the strangely secretive golem-making cognate with their contraband books as she slid down from Appleslayer's back in front of the open iron gate. Just the thought of being surrounded by so much knowledge and antiquity was making her fingertips tingle. The smoothness of vellum! The suppleness of leather! The sensual topography of embossed and illuminated pages!

"May I help you?"

It should have occurred to Zae that a facility so possessive of its contents might have guards stationed within and around its borders. It hadn't, but it should have. She felt herself blushing, and smiled up at him as pleasantly as she could. His brown leather uniform and cream shirt almost made him look like the living embodiment of a book, himself.

"Thank you, that's very kind. I'm studying here in town and I was hoping to do some research in the library. Is there a ticket stand or a registry to sign in on, or something of that sort?"

The guard showed little reaction, as if he was familiar with these sorts of inquiries and expected them. He gestured toward a tall stone archway. "You'll have to tie up your mount first. Just before the arch." She thanked him politely, patting Appleslayer's flank, and led the dog over to the hitching posts.

"It's just for a little while, Apple." He licked her hand and sat back on his haunches to wait.

The guard towers meshed seamlessly with the architecture of the library, and Zae could only assume they had been built together, with the deliberate intent of giving the library its own security force from the start. She extended her senses as she passed through the arch and felt the unmistakable aura of magic. Despite her curiosity, one thing she was *not* going to do was ask how someone could manage to remove books from the premises under all these watchful eyes and wards.

The reception desk was a crescent-shaped block of black marble, every inch of it carved with artistic representations of books and reading. Some were rather serious: a scroll with a guttering candle; a weathered scribe copying a thick tome onto a similar but empty page; a brace of ornate quill pens. Others were delightfully whimsical: of these, Zae's instant favorite was a carving of bare-breasted mermaids frolicking in a bottle of ink. As a result, when she got the attention of the clerk behind the desk, any hesitation she might have felt had been replaced with a happy, genuine smile.

"Good day," Zae said. "I'm a student at the Clockwork Cathedral and I'm researching the history of detection spells." It was the first thing to come to mind, but she knew she had to have a reason to be here. A library with its own personal guard wasn't going to let just anyone come in and browse the collection for browsing's sake.

The dwarven clerk's blond hair made her contrasting dark eyes look mysterious and deep behind their delicate spectacles. "Please sign in and pay the fee. By entering your name in the register you are affirming that you are not bringing any books into the library, and that you will not remove any. If you want to take anything out, we offer a copying service for a modest fee."

Zae signed her name with a flourish and looked up expectantly. The clerk checked her signature and stamped a small glyph beside it.

"Up one flight, turn left, in the corner along the front wall. Go on in."

"Perfect. Thank you!" Zae continued through the next set of arches. She could sense the magic washing over her skin as clearly as if a gossamer curtain hung across the entryway.

If she'd had longer—a week, maybe, or a year—to browse the library, it still wouldn't have been enough time.

Meticulously organized through some arcane system that Zae couldn't decipher, the collection was so vast that she quickly stopped being able to distinguish individual books and could only take in the overwhelming scale of it all. The ceiling was lost in darkness, making the shelves seem to stretch upward forever.

Zae was tempted to pass at least a few hours gawking like the tourist she was. Occasionally a guard or clerk would pass her, but they left her in peace. Now and then she was tempted to ask the way to a particular section, to see what they had on, say, the history of simple machines, or the genealogy and pedigree of sled dogs, or even just recipes that contained tea. But no, her mission was to remain unfocused and open to Brigh's guidance. What might someone else have been doing in the library? Researching, or hiding in the vast stacks, or having a clandestine meeting, or—

Zae drew up short and knelt. Around her feet were a spattering of reddish-brown droplets.

Or fighting.

Or studying a jar that seeped blood.

Since finding the remains of Kala's bloody garments in the alley, Zae had started adding a blood-detecting spell to her complement of prepared spells each day. With a scrap of parchment from a pouch at her belt and a piece of charcoal, she tried it now. The blood was mostly soaked into the floorboard, but there was enough that the magic should be able to identify its former owner. She touched it, cast her spell, and waited.

The page remained stubbornly blank.

Zae frowned. She rubbed the blood between her fingertips. Smelled it. It wasn't ink, or melted wax, or anything else reddish brown that might have spilled in such a pattern. No, it was blood. Blood that hid its history.

The blood of a dead demigod might not have a history that a mortal would be able to glean, the same way that divination didn't work around the Bloodstones themselves. Gods were probably too powerful for the spell. That could mean the Bloodstone had been revealed here, and recently enough for the blood to still be damp. This was the spot at which Arazni felt it.

She stood, stretching, and surveyed the area. A wide aisle separated a section of the stacks from a study area with long tables and chairs. Fireless lamps provided light for reading.

He had been here. The thief had stood right here with the Bloodstone, and unwrapped it from the container that kept it undetectable, and Arazni had felt it and told her guards. But why here?

Zae looked around at the tables, but saw none with books still stacked on them. Just her luck that the largest library in the world had to be the most efficient, as well. There were islands of tables throughout the whole floor of the building, and there was nothing particularly private about this one. That meant that if the thief *had* come here to read up on something—the best guess Zae could make so far—the shelves that interested him must be nearby.

Zae considered the shelves, her awe now flavored with dismay. Even if she could reach to see the upper shelves, there were far too many books in too strange an order for her to hope to stumble upon the right shelf, much less the right book.

If that book had even been put away yet.

She sat at the table, possibly in the same chair in which the thief had sat, and watched the clerks make their rounds. They circled constantly, clearing books and abandoned papers from tables. It seemed each had their own particular circuit, so Zae picked a few books at random and put them on the table next to hers. She got up and rearranged them to look more abandoned, and then took a small bronze ladybug out of her pocket, sat it atop the books, and settled down to wait.

A clerk came by within about ten minutes, wheeling a cart with a generous load of books stacked side by side. She looked young—though who could tell with elves—moderately tired, and extremely distracted. Physically, she was striking. One of her eyes was solid white, and her hair was blacker than any Zae had ever seen. She stopped to take the decoy books, and picked up the ladybug. The touch of her fingers made the figure's wings flutter—and also released a charm spell.

"Excuse me, is this yours?" she asked Zae.

Zae looked up from her book and smiled happily. "It isn't, but it's really cute, isn't it? What's your name?"

The clerk glanced around quickly, but Zae had kept her voice suitably low. She returned the smile. "Stochan."

"Can I ask you a question, Stochan?"

"Usually you go to the information desk when you need help finding something, but I'm happy to help too, if I can."

Zae nodded toward the cart. "Do the rounds get that boring?"

Stochan's lips pressed together into a coy sort of smirk. "I'd hate to call them boring, exactly, but . . ."

"But you'd rather be studying, or out for a pint?"

The clerk's demeanor softened. Charm spells had a way of making people feel that someone understood them. "Yes . . . Or anything, really. It's a long and complicated family inheritance story, but I have to complete a course of study before I can go off and travel. I'm doing a dissertation on druids and their interaction with the land. It's not a bad job, though. I shouldn't complain. They're paying me to learn my way around this place, and that's been very helpful."

"That's a good arrangement," Zae agreed. "Do you work all day?"

"I started before dawn this morning. I'll get to go home soon."

"Even better. You must be looking forward to finishing up and spending some time outdoors. This place is so deserted—has there even been anyone in this room today? Or am I the first?" While she spoke, she eased the chair next to hers out from under the table. Without putting much thought into it, Stochan took the invitation and sat.

"You're not quite the first, but I don't really notice people. Just books. If someone was doing something unsafe or prohibited, I would notice, but usually all I see are the tops of their heads bent over books when I come by."

"Have you put away many books away from these tables today? I'm always so fascinated by the combinations of books other people read. Aren't you?"

"Oh, always!"

"Anything interesting this morning?"

Stochan tilted her head and twirled a strand of hair around her fingers. "Myths and legends."

"Oh, I love myths and legends," Zae gushed. She was momentarily concerned that she had overacted, but the elf didn't seem to notice. "Which ones?"

Fueled by Zae's interest, Stochan perked up considerably. "I still have them on the cart. Would you like to see?"

Zae beamed. "Why, yes. Yes, I would."

23

THE GRAND TOUR

KEREN

Outside the warehouse, Keren got her bearings by sighting the Starstone Cathedral. Grim and determined, she made her way toward it. Zae had healed her, but she still wore her blood on her skin and in the fabric of her clothes. She had no idea how she looked, only that she was probably far from presentable. For her purposes, it was better that way. She was frayed, and she wanted that fact to be noted and taken seriously.

One of the guards was familiar, but the other was new. She bowed her head to both of them; they returned the gesture solemnly.

She found Evandor praying in the chapel, wholly healed, his armor scarred but clean. He greeted her in silence, with just a nod of his head.

The altar to Iomedae was an oasis from loss as much as a reminder of it. On it lay a short sword polished to a blinding gleam. In her mind's eye, Keren recalled Evandor's rage and inaudible scream as the rivulets of what was left of Sula etched tributaries in the stone underfoot. She felt her grief for him and for the order, recalling the way Sula had so easily shown herself worthy of Appleslayer's trust.

After a few moments, he looked up from prayer. She straightened at his side. "Sword Knight Malik, I have developments to report." He motioned for her to lead, then fell into step beside her, and didn't seem surprised that their destination was Yenna's study.

Once inside, there was still no mention of Sula, and Evandor's hard eyes warned Keren away from opening the wound of his loss. Keren sketched out her night and morning's ordeal, as well as the previous day's explosion at the Clockwork Cathedral and how it was related. She answered questions, and showed them the recovered financial sheets and list of names, and told them about the sudden change of plans when her captors discovered the Bloodstone was again in play.

They took her seriously. Yenna summoned a pair of Sword Knights and gave them the list and instructions to track down all the names on it. Another pair she sent to the warehouse, with Keren providing directions.

When the rush of deployment quieted, Yenna sat back with a frown.

"What is it?" Keren asked.

"These clues are useful, but they don't fit the behavior of the thief as we observed it in the vault of the Bloodstone."

"What's different?"

"Whoever our thief was, he knew our defenses and evaded them all. That sort of premeditation and research suggests a very specific interest in the Bloodstone, and a purpose for it once the theft was done. It doesn't match with someone who comes here afterward and lingers, unwrapping the Bloodstone all around the city. If he had a buyer, it would have changed hands by now. If he had a use for it, he would have used it."

Keren leaned forward. "Will you let us see the vault? Maybe by combining your clues with the Gebbites' clues, we can piece something together. If innocents are being killed because of our actions, please at least let our actions count for something."

Yenna shook her head. "Our investigators—"

"Haven't seen what we've seen." Keren forced herself to stay perfectly still, meeting Yenna's gaze.

For a long moment, Yenna and Keren studied each other in silence. At last the priestess bowed her head and sighed. "So be it. Gather your companion, Crusader Rhinn. I'll take you myself."

The slight disorientation of teleporting was nothing compared to the disorientation of the sudden shift in climate. Where Absalom had been breezy and a bright sun had shone overhead, Keren now found herself in a barren wasteland. Uneven rocks made footing treacherous, and the air was completely stagnant, with no hint of breeze to soothe her skin or moisture to wet her lips.

"What *country* is this?" Zae breathed.

"Come." Yenna started off in what seemed an arbitrary direction. Zae climbed up into Appleslayer's saddle, and the dog and Keren walked side by side, picking their way carefully over loose stones that seemed to be entirely without dirt or other foundation to hold them in place.

Zae had updated them with her findings at the library, but that had only concerned Yenna further. If such planning had gone into the theft, why was the thief—or the thief's buyer—researching it now?

"Shields, wards, and camouflage from ground and air," the priestess said. She sounded almost bored, as if she were showing a vacant house to a prospective buyer. For a moment, Keren felt uncomfortable about their insistence upon seeing the vault. But only for a moment. They were neck-deep in this, after all, so it was only right.

At a grand gesture from Yenna, golden light poured across the ground like a liquid sunrise. In its wake, golden glyphs remained, shimmering on four of the rocks. She stepped on them in a particular order, and before them a pathway began to sink away from the surrounding stone, creating a ramp downward until a human standing at its end would be faced with a smooth wall of stone and dirt taller even than herself.

"The thief had to be able to call holy energy?" Keren asked.

"In principle, the stones can be activated in order without it, but they would be quite difficult to find. The stones are only the first half of the trap. Here at the entryway, there is one chance to activate the lock. If it is not activated within a certain time, or a first try is unsuccessful, the stones give way to a pit filled with holy water. Please stand back until I open the door."

Keren watched carefully, but Yenna was equally careful to block the mechanism with her body. Though the vault was empty, and perhaps could not be used again now that it had been breached, the priestess still guarded its secrets. The door, with its facade of rock and dirt, swung inward, and Yenna gestured for them to follow.

"How many people, besides the guards, know how to get in here?" Keren asked.

"Five," Yenna answered. The door swung closed behind them, plunging them into momentary darkness. Zae's eyes adjusted first, and she made a small, curious noise. When Keren's vision followed, she could see three stone steps down, leading to a well-lit path straight ahead, roughly the same width as the doorway through which they had entered. A smaller, unlit dirt path branched off to the right.

"All of us who know are sworn to Iomedae. If any key-keepers or guards had turned, they might keep secrets from their fellows, but not from their patron goddess. We renew our sacred oaths each day. I'm confident that the breach came from outside."

Her tone invited no argument; one was on the tip of Keren's tongue regardless, but she kept her silence. In a place as dangerous as this, she wasn't about to argue with her only guide.

"Ahead, the path leads to a door with a complex lock. The door is a decoy. Behind the lock is not floor, but a pit, and within the pit is death. But first, the stairs must be traversed and then deactivated. They contain pressure plates that must be pressed; to circumvent the stairs triggers a trap, and to fail to deactivate the stair also triggers a trap. Come, all of us abreast."

Zae dismounted and they obeyed, stepping deliberately on the three stone stairs. When they were at the bottom, Yenna turned and crouched, lifting the top off the second stair and manipulating a mechanism within. Keren turned her gaze upward. A section of the ceiling was textured differently from the rest; borrowing Zae's goggles off her head and holding them up to her own eyes with the magnifying lenses engaged, Keren saw the texture resolve to a dense forest of close-placed spikes. It swayed a bit, as if by some unnatural breeze.

Yenna summoned three dancing lights to guide her way and led the companions down the side path. It was narrow enough to require them to walk single-file, and had a disused, undisturbed air about it. Appleslayer lingered for a moment, sniffing, but continued on before Zae had a need to nudge him.

The path opened up into a large rectangular room—a folding screen partitioned off the section of it in which they stood as a common room for the guards who lived here, and it contained books, musical instruments, cards and dice, and other such amusements as might occupy a guard during his idle time. Most of their time had been idle, Keren supposed, since their task had been simply to live down here with the Bloodstone, should anyone happen to bypass the vault's tricks and traps. Not that their presence had done the artifact any great service when that intrusion occurred.

"Where were the guards . . . found?" Keren asked.

"Neatly disposed of in one of the pit traps," Yenna answered. "Mutilated in a precise and careful way."

As if the thieves intended to cast scorn on the trap, and proclaim themselves too smart to be fooled, Keren thought. She cleared her throat. "Have other attempts on the Bloodstones been made?"

"Of course. They've been under our guard for nearly a thousand years, after all. There's only so much ground in the world, so it's inevitable that some might stumble upon the vaults, or have their suspicions about where they might be. The guards retrieve the bodies and alert us to the nature of the intrusions. None have ever been great enough threats to cause us concern. Most wander ignorantly around on the surface. A rare few have activated the stones up top. Of those, most are dispatched by traps before the guards need even rouse themselves. Only once, I believe, did a guard need to slay interlopers, and that was for the heart's stone, in a different vault than this."

Keren held herself back from the question in the hope that Zae wouldn't be able to resist asking. She was not disappointed. "Which Bloodstone was housed here?"

"Here rested Arazni's Glory—her liver."

Zae opened the cover of one of the books and fluttered through the pages. "Do the guards serve here until they die, or do they retire somewhere?"

"They have the option to retire. Some of them prefer to serve out their days here."

"There have been several generations of guards by now, I imagine." Keren tried to phrase this delicately, to avoid suggesting that replacement guards may have been agents biding their time, but from Yenna's frown she could see that she hadn't succeeded.

"All of whom are loyal to Iomedae to their last."

"But, force? Or coercion?" Zae ventured.

"You are not of our order and, with respect, you're already seeing more of our secrets than an outsider ever sees. Be assured, they are carefully screened and their vows are under constant watch," Yenna said, and that was the end of that. "Come. There is more to see."

They followed Yenna back out of the common area and along another brightly lit hallway carved out of the rock. It had smooth walls and a high ceiling, for all that it was fairly narrow. "Down this way is the vault itself. We will pause here at the door."

The door was a thick, wooden affair, carved with three faces, eyes upraised and mouths open in song. Shadows deepened their creases and the light flickered in ways that almost gave them life, making them angelic and terrifying at the same time. Zae hopped up on tiptoe, but there was nothing to see; no light emerged at the far end of the mouth holes. They were arm-sized tunnels; a person would have to reach her entire arm into the alcove in order to manipulate the lock. And that meant . . .

As she realized it, Yenna confirmed it. "Each alcove has a keyhole at its end. The first door we entered, and the decoy door to the dead end, also have this configuration. Reach into the wrong keyhole, and a guillotine neatly removes the offending arm. Poison on the blade keeps the wound from healing. There is a pressure plate underfoot—it's been disabled, don't worry—that gives way to a pit if someone stands before them deciding for too long."

The priestess slipped a signet ring on her finger, and produced a key from the folds of her robe. "Even getting the correct keyhole has its penalty. Unless the hand which opens the lock bears a sigil of Iomedae, reaching into the alcove triggers a weakening spell, and opening the lock triggers a curse. It's a harmless thing to one with no ill intent—any priest of Iomedae will gladly remove it, and there's at least one priest in every watch. But for anyone who intrudes with theft or murder in mind, it can create a great disadvantage, especially if the same thief successfully unlocks each lock. Their success will come at the cost of the ability to defend themselves."

Yenna reached confidently into the middle keyhole, and a moment later a deep click resonated from within the door. It swung smoothly open, revealing a perfectly round room. In its center, on a pedestal, was a stone jar with its lid carved into a bust of a grotesque creature. Surrounding the jar was a glowing blue circle of power. Nothing here looked as though it had been disturbed. "Obviously, this is not the actual Bloodstone."

Keren stared, awed. She had expected defenses, but not multiple decoys upon decoys. "So . . . This whole vault is false, and it's a trap?"

"Indeed."

"And the thief knew this?"

"Apparently. I'm showing you this so that you understand the depth of knowledge required to carry out this theft. And to stress my concern when I say that the first decoy door after the entrance, and this door to the formal decoy vault, were both undisturbed."

Keren cleared her throat. She could see what Yenna had meant about the intricacy of the theft. Now she also wondered what would make so motivated a thief linger around Absalom. Maybe the times the artifact was unwrapped were different attempts to entice a buyer, but who would go to such trouble without a plan for after?

"Arazni can supposedly feel it when the Bloodstones are used?" she asked. At Yenna's nod, she continued: "What counts as 'using' a Bloodstone?"

Yenna looked pensive. "I believe merely having it on one's person triggers the effects. That would count as use. It's also said that she can tell which Bloodstone is active, since they're all different organs and pull at her differently. That's why we're confident our thief must have the Bloodstone in a container that shields it from detection. Otherwise, the Bloodstone would have summoned Arazni's minions to the entrance of the vault the moment the thief surfaced with it; this facility is, of course, shielded as well."

"That's exactly what I was wondering, yes."

Yenna led the way back to the barracks, to the other side of the folding screen that divided the room into sections. This was the bunk room, and what stood out immediately was a gaping hole chiseled out of the wall.

"That . . ." Zae murmured. "That's kind of brilliant."

"What's that?" Keren asked.

"Instead of having the artifact in the big fancy vault, you have it in the barracks, where it's going to be best defended at all times because there will always be guards around it. And it can't be burrowed to from behind because it's so far underground, and it's not on ostentatious display, which it wouldn't need to be—it's not like this is a museum where people come to gaze at it. It's supposed to be hidden away, that's the whole point, so of course it would be hidden someplace where it wasn't easy to access, because who would ever need to pull it out again?"

Keren felt an equal measure of her companion's awe. The first thing to come to her mind, though, was not an affirmation of that awe. It was a deep, cold fear that drilled at the pit of her stomach. "Where's Appleslayer?"

24

Trail's End

Zae

Zae found she couldn't pinpoint the moment when Appleslayer had wandered away from her side. She had faith that the dog was, in general, more than smart enough not to wander where he shouldn't, but this was not a general case. This was a literal minefield, and she wasn't sure of her step even *with* the expert guide.

Apple wasn't among or under any of the bunks, or in the galley, or the privy, or in the common room. Zae whistled sharply and heard his muted bark in response. With a look toward the others, she stepped into the doorway. "Is it safe to traverse the paths we've already seen?"

"Yes, as long as you don't try to open any doors or go up the stairs," Yenna answered. That was good enough for Zae. Carefully, minding her steps, she followed the echoes of Apple's bark and the sparse drifts of shed white fur. It hadn't been a pained noise, or a worried one, so she wasn't panicked, but she also didn't know what sorts of trouble he might yet get himself into. The others trailed behind her.

They found the dog in the entry corridor at the base of the three stairs, pacing the well-lit passage between the rigged steps and the first locked decoy door. He was sniffing wildly, nearly losing his balance staring up at the cavern's ceiling as he paced and circled. When Zae approached, he reared up on his hind legs and pawed at the air.

"His response isn't unique. We brought our own tracking animals through, and they also caught the thief's scent in the barracks, and lost it here when he exited successfully. We think he obscured his scent and appearance at this point, in case anyone might have been outside."

Zae, resting a hand on Apple's flank, looked upward with him. The spiked platform loomed menacingly above, waiting to be released by the trigger in the second stair. As soon as Zae joined the dog in contemplating the ceiling, he calmed. She knew this behavior: it meant that he had observed something and was now content that others were checking into it. The gnome considered for a moment. "Is there any way we can get the spikes down gently?" she asked.

Yenna seemed surprised by the request, but moved obligingly to the stairs. "Wait in the common room until I call for you. It's dangerous, and it might also stir up a lot of dust."

Zae and Apple followed Keren to the other room, where Apple whined an inquisitive noise and wagged his tail expectantly. "You're a good boy," Zae told him, rubbing his ears. "Be patient, and we'll see what you found."

At Yenna's call, they returned. The priestess had lowered the spiked drop-ceiling so that its wicked points hovered just above the ground, putting its platform at the level of Keren's chest. There was something on the platform, but Zae's attention was on the spikes, which were taller than she was. For the first time since she'd entered the vault, she felt queasy. Fortunately, she had to back up from the spikes to see onto the platform that held them, and that sight distracted her from the flutters in her stomach.

"That doesn't look like a guard," Keren ventured.

From Zae's low vantage, she could see only crumpled black cloth and dried blood. Keren and Yenna circled the platform, pausing to inspect it from all angles.

"What do you see?" Zae asked.

"Cloth and blood. No body. That explains why none of us noticed a smell. The surface is corroded and pitted, but there's still some blood. One moment, and I will be able to tell you more." Yenna pulled a curl of parchment out of a pouch and flattened it on the wood next to the corpse. Then she took a vial from a pocket in her robe and allowed two drops to fall on the blood, reconstituting it. She narrowed her eyes in concentration and murmured a spell, reaching out to touch her fingertips to the bloodstained platform; the same spell Zae had attempted in the library.

The spell had not worked on the blood Zae had found, but when Keren leaned over to look at the parchment, the surprised look on her face was enough to tell Zae that writing had begun to appear on it.

"His name was Ferrin Tark," Yenna read from the parchment. "He's been dead a week, weakened in battle and then stabbed in the back. He was a necromancer from Ustalav. Our investigators assigned to the Whispering Way might well recognize his name. It seems that they were the culprit after all, not that that helps us now." She rolled the paper tightly and tucked it back into her pouch.

"Was he our thief?" Zae asked, at the same moment as Keren said, "But if he's our thief . . ."

"Then where is the Bloodstone?" Yenna finished. "Indeed."

"What if all the times it's surfaced, it's been changing hands?" Keren asked.

Yenna shook her head. "That doesn't matter. It's still in the city, and therefore we still have a trail to follow."

"Stabbed in the back . . ." Keren mused. "Even if a guard had stabbed him in the back, a guard wouldn't have moved him and left his cloak like that. It's like someone tried to hide the body and then the body, what . . . ?"

"Took care of itself, like the Arazni cultists do? Maybe whoever killed him did something to the body after he died," Zae said. "But the stab in the back was what technically killed him."

"And someone who was with him decided to take the treasure and run?" Keren added.

Zae frowned. "Would that make him the mastermind or the minion?"

Yenna brushed flecks of blood from her fingertips. "Well, now that we have his name, we can find out. More importantly, he was weakened in battle. Our thief likely let the necromancer and the guards weaken each other, and delivered the final blow to him here, right before the entrance. Then, in his haste, he didn't disarm the final trap. The spikes fell, but he managed to survive them. Then he thought he would hide the necromancer's body here and raise the platform, but he destroyed the body first, so that there would be little to find and trace back to him." Her brow creased. "So now we have a new avenue: we will track down our departed Master Tark and see what we can learn about him, about his associates . . . and about how he learned to bypass the secrets of this vault. His trail should lead us to whoever has the Bloodstone now."

Yenna stepped around the block of spikes and manipulated something near the stairs. She paused. "We've been over this vault repeatedly; I didn't think anything would come of visiting it again, but I was wrong. We should return to Absalom."

"Will you use this vault again?" Zae asked. "I notice you're taking care to keep the traps and locks functional."

"We won't return the Bloodstone to this location, but we may use it for something else in the future. We will have to see how widely the knowledge of its location has spread. It may even be useful to have an empty vault to serve as a decoy, with plenty of traps yet no treasure at all."

Zae skirted around the giant spikes. "I think that would be extremely deterring. I would ask you to reset this one, but I don't know if I'm bothered more by seeing how large these things actually are, or not having to see them but knowing that they're hovering over my head."

"I will have the remains removed and returned to us, so the spikes will stay down for now. Come around carefully, and we'll be on our way."

They emerged into a hot, barren twilight, and Yenna transported them back to Absalom, where the afternoon sun was still in the sky.

She gave orders for the necromancer's remains to be collected, and checked in with the people she'd dispatched earlier. All but two names on the list had been accounted for; they were all members of different institutions or organizations around Absalom. The Arcanamirium. The Scriveners' Guild. The dockworkers. The theaters in the Ivy District. The courtesans in the Petal District. A seller in the Grand Bazaar. A guard at Azlanti Keep. An errand boy in the Puddles. Ruby at the Clockwork Cathedral. And on, and on.

"So they're spies, then," Zae said. "They must be. They wouldn't pick one suspect at each location, but they would plant one set of eyes and ears with nearly every group in the city, so that they'd be sure to find the thief no matter his affiliation."

"That's how it looks, yes."

They were silent all the way home. Zae rode Appleslayer at a walk, and Keren strode beside them with a hand on Zae's shoulder. Zae had never been happier to hear the sad trickling of the lumpy orange fountain. Even the inexhaustible dog was dragging his paws, but he rallied a last surge of energy as they turned on to their street.

Zae built up the fire and put the kettle on. Once the flames were flickering in the hearth, she sat on the kitchen floor with Appleslayer, removing his saddle and brushing him while she waited for the water to boil. Generous snowdrifts of fur collected in the wire brush. Back in Vigil, Zae had collected the fur and sent it to be spun into fine thread. Her favorite formal gown, stunning white with bell sleeves and cobalt jewels, was made from Appleslayer's own coat. As for the dog, he glowed under the attention. His tongue lolled happily, and his left ear drooped the way it only did when he was deeply relaxed.

Keren padded out to join them wearing her jade silk robe.

"So, what now?"

"I don't know. You visited all the sites. Yenna's people tracked down every name on the list."

Zae thought of Ruby, her kind and gentle demeanor. Then she thought of Rowan and her stomach soured. His name had not been on the list, but that greenish metal she'd been trapped under had been enough to show her where he stood. "I'd like to think they're not really accomplices, that maybe they're just being used, but . . ."

"Possession and scrying, you mean? I suppose it's possible, but there were a lot of names on that list. It would be a lot of work and constant vigilance to monitor all those people all the time. The simpler explanation is that they're willing accomplices—but they might not be really willing. They might have been coerced into cooperating."

Zae smiled weakly. "I appreciate that. Trying to soften it for me, I mean. But if Ruby's in on it, then she's in on it. Maybe that's why she's so nice. She's cozying up to the academy because she wants to earn the trust of anyone with something to hide. And she does blood magic," she added, remembering the healing spell Ruby was applying to a saw on Zae's first day.

Keren sighed. "Sorry, Pixie. It does make sense."

"More sense than anything else. What about the blood in the vault?"

Keren handed a mug down and joined Zae on the floor. She took a turn at brushing Apple's flank while Zae sipped her tea. "Yenna will let us know when she receives word. What about the circles on the map?"

Zae inhaled steam, ordering her thoughts. She'd been tumbling over herself to tell Keren everything when she arrived at the Seventh Church, but she'd had to keep it all packed down for so long that other thoughts had become stacked on top of it all and now had to be shifted aside. "All right. Let me go over it again. At the other sites, I couldn't figure out what the circles were actually meant to be circling, but at the Forae Logos I found nearly fresh blood whose owner couldn't be divined, and a very nice clerk showed me what had been researched just this morning at the table next to the blood." She had shared this much already, but she didn't recall exactly what she'd said, so it didn't hurt to say it again. "Whoever sat next to the blood was reading books on religious artifacts, all of which contained entries on the Bloodstones. Folklore and legends about them. Things like that. And she remembered him moving from one section of the library to another. At the other place where he sat, there was another stack of books, but that was someone else's section. She's not sure she'll be able to find out what he'd been reading there. She offered to try to sweet-talk the clerk who reshelved them, but she might have changed her mind once my charm spell wore off."

"He was looking up multiple things in different places? Or he wanted to make sure those two stacks didn't look like they connected to the same person? Why does he care?"

"I didn't connect it earlier, the two stacks, but this makes the odds good that it wasn't a hand-off or a sale. The same person was in both places, and he was researching the Bloodstones, *and* something else. Maybe he just switched seats to be closer to wherever the other topic was shelved. So whoever has the Bloodstone and whatever they're using it for, I don't think that's worked out for them the way they planned it. Something's gone wrong that they need to try to research again."

"Do you think that's where the Araznians were planning to go when they left us?"

"I'm pretty sure. The blood was fresh. But they didn't get to the library in time and the thief was already gone and the trail was lost. I don't think they even went in. I'm sure the librarians would have still been talking about it if a bunch of bandits had tried to storm their guards."

"Or maybe they homed in on a different building? You said that the other sites were too vague to yield anything. Maybe those sites were only too vague to you. What if you only focused on the library because you were thinking about the stolen books hidden in the workroom? At least now we know *they* weren't involved. Even though it means those inventors died for nothing . . ."

Was it possible her own bias turned her toward the Forae Logos? Maybe. "I'm not disagreeing. But that circle looked like it really was centered on the library. The other circles were more vague; they covered more than just one main site."

"So. What was in those other areas?"

Zae set her mug down and traced her thumb along its rim. Apple perked his head up and sniffed at the contents, then settled his chin back down on his paws with a quiet huff.

"The one in the Coins could have been a hostel or a slave auction hall, a dead end street, or any of about five market stalls."

"What did the stalls sell?"

Zae closed her eyes, focusing on recreating the visual memory. It wasn't that she hadn't paid attention; it was that she'd assumed the information unimportant and discarded it. "I think . . . food sellers, and a fortune-teller or two."

"That would make sense, a few steps away from the door of a hostel. Maybe the thief was staying there."

"Maybe."

"What about the other site?"

"The Foreign Quarter? There, it could have been any number of taverns or gambling dens. Maybe the thief tried to sell it to a fence when he realized he was being chased for it."

"Except that if he went to all that trouble to get it out of the vault in the first place, he'd already expect to be chased for it."

"Well, yes. I was thinking if he was trying to sell it, he'd have to unwrap it to prove it was real. So, it was a lot of taverns and gambling, and a combat arena—the Irorium, it's called. With such a big betting industry built up around the arena, the thief could have tried using it there, with a few well-placed bets . . . but again, no one smart enough to pull this off would go to that much risk for something priceless and then turn around and use it for such a relatively small . . . reward. Keren . . . ?"

The knight's gaze had gone distant. "The Irorium?"

"Yes. It's where the—"

"—devoted followers of Irori train and practice." Their eyes met. "I'm so stupid," Keren whispered.

"Why? What is it?"

"He said he went to a fortune-teller. He's been hanging around the Tempering Hall so much to see if they're onto him, and meanwhile he's watching them fight and learning how to beat them. The Bloodstones don't do very much for mortals, but 'divine tools for divine goals.'"

"Wait . . . Who said? What goals?"

"You know what's worth that much risk for something priceless? Trying to become a god."

25

An Abundance of Not-Lies

Zae

Y ou're okay! I was worried!" Rowan spun Zae by the shoulders in order to hug her properly. "Everything exploded and then you were gone, and when you didn't come in today I started to think the worst."

Zae endured the hug, mumbling quietly, but didn't return it. She pulled him over to a quiet corner of the tea shop's cellar, eyes blazing with anger. He felt her heat, and it slowed him. He drew back a step, swaying on his feet as if he was ready to bolt. "What is it?"

Zae pressed her lips together, missing the feeling of the metal ring to center her. "Your net. Your bronze-damned net that *I* helped you make."

Above them in the rafters, the clockwork hummingbird preened.

"My . . . what about my net? I turned it in, I got paid, I tried to find you to give you your share!"

"Your net was used on me. I was under it in a store room all night. I liked you and I trusted you, and you betrayed me like . . . like a squirmy little betraying thing!" Instead of shouting, her voice got lower and lower as her anger rose, until it was barely a hiss. Zae whispered a few last choice words, then turned and stormed out, making sure to stomp her way up the stairs.

Several doors away, in the back room of a quiet bookshop, she waited. It was only minutes before Rowan joined her. Keren browsed in the next aisle, and when the halfling entered, she slipped around, book still in her hand.

"What was that about?" Rowan asked. He looked close to tears. "You said to meet you here so I am, but—"

Zae hugged him properly now. She should have been upset, but seeing his genuine distress had melted her anger away; having a chance to vent it, even if it had been partly an act for the sake of Ruby's familiar, had been punishment enough. "I'm going to cast a lie-detecting spell," she said into his shoulder. "Is that okay?"

"Y-yes, of course." He pulled away. "Why wouldn't it be?"

Zae closed her birthmarked hand around her gear and murmured the prayer to Brigh. "Because I wasn't lying about the net. I spent last night trapped under it, and between Keren and me, I'm the lucky one. So I'd like you to tell me who commissioned it, exactly, and how it happened. Because it wasn't the district council, I can promise you that."

"I am so, so sorry," the halfling said, encompassing Keren in his apology and rubbing his hands over his face. "I had no idea." His aura didn't waver.

"Tell me how you got involved in this," Keren said.

Rowan turned his big eyes to Zae, but she only nodded. She believed Rowan, or wanted to, but that did *not* mean Rowan was in the clear.

He slumped against the shelf, gathering his thoughts.

Zae prompted him sharply. "From the beginning, if you would."

"I . . ." He cleared his throat. "A well-dressed lady, a district councilor named Vinian Kerr, offered me a commission to build a prototype net that could detain magic-wielding suspects without harming them. She gave me a generous advance, and then again when I showed her the drafted plans, and I swept up a good bit of the cognate into helping me fabricate it. I turned it in and got paid, with a bonus for quickness. That's all I know."

"And then," Zae appended, "some less than savory characters used it for less than savory purposes."

"I swear, I believed her that I was building it for the city, to help save lives."

"Where did you meet her?"

"Her assistant sent for me at home, and brought me to her at a very stately house in the Merchants' Quarter. The weather was nice, so she met me in the side garden. That's where I met her both times I went back."

Keren pursed her lips. "So, a well-dressed woman had you come to a house she said was hers, but never actually let you inside."

"Well yeah, I . . ." Rowan slowed as realization dawned. He dragged a hand through his disheveled hair. "She wasn't really Councilor Kerr, was she? She was either a servant at that house or she'd bribed one of them to let her use the garden. I'm usually so much more careful. I don't know what happened. I guess I let my eagerness get the best of me."

Keren looked toward Zae, who nodded. "All true. Or at least, all non-lie."

Rowan made a wounded face. "Ouch. But yes, all right. I deserved that."

The door chimed. Zae glanced around, but saw no one. "Tell me about the cognate. Is everyone okay? How bad was the damage?"

"Our projects were ruined, but nobody in our cognate was seriously hurt. Not now that you're accounted for, I mean. Today we started over on the dual-schematics project in the tea cellar. Nobody felt like going back into the workroom."

"Who'll clean up in there?"

"The Thumpers take care of that. It's probably already clean, and at least halfway fixed."

"Do they know what happened to the machines?" Keren asked.

"The administrators might, but they don't mix with the likes of us." Rowan shrugged. "I've heard that there were bombs, that there was an overload of magic through the system, that the building just decided to pop all its gaskets for no apparent reason . . . Some people are saying that the Assembler didn't like what some group was doing in there, and decided to punish them. That last one's the only one too implausible to have any truth to it. The Assembler has never been seen by anyone, and there've certainly been much more volatile experiments going on in that building without any incident at all."

Zae exchanged a look with Keren, and nodded. "No lies. We can trust him, I'm sure of it."

She expected Keren to be skeptical of her quickness to trust, and was surprised when Keren nodded, following her instincts without complaint. The lie-detecting spell must have helped.

Far more succinctly than Zae might have managed, Keren summarized the disappearance of the Bloodstone, the use of the net in their capture, and their concern over Ruby's allegiance. As Zae listened, she remembered she still needed to find Glivia and apologize for losing the shard of metal from her finger.

Rowan whistled through his teeth. "Now I see why the big show in the cellar," he muttered.

"Her bird was buzzing around us the moment I got there," Zae said. "If she knew that her people captured us and we escaped, she would have been expecting me to storm in and turn on you for that net, no doubt. And I did, so now she'll think she's successfully framed you."

"And that helps us how?"

"Because we need her confident enough that she stops paying attention to us, because now we know who the thief is, and her people can't be allowed to get to him first."

"Who's the thief?"

"We think it's Omari. We think he's going to try to use the Bloodstone in his ascension test."

Rowan's whole demeanor changed, from defensive and defeated to alert and hard. "Omari? Omari the 'I want to commission a bard for my epic ballad' Omari?"

"Yes. Why?" Zae asked.

Rowan swallowed and squared his shoulders. "Because Pendris took him up on that commission. She's on her way to meet him right now."

"I should have followed her," Rowan said, not for the first time.

"And if she'd spotted you?" Zae asked.

"Then she'd have seen me keeping her safe." The halfling frowned. "I don't like this."

They arrived at the Duck and Castle and Rowan pushed his way inside. "Nothing," he reported a moment later. "They're not here."

"Are there private rooms they could be in, or . . . ?"

"No, they were going to meet here and then go somewhere quieter to work."

Zae bit her lip. "You don't have anything of hers on you, do you? Apple could track her."

With a faint blush, Rowan withdrew an embroidered handkerchief. Zae held it under Appleslayer's nose."

The dog sniffed, Zae gave him the command, and he whuffed under his breath. He sniffed around the tavern's entrance, then perked up and barked.

"He's caught her scent. I'll try to keep him from breaking into a full-on run, but . . ."

"No, give him his head," Rowan said. "I'll keep up."

Zae hesitated, nodded, and spurred the dog onward. "Find her, Apple!" He lifted his muzzle, sniffing the air, and sprang into action.

The trail led southeast, weaving through merchants' buildings and residential streets. Zae found herself riding without paying attention to where she was going, making sure Keren and Rowan were keeping up more than watching the lay of the streets, so she was surprised to pull up to the steps of the Clockwork Cathedral. More surprised to realize that anxiety and anger had fueled the journey without any sense of time passing.

Zae dismounted at the top of the stairs. When her companions caught up, they all entered together in silence, their progress accompanied by the clink of Keren's armor and the click of the dog's toenails on the marble floor. Rowan, not surprisingly, walked the familiar hall without making a sound. Zae drew up short at the entrance to one corridor, holding up a hand. Apple obeyed the signal and stopped, ears perked tall. Keren halted as well, closing her eyes to sharpen her hearing. There were definitely voices. One was a confident rumble in a male-sounding register. The other was female and rich in timbre. Keren opened her eyes and exchanged a glance with Zae, who nodded and signaled for Appleslayer to lead the way.

"A minor key through here, I think," Omari said as they neared. Zae peered around the doorframe and saw only his shadow, dancing around the room. "A dirge, mourning the great necromancer Ferrin Tark, who was no more. Then the melody should be a bit more lively as we turn to his bodyguard, who now guarded his body from the possibility of resurrection by melting it bit by bit."

"But—"

"Yes, yes, I know he could still be resurrected, but he wasn't, and I like the symmetry of the line. Moving on: I should have known then how useless the artifact would prove, when it saved him not from the blade I slipped between his ribs. Did you get all that, good lady? 'It saved him not . . .'?"

"It saved him not from the blade you slipped between his ribs."

"Just so. Now . . . The guards were disposed in similar fashion, in their own watery pits. And so on. Feel free to make that part fancy. Using a weapon wasn't my preference—true perfection requires only the strength and skill of the body—but it had to draw suspicion away from me, as well."

"But if perfection means only using the strength and skill of the body, then . . . why use the Bloodstone for your ascension?"

"Mortal magic may taint the purity of the attempt, but *divine* magic is different. Because I'm meant to be a god, I can use the magic of the gods. And I don't intend merely to hold the jar under my arm. I intend to consume its contents and let them merge with me. Aroden's legacy and Arazni's power will both be a part of me. The Starstone will recognize its own, and likewise recognize my divine right. Now, if you please. I find your curiosity flattering, but you're getting ahead of the tale."

Zae clasped her hands firmly over her mouth. She looked toward Keren, whose expression was as incredulous as Zae had ever seen it. Keren put a hand on her shoulder. She seemed to be fighting a rising gorge instead of mere surprise. Omari intended to *eat* Arazni's thousand-year-old desiccated liver?

Keren drew her sword and stepped into the archway. "How does Act Two begin? Arriving in Absalom, hiding like a coward, and watching the devoted of Arazni wreak havoc in your wake?"

Omari sketched a graceful bow. "Why, it's Crusader Rhinn." His smile was crooked. "What a pleasant surprise."

26

A DELICATE DANCE

KEREN

Keren had thought to loiter in the shadows while he revealed more of his plan, but anger had broken her silence. Now she trusted Zae to hold Rowan back and keep him out of Omari's line of sight.

"Hardly hiding," the monk said. "You yourself spoke with me on more than one occasion. The first day we were introduced, in the training hall and then on the avenue, I had the Bloodstone on my person, right under your nose. Did Evandor already have you seeking it then? What an amusing coincidence!"

Omari wore loose-fitting pants and a simple shirt, both of white cloth, with a brown sash at his waist. His feet were bare and he was unarmed, though that made him no less of a threat. Behind him stood a large pillar-like sawing machine, with Rowan's bard friend chained to it by her wrists. Pendris sat tall and calm, unafraid. The skirts of her long green dress had been tucked up under her to show off her metal-bound ankles, demurely crossed. Her expression was difficult to read, but her facial muscles looked relaxed. Her lute was on one of the worktables at the far side of the room, safe but out of reach.

"Are you all right?" Keren asked Pendris. "Aside from the obvious, I mean?"

Pendris gave a wan smile. "I'm not harmed."

"You should caution your diminutive friend against the use of magic," Omari said smoothly, pacing a deliberate circuit around the central machine. "I know you wouldn't have come without her. The snake construct binding our minstrel's ankles together is especially sensitive to magic. I think it likes her, but the slightest whiff of magic or attempt to remove it will make it nervous, and when it gets nervous, it bites. I assure you, its venom is quite deadly. It would be a shame to lose a talented songstress when she still has my epic to write."

What Keren had assumed was just a spiral of metal resolved on closer inspection to an iron serpent. Its eyes were sparkling red gems, and its jaws were spread wide around Pendris's calf. Sharp fangs dimpled the skin, more than merely poised to bite.

Keren lifted her hands to show that they were empty, and hoped he wouldn't be suspicious about the powers of the permanent but inert shields on her palms. "No magic. Let's just chat. Are you really planning to eat that thing?"

He paid no heed to the marks on her hands, but instead drew close enough to threaten her. "That 'thing' is a piece of a god. You might want to refer to it with the respect it's due."

Zae spoke from the doorway. "You want to pulverize it in your teeth and send it through your intestines, and *she's* the one not showing proper respect?"

For a moment, Keren wondered how quick the monk might be to anger. While he had seemed perfectly placid on their last meeting, much less had been at stake for him then.

"You should be pleased with my plans," he said in Zae's direction, then turned back to Keren. "You most of all, Crusader Rhinn of Ozem. Once I do what I mean to do, the organ can never be returned to Arazni. She will never be able to seize all four Bloodstones. I'm saving you from a terrible fate. You could at least thank me for that."

"I could," Keren agreed. "But I somehow don't think it's going to go the way you expect it to. Eating it could kill you. Or Arazni could send a graveknight after you to rip it from your body."

"Concern for my well-being? I'm touched. But I suspect it won't do me harm. I've already tasted her blood with no ill effects—why would the stone weep blood, if not for me to drink? I'd gone decades without tasting flesh or blood, all cleansing me to lead up to this. I gained no power from it, unfortunately, but no illness either."

"The blood in the library . . ." Zae said, stepping into the room. "I found the spot where you dripped it."

He waved, an absent gesture. "And as for the graveknight, I will have ascended before it returns, so it won't be able to touch me. I've been paying attention. It takes a graveknight at least a day before it can return to Absalom, and when it does, a squadron of Iomedae's knights and city guards helpfully distract it for me."

"You've thought everything through, haven't you? So, why capture Pendris, Omari? And why bring her here?"

"Ah!" He turned to Zae with one finger raised. "Why indeed? For the poetic justice inherent in thwarting Arazni's thugs. You witnessed the destruction they brought down upon this building just because they thought the Bloodstone might be here. It made me realize I have the power to raze any part of the city I wish to, just by spilling a drop of a dead god's blood. What better place to hide it than a place they've already ruled out? And this is familiar ground for me. I trained here too, remember. There's a chance I know this building's schedule better than any of you."

"I think I missed the part of the story where you had any reason whatsoever to apply here," Zae answered.

"To better myself, of course. The same reason anyone studies anything, anywhere. It was the study of many skills that led me to my true calling."

"Godhood," Keren said dryly.

"Precisely. Ozem has closed in on Arazni, and though it's amusing to watch the two factions shuffle you around as their pawns and even help each other unwittingly, soon both groups will close in to watch me. Arazni's people will find me through the Bloodstone itself, and Ozem has found me by tracking down the fool necromancer. Somehow, one of your investigators got hold of his name. So. I've completed my tests on the blood and determined the organ safe to eat. I've seen the graveknight summoned this morning, so I know it can't interrupt me now, and my first disciple has approached me to spread the word of the new god throughout the lands. If you're properly worshipful, I might extend my boon to you as well."

Keren's head spun. Omari had brought Pendris to the Clockwork Cathedral because he had hidden the Bloodstone here. It was here now. And while he didn't seem surprised that they had been on the trail of the Bloodstone and had found him, he didn't seem to care. He wasn't interested in hurting them, nor was he at all concerned that they might stop him. To him, Pendris's predicament was just a way to ensure that bodies were filling seats in his audience, nothing more. Keren wasn't sure at this point whether he was arrogant, as she'd first presumed, or fully delusional.

She took a step backward, but the movement caught his eye. "Oh, I wouldn't, if I were you. If you were to leave, my snake might get jumpy." Omari tilted his head, as if listening to something far away. "And sadly, our time is up. Do you have enough to work with?" he asked Pendris, drawing near to ease a lock of dark hair out of her eyes. The gesture was so tender as to be patronizing. He touched her cheek. "If you need any help during the writing, all you'll have to do is pray. I'll come back and release you, after. Have faith, and you'll be rewarded. I'm sorry that you'll have to miss the spectacle, but it's important to keep you safe. Returning for you will be my first miracle!"

Keren had not seen the monk in motion before, and was dismayed to see the speed at which he moved. He was past them and through the doorway before either she or Keren had a chance to block his path, leaving them with the choice between freeing Pendris and chasing after him. Before she could phrase the choice into a question, she felt the faint rumble of machinery. Her stomach sank and panic flooded her veins.

"The gears!" Rowan cried from across the room, lute in hand. Keren blinked. She hadn't seen him sneak along the walls. "We're about to be locked in. He'll get away!"

Keren raced to Pendris, examining the chains that held her to the machine. "How long before the hallway closes?"

"Moments," Rowan answered. Urgency buzzed in Keren's ears like angry bees. "The gears move slowly, but once they start there's no stopping them."

Zae closed the distance, joining Keren at Pendris's side. "We're not leaving you here," she said firmly, resting her hands on Pendris's calf.

"No! We don't know what the thing will do to her," Keren objected.

"Yes, we do." The gnome smiled. "Get ready to chop it when I say. Oh, the viper's fangs did sting, but they were no match for the knight, who steeled up her courage and on the count of three . . ." She held up a hand that was already glowing faintly with energy. "One . . . Two . . ." Zae pressed her glowing hand to into Pendris's skin. The fangs snapped down and the bard screamed, writhing against her bonds. Keren hacked the snake-thing in two, then did the same for the chains on Pendris's wrists and hefted her over her shoulder. Then they ran.

At the end of the hallway, where it met the main corridor, the large black gear was already inching down across the doorway, blotting out the light from the hall like a moon in partial eclipse. Keren lowered Pendris to the floor and pushed her through the opening. Zae ducked through immediately after, followed by Rowan with the lute. As soon as they were through he gathered

Pendris into his arms. Blood pounding in her ears, Keren dove through the narrowing gap, her armor screeching a high-pitched whine against the marble floor. Keren turned onto her back and tucked her feet up, pushing off against the lowering gear itself to propel herself clear of it. She stared at the giant mechanism, panting, mesmerized by its inevitable orbit along its path. Keren had squeezed through by mere inches, and while the thought of it hadn't swayed her in the moment, it left her a bit lightheaded now.

The gear locked into place, and an impatient, muffled bark snapped them out of their trance. Appleslayer paced anxiously at the entrance of the cathedral. He had something snatched up in his mouth—she couldn't tell what it was and didn't have time to worry about it. Zae vaulted into the saddle, said a quick prayer, and shouted Apple onward. Keren gently took Pendris from Rowan, scooping her up and securing her over her shoulder to follow them. She didn't see Rowan but she assumed he was with them.

They already knew where Omari was headed; what they hadn't counted on was his speed. One moment, they were gaining on him, and in the next he had simply vanished. Keren swore.

Streets blurred past in flashes of color and bursts of overheard conversation. Appleslayer quickly outpaced Keren, but when he and Zae reached the edge of the God's Market they slowed to a walk, Apple with his nose to the ground.

"That was a hell of a gamble you took," Keren yelled across the distance. She set Pendris down onto a bench and Rowan was immediately beside her, already starting to work on disengaging the iron snake around the woman's ankles. Blood dribbled from under the construct, black against the pale of Pendris's skin, but the bard was conscious and watched Rowan with lucid eyes, reaching down to push his hood back and ruffle her fingers through his hair. She didn't seem to be in pain.

"He said venom, so I knew it was poison!" Zae countered. "It wasn't a gamble. The spell I cast gave us hours to get her an antidote. We can't worry about it now. Come on, we've got to find Omari before he does this thing."

"You mean we have to find him before *they* do." Rowan gestured with his chin. What looked from a distance like a band of street thugs proved, at a closer distance to be . . . a gang of street thugs. Arazni's patrol.

Keren recalled what Omari had said—that if he was able to ingest the contents of the Bloodstone and ascend, Arazni would never be able to assemble all four organs. She had no expectation that he would be able to succeed at the test, not when he seemed so overly confident, and those who failed never actually returned. It would get one Bloodstone out of the way. As solutions went, it did seem to be a tidy one.

But her order lived in hope of being able to retrieve and restore Arazni someday, and for that the Bloodstones had to be intact and in their possession. It pained Keren to think of her order's former patron trapped in undeath and deaf to the lure of freedom.

It would be easy to just let Omari go through with his plan and wait for the Starstone Cathedral to kill him, but it wouldn't be enough.

Rowan glanced up from Pendris's metal serpent. His tools were laid out in a leather roll at his side, along with a pad of bandages. "Do you see Omari?"

Keren shook her head. "No. Not yet. But we know two things about him: he's sneaky, and he's vain. He's probably waiting for both sides to amass so that they can all witness his show. Evandor said that when a hopeful tries for the test, it's a big deal. They gather people down the Avenue, to come and watch. I can't see him organizing an entire parade, but I also can't see him denying himself the spectacle."

"Or he's waiting for them to fight each other out over him. At the most, he'd only have to pick off the few who remain," Rowan added. With a grunt of effort, a sturdy file, and a wicked looking little saw, he sprung the construct open with a sharp snap. Pendris stifled a yelp into her sleeve. She looked pale, but no worse for the removal of the metal fangs. Zae assisted Rowan in unrolling medicated bandages and pressing them onto Pendris's puncture wounds.

Del, the man who had interrogated Keren, was near the lead of the Araznian pack, along with a well-dressed man who looked like he'd been diverted on his way to the opera. A few paces behind them was Ruby. The gang behind them pushed spectators out of the way, overran carts, and destroyed merchandise without a care. Keren estimated about two dozen, some of them walking with a strangely lifeless stride. It wasn't a shamble, but it lacked something Keren couldn't describe—emotion, perhaps.

"The procession draws near. Half of it, anyway."

Keren drew her sword. "And here comes the other half."

Evandor, in full white-and-gold armor, led a squadron of about twenty Knights of Ozem along the perimeter of the chasm. Weirdly, he appeared to be following some sort of floating, spectral hand. The two groups, each on its stately course, would converge right at the edge of the market where Zae and her companions were currently standing. The usual foot traffic still milled about at the near end of the market, browsing wares and haggling for souvenirs, but the two processions were beginning to gather attention. Visitors were abandoning their shopping to line the avenue, pushed aside by the crude swarm of Arazni's followers. Now the chatter was made up of murmurs about who the aspirant might be.

"Get ready," Keren said. "There he is."

One of the market stalls at the end of the street was more a sturdy wooden pavilion than a tent, and it was on this that Omari stood to watch the crowds gather. He let out a fierce battle cry and lifted his arms in premature triumph. Only the nearest handful of people needed to notice him. Once they murmured among themselves, word spread through the crowd like a hungry flame. The wave of it spread outward and devoured all other conversation in its path.

"People of Absalom!" he shouted. His voice wasn't amplified in any magical or mundane way, but it still reverberated majestically off the buildings and stonework. "Meet your new god, and know me."

Pendris stood, hand on Rowan's shoulder for balance, and kicked the cobra over the edge of the chasm. Despite knowing better, Keren found that she was waiting for the sound of impact; it didn't come.

Omari proceeded to expound on his own numerous virtues, but his raised arms were not enough to silence the two militias that had marched to compete with each other at retrieving the Bloodstone from him. If anything, he only riled them more, dangling the knowledge that the object of their search was before them. The living among Arazni's mob looked even more bloodthirsty than the undead. Zae started a prayer under her breath. They were almost near enough for her to hit.

"Keep him engaged," Evandor roared. Keren nodded, but it was Rowan who sprang into action, melding into the shadows behind a vendor stall and slipping away into the shadows.

Omari would be expecting the two bands to fight each other, while he took advantage of their distraction and got away with the Bloodstone. Keren knew he was nimble and fast, and that he fought unarmed, but she didn't know what tricks he had in reserve.

"He's standing *right there*. Why doesn't everyone just go after him?" Zae asked Keren.

The knight shook her head. "Because it matters very much which of us get to him first."

Even though Keren was looking for it, she barely saw Rowan's arrival on the rooftop behind Omari. She bit her lip as the rogue lifted his dagger, but just when she thought a backstab to Omari's kidneys was all but assured, Omari whirled and kicked at Rowan's wrist with his bare foot. Rowan's knife flew out of his hand. The monk followed up with a punch and the halfling dodged, rolling to the edge of the roof and bouncing there on the balls of his feet, inviting Omari to charge. He brandished a new knife in his hand.

Between Keren and the wooden market stall, Arazni's militia surged and met the knights' shield wall like water colliding with stone, sending up clouds of greenish poison as undead fighters used their secret reserves to threaten groups of knights in close quarters. As the crowd of fighters shifted away from the deadly air, they created a perilous shoreline that Zae and her companions would have to wade through to reach Omari and Rowan.

Lute strings played at the edge of Keren's consciousness. Pendris had her instrument up, and was picking out an archaic dance on it. Magic surged through Keren; she felt stronger and more confident. She nodded to Zae, lowered her visor, and charged into the battle with Appleslayer at her side, carving a path toward the man who had been her primary interrogator. Her adversary wore armor of studded leather, but it could only protect so much of him.

Shouting with the primal joy of finally having an obvious enemy to fight, Keren swung hard, eager for blood.

27

In the Fray

Zae

R owan won't be able to keep him occupied for long," Zae said, raising her voice to be heard. "Can we get around the back of the knights' line?"

Pendris shook her head. "Look." One of the undead turned to smoke as Zae watched, reforming into human shape behind the knights' front lines. Others followed, sending what remained of the ordered formation into chaos. "And there's that small matter of the bottomless pit."

"Then we'll have to do our best from here." The gnome scrambled up onto the bench and then, with Pendris's offered shoulder for balance, to the back of the bench. Here she had a vantage slightly higher than a human's line of sight. It wasn't much of an advantage, but it was the best she could do for now, and it was enough to let her see over the heads of most of the combatants.

There were more servants of Arazni on the trail of the Bloodstone than Zae had realized, but then, they'd had time to arrive from elsewhere. And if Ruby was among them, it was a safe presumption that the forces were bolstered by some of the other names on the list they had found. They fought without order or elegance, but with the enthusiasm of malice and bloodthirst. The living called insults and battered at Iomedae's forces, while the few undead among them rushed the knights with tooth and claw. The knights rained glowing columns of holy light on the swarm of Arazni's followers like a field of blinking suns. The undead faltered, but they were intelligent and resourceful; one grabbed a brave shopkeeper who had been blocked in before she could abandon her stall, and drained her to renew his strength while chaos clashed around them. Relics spilled and potion bottles shattered, and the clashing forces stomped them all into a faintly magical paste underfoot.

Arazni's followers were near enough now, and Zae called down her own holy energy onto them. It pleased her to see them stagger. Ruby turned toward the soldier she fought beside, touching his shoulder and bolstering him. Zae didn't want to have to hurt Ruby, so she kept her focus on the others, sending a ray of holy light at the Araznian undead who looked most wounded. He let out an unearthly scream and swayed on his feet. One of Iomedae's knights cut him down where he stood.

All around, the clash of steel and the sizzle of flesh had replaced the sounds of the market. Up on the stall's roof, Rowan and Omari still sparred. The monk was ducking and dodging the halfling's strikes; he was smiling, as if this were just another casual workout with a friend. Rowan looked set and serious, and wounded to boot—a bruise had already bloomed across his cheek, and blood painted his lips and chin. Zae focused on him, sending him and the knights courage from afar. Then Omari's expression turned sour, and he spared a hand to swat at the air. He did this a couple more times before Zae realized what he was actually doing: catching arrows and batting them away. Behind her on the opposing market stall's roof, an archer in Iomedae's livery shot over the crowd, hand blurring with a speed that even Zae's sharp eyes could not follow. While it might have been only an annoyance to Omari, it still was a distraction that could give Rowan an advantage.

Keren was holding her own against her foe. One of Arazni's other fighters, a thick meat-slab of a man who likely had some orc blood in his ancestry, caught sight of Keren and let out a battle roar, rushing to the defense of his companion.

But behind him came Evandor, resplendent in his gleaming armor. He cut the large man down in a single stroke, before Keren even knew there had been an adversary angling to take a chunk out of her back. With him at her side and Apple going for his calves, Keren's interrogator went down quickly. One moment, he was fighting Keren, and the next, there was a hole in the sea of people where his head had been. The crowd flowed to fill in the gap so swiftly that Keren had no time to rest before facing off against another foe. Evandor handed her his shield and held off the nearest adversary while she secured it. Zae scanned the melee for her allies.

Yenna Quoros had found herself a spot out of the way, under the stall where Omari and Rowan still sparred. With a table upended as a barricade, she channeled holy energy against the undead, with much more power than Zae could have matched, while a foot soldier at her side threw fragile flasks into the thick of Arazni's forces, scorching the few remaining creatures with holy water and showering glass shrapnel underfoot.

Keren was still full of vigor, and it didn't look like any of the blood smeared across her armor or Apple's white fur was their own. The two of them and Evandor were on the move, slicing their way through Arazni's minions toward Omari. The monk wore a satchel much like Zae's slung crosswise over his shoulder. The Bloodstone, undoubtedly, was in there. He would need to be parted from it.

Below the monk's perch, Ruby faced off against Renwick. That startled Zae—when had the dwarf arrived? Moreover, how did he even know to come here? Had he been keeping tabs on them, or on Ruby? She supposed it made sense, though—of course he would have wanted to investigate the sabotage in the cathedral himself. She hoped he had brought others with him and felt momentarily guilty; he looked as though he'd rather have been anywhere else in the world than opposing his student in combat.

Zae wormed her way closer to Renwick. Though Ruby was subordinate in the workroom, here they were equals. Every spell

Ruby could cast, Renwick could counter—yet he gained no ground on her, either. Zae prayed for a spell to make her falter, and then one to give Renwick an advantage, touching his sleeve. Sinuous coils of Ruby's hair writhed out to grasp at him, but steaming flames flowed brightly from his mouth to singe the tresses away. She screamed, a sound of anger more than fear or pain. While she was distracted putting out the flames—with a flask of water, produced from her cloak and upended over her own head—Zae dug a device out of her bag. Before she could activate it, though, Renwick closed in. Without Ruby's hair to keep him at a distance, he swept at her midsection with a short-handled hatchet.

It connected. Ruby staggered, hair cindered and steaming, clutching her belly. The witch wove in place, then crumpled, gasping, to the sticky ground.

Most of the fighting had moved on, leaving the path to them mostly clear. Zae ran for it, pulling to a halt beside Renwick where he crouched over Ruby's form. The rugged dwarf's face was full of remorse; Ruby's was utterly calm.

"Cheer up, old man," Ruby said. "You couldn't have known."

"That may be," he answered. "I should've, though."

A shout from the rooftop turned Zae's attention away from them. Omari was herding Rowan off the edge of the roof toward Geb's remaining forces.

Zae tried searing Omari with a spell, but he seemed to be too fluid for even Brigh's might to latch onto him. Despite all his talk of natural combat, she suspected he must have some unnatural resistance aiding him in order to evade her magic. She saw no way to wade safely through the combat, but she could still aid her allies.

Omari's punch connected with Rowan's face. The halfling tumbled off the roof's edge.

Keren fought her way through to Rowan and shielded the fallen halfling while she hauled him to his feet. Then she lifted her chin and shouted a challenge at Omari. "Is no one paying attention to you? Come down here and join your own party, coward!"

Omari, grinning as if humoring Keren, sailed down from the roof with a flying leap that caught her square in the chest and knocked her off her feet. Zae's breath caught in her throat, but Keren struggled upright again. Omari's foot struck out faster than Zae's eyes could follow, a solid kick to the side of her helm, yet she remained standing, if only barely. She slashed, he dodged, and Zae realized with horror that he wasn't truly fighting her—he was herding her toward the edge of the pit. The distance between Keren and the abyss dwindled as she backpedaled, barely managing to avoid the monk's attacks.

Zae surged forward, knowing she was already too late.

28

THE CHASM'S EDGE

KEREN

Omari's face twisted in concentration. Keren was panting, her hair stringy with sweat that dripped down her back and soaked the layers under her armor, but still she pushed him, forcing him to dodge and jump and spin to avoid her blade. A few deep cuts on his chest and arms attested to her ability to hit occasionally, but he moved without fatigue, as if unaware of them.

Keren drew Omari sideways, still too close to the pit but putting more distance between her feet and the edge. She couldn't take the chance of the Bloodstone going over with him.

He crouched, shifting balance from one foot to the other. She didn't know whether he was going to lunge or leap, but she wasn't going to wait around to find out. She swung instead, feinting for his head and then dropping her wrists to move that momentum to his leg. He pounced forward, she turned aside but not fast enough, and he knocked her down onto her back. Armor hit stone and punched the wind out of her. Straddling her, he pulled at her helm. He might have been aiming to remove it so that he could reach her vulnerable face, or use it as a tool to smash her head against the pavement. She struck at his side with her fist, and at his other side with her sword pommel. At least she still had her grip on the sword. He had to have kidneys, and they had to be in the same place as everyone else's—and unlike her, he wore nothing to protect them. No matter how perfect he was, armor was still harder than flesh.

A moment's respite told her he'd given up on removing her helm, but a moment was all she got. Something immensely hard cracked down on the center of her forehead, sending her vision swirling red and black. Had that been his elbow? She couldn't breathe *or* think now.

Her visor lifted. Keren caught sight of the great Starstone Cathedral looming large behind Omari, its spire stretching high into the heavens. It glowed, haloed in the first golden reds of dusk, and Keren thought again of Iomedae's ascension; her god's heroics on this very spot. A fitting last sight. As Omari drew back his fist, she forced her eyes to stay open, fixed on the tip of the cathedral's spire. And she prayed.

A nimbus of glowing light surrounded and filled her, red and gold like leaves glowing under an autumn sun. Something deep within her clicked into place. She felt invincible. She felt like justice.

Omari leaned over her, blotting out the sky. His fist became the world, and in slow motion she felt the crunch of bone shattering in her nose. She knew it would hurt, but it didn't yet. She gasped, but still couldn't take a full breath. That was all right. She only needed to *be*. The light, Iomedae's light, would take care of the rest.

The weight on her shifted and slumped, giving her the sky and the spire again. She drew on her last reserves and sat up, grasping for her sword and struggling to her feet. Omari remained where she'd left him stunned and unmoving, eyes staring past her and shining with the reflection of that golden light. Zae was at her side, steadying her arm. Apple was close behind her. His sharp teeth latched into Omari's leg and his strong jaw shook the limb in rough jerks.

Blood poured from her nose now that she was upright. She curled her fist and punched Omari in the face with her gauntlet, just as he'd punched her. Blood flew, his eyelids fluttered, and his pupils rolled back in his head. Zae moved around behind him and slid the tip of her blade under the strap that crossed his shoulder, severing it with a twist of the knife.

There was a moment, paused in time, perfect and golden, when it seemed as if it would be that easy. But then time resumed, and Omari's elbow shot out, catching the gnome under the chin.

Zae fell, momentum knocking her away from him and toward the edge of the pit. The gnome curled tightly around Omari's bag, and only at the last second seemed to realize that it came at the cost of slowing herself. Keren dove after her, but time felt slippery, both too fast and too slow at once. She didn't know whether she would make it to Zae, but she put everything she had into trying, praying to Iomedae for the strength. Lunging to reach out over the chasm, she *was* the bridge she had been unable to visualize in practice.

Warmth filled her, lending her confidence and hope. Her hand closed around a slender leg. She pulled.

Keren couldn't see more than rough shapes now, between the blood in her eyes and the pain, but she held on tightly, easing back onto her knees. She felt strong arms around her sore ribs, pulling her back while she pulled Zae. Who—? Evandor?

Keren wiped the blood and sweat out of her eyes. Renwick. He handed her a potion, already uncorked, and she drank it down without hesitation, handing Zae over into his care. The gnome was wild-eyed and trembling, but alive.

Keren retrieved her shield and sword. Yenna was casting magic at Omari from a wand and Evandor, Rowan, and Appleslayer had him surrounded on three sides, slashing and biting. His attention was strained, juggling four attackers at once.

The world turned sideways as Omari took his one avenue of escape and tackled Keren, following her to the ground again, using her armor as his own shield against her allies. He was too close for her shield to help her, and with her sword trapped under her she couldn't use it, either. But she didn't need a weapon. With Iomedae's grace inside her, she was a weapon. She prayed, and spikes grew from her armor, their sharp points sliding into Omari's skin.

The monk stiffened and screamed, pushing against her now. But the advantage was Keren's and she took it. Keren rolled onto him, letting the weight of the armor force the spikes into him and pin him to the ground.

His dazed pupils nearly engulfed the prized violet of his irises. "Your mortal laws don't apply to me and your mortal walls won't hold me. All you've done is shown me what sort of god I'm meant to be."

She had him for now, but Keren knew she didn't have much time to consider her next action. He would be deadly fast once he recovered himself.

She punched his broken nose to delay that recovery, then pushed herself to her knees, bracing him on the ground to peel him off her spikes. She held out a hand and Renwick took it. The few straggling members of Arazni's forces were fighting their way toward Omari—and toward Zae, who held the Bloodstone in its shielded bag—but her friends were stronger in number and they were keeping the desperate cultists back.

If she let Omari up, he would try to take the test. Most likely, he would fail and die all on his own. But there was always that sliver of a chance that he would succeed, and even a sliver of a chance was irresponsible to discard. She could let the city have him, but no cell or exile would hold him for long. She took up her sword. She was sworn not just to defend against attacks on her faith, but to seek them out and eradicate them. Any man who would claim superiority over her god was certainly such an attacker, and she could not give him quarter. Her path was clear; as Iomedae's divine instrument, she knew what she had to do.

Keren rose, planting a foot against Omari's side. "Good luck meeting your god," she said, and nudged him off the edge and into the endless chasm.

In the wake of the chaos, order was relatively quiet. Graycloaks walked the grounds together, arresting anything living and sticking swords into anything that was dead but still twitching. Renwick crouched over Ruby's inert form. Zae and Keren paused long enough for him to acknowledge them with a somber nod.

Rowan joined them, dropping something metal and inert onto Ruby's body. Her hummingbird was mangled, full of tooth-sized dents. "I think it lived long enough to tell Ruby where we were, and then your dog got hold of it. He brought it all the way here in his mouth."

Zae stroked Appleslayer's ears. "Will you be all right?" she asked Renwick.

The dwarf inclined his head. "In time. Never had to kill my own student before." He rose to his feet, groaning with protest. "Thank you for asking, though. I reckon I'll take you up on a stiff drink soon enough."

"We'll all need one, after this," Keren said. "I'm going to drink until I feel it."

"I'll clear my schedule," Zae responded, not entirely in jest. With Keren's tolerance, that much drinking could take a while. The gnome hesitated, then said, "You know, you could have just given Omari to the guards and gotten him sentenced to prison. Did you have to push him off the edge?"

Keren hadn't stopped churning that over in her mind, either. "Yes. I think I did. He wasn't going to stop trying for ascension, and if he could steal a Bloodstone, could any cell have held him? Who knows what else he would have done or how many others he might have hurt along the way."

Yenna and Evandor had rejoined the rest of the order, what few of their hastily assembled force remained. Keren wondered if reinforcements would arrive, now that everything was over. Evandor's breastplate was rent with a long, scorched scar from his earlier battle with the graveknight, but he seemed mostly whole.

Zae shifted the bundle in her arms, pulling out a rough-hewn stoneware jar. Its carved lid sported a filial of some sort of grotesque creature, like a gargoyle on a gravestone. Though it seemed thoroughly affixed, a slow trail of viscous blood pushed its way out of the jar as Keren watched. Its descent was mesmerizing, but then Keren recalled Omari's talk of drinking it. She had to shudder and turn away.

Yenna opened her arms for the jar, and Zae passed it to her, holding it as gingerly as she might cradle a patient's beating heart. Yenna took it from her, grasping it carefully by the wrappings to avoid touching the stone or the blood.

"I will draw this away from Absalom, and then return." Yenna met Keren's eyes, and bowed her head slightly in thanks. Keren did the same, and stood aside. The priestess took several steps away from them, paused, and vanished from sight.

29

THE WORST PATIENT

ZAE

Would you sit already?" Zae demanded. The curtains at Lumpy Orange Crescent were already closed, but Keren made a point of checking every room. Zae trailed along behind her, frustration rising to a simmer. When the whole small house was proven free of spies, monsters, and whatever else might have legitimately enabled her to further stall, Zae put her foot down.

"Keren Rhinn. Chair. *Now.*"

The mottled plum-colored bruise spreading under her eyes may have, to anyone else, added a certain degree of imposing menace to the knight, but Zae was unmoved by Keren's glower. Keren loitered just long enough to show Zae that she, too, was unmoved by intimidation. Point made, she relented with a grimace and a sharp intake of breath, easing into the seat. She leaned forward with a gasp and tugged at her chainmail tunic to let it rumple off over her head with a loud chink of rings. When it was a steel puddle on the floor, she sat up with great effort, which she no longer bothered to disguise.

"How many broken, do you think?" Zae asked.

Keren, who was no stranger to such things, answered without a pause for thought. "Three over here. One on this side." Only after speaking did she reflexively palpate her torso, confirming her prediction.

"Yenna could have healed you. Anyone at the church would have healed you."

"I know. I wanted you to do it. I wanted to walk with it. To them, it's impractical to wait. To me, it's too important to just erase like it never happened. I needed to feel it first."

Zae started water boiling on the hearth. "You cast spells. I saw it!"

"I did." Keren took a deep breath, then cursed herself for it. Zae winced in sympathy. "Shallow," Keren added. "Shallow breaths, slow movements. I know."

Zae pulled over a mug and drizzled a dark brown syrup inside it from one of her many glass vials. She added cold water to the mug and swirled it. "First order, something to prevent you from coughing."

"Oh, bless you. I love you." She took the mug and swallowed the contents in one bitter gulp.

"I love you too, Inquisitor Rhinn."

Keren had the foresight to press the mug to her side *before* she laughed. "Yes, all right. You were right, if that's what you're waiting for."

"No, I'm waiting to congratulate you, is what I'm waiting for. You did it. Iomedae worked through you. You were part of the great machine. It all worked."

"Yes. And, again, you were right. It was exactly like you said it was supposed to be. I offered myself as her conduit, to do something for her that I couldn't have done alone, and she filled me and worked through me and made it possible."

"How did it feel?"

"A damn sight better than a kick in the ribs."

Zae lifted Keren's undershirt to her armpits, surveying the violet garden of blooming bruises across her skin. "That guy had hard feet."

"Not nearly so hard as his head," Keren grumbled.

"That's a good thing. Anyone else, with less arrogance and willpower and all-around stubbornness, would have used the

Bloodstone right away. Nothing to retrieve." Zae still wasn't entirely convinced that the permanent loss of a Bloodstone would be so bad, and she knew Keren felt the same, but if there was even a glimmer of hope that the order's former god could be restored, Zae understood their need to cling to it.

"So," she continued. "Can I please heal you now? Or do you want me to summon a portrait artist to capture these bruises for you before you let them go? They're very impressive. Purple suits you as a skin color. Maybe you should dye yourself completely."

Keren made a face, but didn't laugh again. "I've always hated sitting for portraits. Sister Zae of Brigh, would you please give me the honor of the Bronze Lady's healing light?"

"I thought you'd never ask."

Technically, it didn't matter where Zae laid hands on a patient, as long as she came into contact with them. Channeling healing energy worked by touch because touch told the magic where to go. Zae spoke her spell aloud instead of in a whisper. Bones knit and blood vessels mended, bringing Keren's internal systems back to working order. Cupping Keren's breasts in her palms didn't send the healing to her ribs any more directly, but Keren's reaction was even more magical than the spell. Everything felt right with the world when Zae was done; all parts clicked into place. Zae let her hands remain where they were.

"Am I the worst patient?" Keren asked her.

Zae nodded solemnly. "The absolute worst. Terrible. Stubborn. Always going out and getting injured again. Shameful, really. I'm glad you insisted on me. I wouldn't dream of inflicting the burden of healing you on anyone else."

Keren bent to kiss the gnome softly on her lips, then squeezed her hand so that the rings they wore touched with a faint click. The water was boiling, so Zae reluctantly parted from Keren's skin to make tea, adding a drop of this for soreness and a drop of that to strengthen the blood. A healthy dose of soothe syrup, a soporific, would help the knight sleep; a drizzle of honey would make her dreams sweet.

"You need rest," she said.

"I need rest," Keren agreed. "And you? What do you need, Pixie?"

Zae smiled.

ABOUT THE AUTHOR

Gabrielle Harbowy first introduced the characters of Keren, Zae, and Appleslayer in the short Pathfinder Tales story "Inheritance," available for free at **paizo.com**. In addition to her Pathfinder work, she's also published the novel *Hellmaw: Of the Essence*, as well as short stories in such publications as *Carbide Tipped Pens* and *Stars of Darkover*. As an editor, she's worked for publishers including Pyr, Lambda Literary, and Circlet Press; spent a decade as the managing editor at Dragon Moon Press; and is a submissions editor at the Hugo-nominated Apex Magazine. With Ed Greenwood, she coedited the award-nominated *When the Hero Comes Home* anthology series, as well as *Women in Practical Armor*. For more information, visit her on Twitter at **@gabrielle_h** or check out her website at **gabrielleharbowy.com**.

ACKNOWLEDGMENTS

So many people have helped to make this book a reality. Matt Harbowy, Fanny Darling, Steve Bornstein, and David Szarzynski, thank you for the full myriad of everythings: love, support, caffeine, and inspiration.

Thanks to Dave Gross, who put me up to it, and James L. Sutter, editor, for guiding me through.

To Chris Jackson, Erin M. Evans, Liane Merciel, and Mitchell Anderson for helping me chart the Pathfinder and RPG tie-in waters. And thanks especially to Venture-Lieutenant Andrea Brandt (Ret.): friend, Zae fangirl, GM extraordinaire, and trusted advisor. And to Brian Cortijo and Dennis Baker, for providing me with some cool tinkering devices.

To my band of fellow adventurers: Jonathon Schultz, Riah Evin, Kristin Lennox, Jordan Toth, Lady Jordan, and James Nighswonger, for reminding me to play in the world, not just write in it. Likewise the Pathfinder Societies of Oakland and the Central Valley.

To the creators and maintainers of Syrinscape and Hero Lab, two independent products which inspired and streamlined my writing process.

Appleslayer is a composite of three wonderful dogs: I owe a great debt and many apples to Ruby Talbert (RIP), Rufus Tobey, and Bronson Evin/Dehlinger for canine inspiration.

GLOSSARY

All Pathfinder Tales novels are set in the rich and vibrant world of the Pathfinder campaign setting. Below are explanations of several key terms used in this book. For more information on the world of Golarion and the strange monsters, people, and deities that make it their home, see *The Inner Sea World Guide*, or dive into the game and begin playing your own adventures with the *Pathfinder Roleplaying Game Core Rulebook* or the *Pathfinder Roleplaying Game Beginner Box*, all available at **paizo.com**. Reader specifically interested in the city of Absalom should check out the Pathfinder Campaign Setting supplement *Guide to Absalom*, while those interested in the faiths of Iomedae and Brigh should see *Inner Sea Gods* and *Inner Sea Faiths*.

Absalom: Largest city in the Inner Sea region, located in the middle of the Inner Sea.

Acts of Iomedae: Eleven miracles the goddess Iomedae performed while still a mortal, demonstrating Aroden's might.

Arazni: Former demigod and herald of Aroden who was slain and then turned into a lich. Currently the ruler of Geb.

Arcanamirium: Prestigious school of magic in the city of Absalom.

Aroden: God of humanity, who died mysteriously a hundred years ago.

Ascendant Court: District in Absalom surrounding the Starstone Cathedral, and which holds myriad temples and markets.

Azlant: First human empire, which sank beneath the waves long ago in the cataclysm following the fall of the Starstone.

Azlanti: Of or pertaining to Azlant; someone from Azlant.

Belkzen: Region populated primarily by savage orc tribes.

Bloodstone of Arazni: Arazni's internal organs, which were removed and stored in canopic jars, becoming powerful artifacts linked to her former divine power. Stolen and hidden long ago by the Knights of Ozem.

Brigh: Goddess of invention and artifice.

Bronze Lady: Another name for Brigh.

Calistria: Also known as the Savored Sting; the goddess of trickery, lust, and revenge.

Calistrian: Of or related to Calistria or her worshipers.

Castle Overwatch: Famous crusader fortress in Vigil.

Cathedral of Sancta Iomedaea: Enormous temple to Iomedae in Vigil.

Cayden Cailean: God of freedom, ale, wine, and bravery. Was once mortal, but ascended to godhood by passing the Test of the Starstone in Absalom.

Clerics: Religious spellcasters whose magical powers are granted by their gods.

Clockwork Cathedral: Legendary college for engineers and artificers in Absalom, founded by a mysterious figure called the Assembler.

Coins: Mercantile district in Absalom.

Construct: Mechanical creature given life through magical means.

Crusaders: Warrior societies who battle the various evils plaguing the Inner Sea Region, including those guarding against the orcs of Belkzen, the demons of the Worldwound, and the Whispering Tyrant.

Crusader War College: Military academy in Vigil focused on teaching tactics and strategy, as well as battle magic and siege warfare.

Demigods: Semidivine beings, not quite as powerful as true deities, but able to grant spells to their followers.

Demon Lord: A particularly powerful demon capable of granting magical powers to its followers.

Desna: Good-natured goddess of dreams, stars, travelers, and luck.

Dwarves: Short, stocky humanoids who excel at physical labor, mining, and craftsmanship.

Elven: Of or pertaining to elves; the language of elves.

Elves: Long-lived, beautiful humanoids who abandoned Golarion millennia ago before the fall of the Starstone and have only recently returned. Identifiable by their pointed ears, lithe bodies, and pupils so large their eyes appear to be one color.

Forae Logos: Largest library in Absalom.

Foreign Quarter: District of Absalom containing the largest foreign population, as well as the headquarters of the Pathfinder Society.

Geb: Primarily undead nation that takes its name from its necromancer founder.

Ghouls: Undead creatures that eat corpses and reproduce by infecting living creatures.

Gillmen: Race of amphibious humanoids common near Absalom.

Gnomes: Small humanoids with strange mindsets, originally from the fey realm of the First World.

God's Market: Street in Absalom's Ascendant Court where many merchants sell holy items, such as divine icons, religious texts, and vestments.

Graveknights: Powerful undead warriors whose spirits are linked to their armor.

Graycloaks: Atheist guards assigned to Absalom's Ascendant Court, tasked with keeping the peace.

Half-Elves: Descendants of unions between elves and humans. Taller, longer-lived, and generally more graceful and attractive than the average human, yet not so much so as their full elven kin.

Halflings: Race of humanoids known for their tiny stature, deft hands, and mischievous personalities.

Harlot Queen: Arazni.

Hex: Magical abilities granted to witches through pacts made with otherworldly patrons.

Holy Symbol: Physical icon that denotes the follower of a particular god or goddess, and can sometimes be used to channel divine power.

Inquisitors: Religious spellcasters whose power comes from a god, and whose skills are particularly dedicated to hunting down enemies of the faith.

Iomedae: Goddess of valor, rulership, justice, and honor, who in life was a member of the Knights of Ozem and helped lead the Shining Crusade against the Whispering Tyrant before passing the Test of the Starstone and attaining godhood.

Irori: God of history, knowledge, self-perfection, and enlightenment. Popular with monks.

Irorium: Largest arena in Absalom, dedicated to gladiatorial competitions and nonlethal combat.

Ivy District: Quiet, wealthy district in Absalom catering to artists and minor nobles.

Knights of Ozem: Military order devoted to Iomedae and based in Lastwall's capital, Vigil.

Kraggodan: Dwarven stronghold.

Lastwall: Militant nation dedicated to keeping the Whispering Tyrant locked away beneath Gallowspire, as well as keeping the orcs of Belkzen and the monsters of Ustalav in check.

Liches: Spellcasters who manage to extend their existence by magically transforming themselves into powerful undead creatures.

Lich Queen: Arazni.

Merchants' Quarter: Financial and business district in Absalom.

Nex: Nation in Garund formerly ruled by an immensely powerful wizard of the same name.

Noqual: Type of skymetal uniquely resistant to magic.

Oathbound: Citizen of Vigil, sworn and magically bound to support its crusade and defend the innocent.

Orcs: Warlike race with green or gray skin, protruding tusks, and warlike tendencies. Almost universally hated by more civilized races for their constant raiding.

Paladins: Holy warriors in the service of a good and lawful god. Ruled by a strict code of conduct and granted special magical powers by their deity.

Pathfinder Society: Organization of traveling scholars and adventurers who seek to document the world's wonders.

Precentor Martial: One of five military leaders who serve under the Watcher-Lord in Lastwall. Also simply called precentors.

Seventh Church: Temple to Iomedae in Absalom and the site of her seventh of her eleven miraculous acts.

Shield-Mark: Magical mark in the shape of a shield, placed upon the palm, binding the bearer to defend Vigil and its ideals while also conferring the rights of citizenship.

Shining Crusade: Historic organization responsible for cleansing the lands of Ustalav and freeing the nation from the rule of the undead Whispering Tyrant a thousand years ago.

Silver Weights: Denomination of currency used in Absalom.

Skymetal: Metal that fell to Golarion from outer space—either as parts of mysterious craft or as meteorites—that has exceptional and sometimes magical qualities.

Starstone: Magical stone that fell from the sky ten thousand years ago, wiping out most preexisting civilizations. Eventually raised up from the ocean floor by Aroden and housed in the Cathedral of the Starstone in Absalom, where those who can pass its mysterious and deadly tests can ascend to godhood.

Starstone Cathedral: Enormous structure built to house the legendary Starstone and the mysterious tests by which it chooses mortals to elevate to godhood. Anyone who enters the cathedral either dies or becomes a god.

Sword Knight: Priest or other ranking official in Iomedae's church.

Sword-Mark: Magical mark in the shape of Iomedae's holy symbol, placed upon the palm, indicating membership in Lastwall's military. When combined with the Shield-Mark, it indicates full rights and citizenship within Lastwall's crusader city of Vigil.

Taldan: Of or pertaining to Taldor; a citizen of Taldor.

Taldane: Common trade language of Golarion's Inner Sea region.

Taldor: Formerly glorious nation that has lost many of its holdings in recent years to neglect and decadence. Ruled by immature aristocrats and overly complicated bureaucracy.

Tempering Hall: Combat school in Absalom run by the church of Iomedae to train those devoted to fighting evil.

Ustalav: Fog-shrouded gothic nation with a reputation for strange beasts, ancient secrets, and moral decay.

Ustalavic: Of or related to the nation of Ustalav.

Vigil: Capital city of Lastwall.

Vigilant: Soldiers sworn to service in Vigil.

Watcher-Lord: Lastwall's ruler and the commander with final authority over all that nation's crusaders.

Whispering Tyrant: Incredibly powerful lich who terrorized Avistan for hundreds of years before being sealed beneath his fortress of Gallowspire a millennium ago.

Whispering Way: Secret organization that promotes undeath as a purer form of existence. None of its lore is written down or otherwise recorded, with all information whispered among its members.

Wispil: Gnome city in the Verduran Forest.

Witches: Spellcasters who draw magic from pacts made with otherworldly powers, using familiars as conduits.

Worldwound: Constantly expanding region overrun by demons a century ago. Held at bay by the efforts of the Mendevian crusaders.

Once a notorious pirate, Jendara has at last returned to the cold northern isles of her birth, ready to settle down and raise her young son. Yet when a mysterious tsunami wracks her island's shore, she and her fearless crew must sail out to explore the strange island that's risen from the sea floor. No sooner have they delved into the lost island's alien structures than they find themselves competing with a monstrous cult eager to complete a dark ritual in those dripping halls. For something beyond all mortal comprehension has been dreaming on the sea floor. And it's begun to wake up . . .

From Hugo Award winner Wendy N. Wagner comes a sword-swinging adventure in the tradition of H. P. Lovecraft, set in the award-winning world of the Pathfinder Roleplaying Game.

***Starspawn* print edition: $14.99**
ISBN: 978-0-7653-8433-1

***Starspawn* ebook edition:**
ISBN: 978-0-7653-8432-4

PATHFINDER
TALES

STARSPAWN

A NOVEL BY Wendy N. Wagner

Shaia "Shy" Ratani used to be a member of the most powerful thieves' guild in Taldor—right up until she cheated her colleagues by taking the money and running. The frontier city of Yanmass seems like a perfect place to lie low, until a job solving a noble's murder reveals an invading centaur army ready to burn the place to the ground. Of course, Shy could stop that from happening, but doing so would reveal her presence to the former friends who now want her dead. Add in a holier-than-thou patron with the literal blood of angels in her veins, and Shy quickly remembers why she swore off doing good deeds in the first place . . .

From critically acclaimed fantasy author Sam Sykes comes a darkly comic tale of intrigue, assassination, and the perils of friendship, all set in the award-winning world of the Pathfinder Roleplaying Game.

***Shy Knives* print edition: $14.99**
ISBN: 978-0-7653-8435-5

***Shy Knives* ebook edition:**
ISBN: 978-0-7653-8434-8

PATHFINDER TALES

Shy Knives

A NOVEL BY Sam Sykes

Daryus Gaunt used to be a crusader, battling to protect civilization from the demons of the Worldwound, before a battlefield mutiny forced him to flee or be executed. Pathfinder Shiera Tristane is an adventuring scholar obsessed with making the next big archaeological discovery. When a talking weasel reveals that a sinister witch is close to uncovering a long-lost temple deep within the Worldwound, the two adventurers are drawn into the demon-haunted lands in order to stop him from releasing an ancient evil. Now both fame and redemption may be at hand ... if they can survive.

From *New York Times* bestselling author Richard A. Knaak comes a novel of exploration, betrayal, and deadly magic, set in the award-winning world of the Pathfinder Roleplaying Game.

Reaper's Eye print edition: $14.99
ISBN: 978-0-7653-8436-2

Reaper's Eye ebook edition:
ISBN: 978-0-7653-8437-9

PATHFINDER TALES

REAPER'S EYE

A NOVEL BY **Richard A. Knaak**

Mirian Raas and her faithful crew make their living salvaging lost treasures from sunken ships along the coast of tropical Sargava. While retrieving riches from the bottom of Desperation Bay, Mirian and her friend Jekka, one of the last of his lizardfolk tribe, unexpectedly run across the wreck of an ancient magical ship. The discovery leads them on a quest for an arcane artifact called a dragon's tear, which may be the key to locating Jekka's vanished people. But a vengeful sorcerer and a zealous agent of the Child-God Walkena also seek the dragon's tear—and they'll stop at nothing to get it. Can Mirian and her crew pass through the legendary gate in the sea and find the tear before it's too late?

From critically acclaimed author Howard Andrew Jones comes a tale of clashing cultures and jungle adventure, set in the award-winning world of the Pathfinder Roleplaying Game.

Through the Gate in the Sea
print edition: $14.99
ISBN: 978-0-7653-8438-6

Through the Gate in the Sea ebook edition:
ISBN: 978-0-7653-8439-3

THROUGH THE
GATE IN THE SEA

A NOVEL BY Howard Andrew Jones

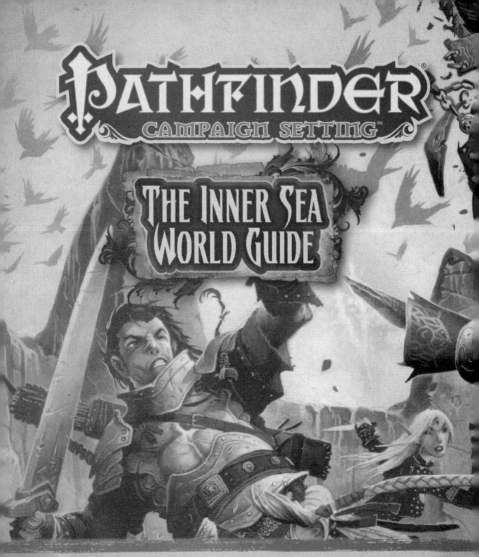

PATHFINDER
CAMPAIGN SETTING

THE INNER SEA WORLD GUIDE

You've delved into the Pathfinder campaign setting with Pathfinder Tales novels—now take your adventures even further! *The Inner Sea World Guide* is a full-color, 320-page hardcover guide featuring everything you need to know about the exciting world of Pathfinder: overviews of every major nation, religion, race, and adventure location around the Inner Sea, plus a giant poster map! Read it as a travelogue, or use it to flesh out your roleplaying game—it's your world now!

EXPLORE YOUR WORLD!

paizo.com